IT
LOOKED LIKE
FOR EVER

IT

LOOKED LIKE

FOR EVER

Mark Harris

McGraw-Hill Book Company

New York   St. Louis   San Francisco
Düsseldorf   Mexico   Toronto

C. 3

1 2 3 4 5 6 7 8 9 F A F A 7 8 3 2 1 0 9

LIBRARY OF CONGRESS CATALOGING IN PUBLICATION DATA
Harris, Mark, date
    It looked like for ever.
    I. Title.
PZ3.H24284It [PS3515.A757] 813'.5'4 79-14423
ISBN 0-07-026720-0

Book design by Marsha Picker.

Portions of this book originally appeared in *Esquire*.

The quotation from *The Boys of Summer* is by permission of Roger Kahn,
The Boys of Summer, Harper & Row; Copyright © 1977, 1972, by Roger
Kahn.

"Provide, Provide" is from *The Poetry of Robert Frost,* edited by Edward
Connery Lathem. Copyright 1936 by Robert Frost. Copyright © 1964
by Lesley Frost Ballantine. Copyright © 1969 by Holt, Rinehart and
Winston. Reprinted by permission of Holt, Rinehart and Winston, Pub-
lishers.

BL

MAY 1 2 '80

For Henry Adam Harris,
who once complained that no book
had been dedicated to him
whereas books had been dedicated to
his very own sister Hester Jill Harris
and
his very own brother Anthony Wynn Harris.

Provide, Provide

The witch that came (the withered hag)
To wash the steps with pail and rag,
Was once the beauty Abishag,

The picture pride of Hollywood.
Too many fall from great and good
For you to doubt the likelihood.

Die early and avoid the fate.
Or if predestined to die late,
Make up your mind to die in state.

Make the whole stock exchange your own!
If need be occupy a throne,
Where nobody can call *you* crone.

Some have relied on what they knew;
Others on being simply true.
What worked for them might work for you.

No memory of having starred
Atones for later disregard,
Or keeps the end from being hard.

Better to go down dignified
With boughten friendship at your side
Than none at all. Provide, provide!

—Robert Frost

The blow had caused a depressed fracture in Chapman's head three and a half inches long. Dr. Merrigan removed a piece of skull about an inch and a half square and found the brain had been so severely jarred that blood clots had formed. The shock of the blow had lacerated the brain not only on the left side of the head where the ball struck but also on the right side where the shock of the blow had forced the brain against the skull, Dr. Merrigan said.

—The New York Times, *August 18, 1920*

I will be the first to know when it is time to quit.

—*189 baseball players quoted from time to time in newspapers and in magazines of sport*

You ain't getting no maiden.

—*Leo Durocher*

After learning that his team will release him from contract, pitcher Henry
Wiggin, rapidly approaching forty, begins a quest, both funny and poignant,
for just one more year in the majors.

1

I was shoveling the snow down the drive way when Holly arrived home from work, climbing out of her car and saying, "Henry, can I see you for 1 minute?" No kiss, no big "Hello," no nothing. Therefore some thing was wrong and I planted the shovel in the snow and went in side the house. 2 days later when we returned the shovel was still in the snow.

"What is wrong?" I inquired. Since all the girls were in the house it could not be any thing too terrible, some thing important but not too important, some thing she heard on the radio coming home, China fell in the ocean, Alaska froze over for ever, or every single United States Congress Person dropped dead. "Dutch died," she said.

My heart jumped up. Why did my heart jump up? Hilary's phsychiatrist inquired, "Why did your heart jump up when you heard that Dutch was dead?"

"I will be the manager," said I to Holly.

"First things first," she replied. "We must go to the funeral."

Hilary went with us. There was no body to leave her with because no body would take her. Her sisters were fed up with her. "I am going to get to see a dead man at last," she said, dancing around the house. She was not *glad* that Dutch was dead, but on the other hand she never attended a funeral before and she was delighted with any thing happening for the first time. We drove in to the city and flew to St. Louis, and every body along the way thought Hilary was the cutest, dearest little thing in the world with her little hands in her little white gloves and her little knees all pink and red. Every body asked her, "And what are you going to get for Christmas, my little lady?" and she replied, "I am getting to see a dead man at last." I my self was 20 years old before I seen any body dead and 20 years old before I flew in an airplane, but every thing I ever done Hilary done many years sooner.

The Schnells lived in a house on Delmar Boulevard. In the old days their house seemed very far out to me, but now it seemed close to town. Hilary was the only kid at the funeral. She stood for a long time looking down in the coffin thinking of some thing she could say that would make the whole place laugh, but she never said it. She was thinking about the Gate Way Arch. Now that she had saw her first official dead man she was thinking ahead to the next thrill on the program. "Bless her," said Millie Schnell, "it is only natural." Millie had give me a kiss at the door and took my arm and walked in the house with me and then give me a second kiss soon after, on second thought, like she suddenly realized how very wonderful I was. In all the years I knew her she never give me 2 kisses in 1 day before, and it was 10 years before she give me any kiss at all. Her grip on my arm was strong but trembling. "Yes," she said, "things loosened up over time. I was always cool to every body. It was how I had to be. He could never afford to become too fond of any body."

"Do not become too fond of any body," said I, "as it raises their expectations." It was what he always said.

"That is it," said she, "to the last word. You and I could sing a chorus together. He could not afford to love young ball players because tomorrow he might fire them. Thank God he was not a general in the war."

He said that, too, "Thank God I am not a general," and the sentence I remember best of all, which he often come out to the mound and said, "Keep the tie run from coming to the plate and you can never lose." While crowds and announcers are speculating on the strategy now under discussion he was saying only that, which was the same as saying "Win" or "Live right" or "Score more runs than them."

Several hundred people were there. Hilary counted 297. He died unexpected on the 7th hole at Pebble Beach playing with Suicide Alexander, the owner of California. He was in the prime of health, still making plans, 2 months short of his 78th birthday. They flew him back to St. Louis still wearing his golf glove on his hand when they carried him in the house, and a police man accompanied them, carrying his golf clubs like a caddy. The score card was stuck in among the clubs, showing he was 2 strokes over par on every hole, which was about right. He was a bad putter. He had no patience for it.

In baseball, however, he had patience for every thing. He was a teacher. "Step aside here with me," he said, and walked off with some ball player to a few square feet in the middle of no place, where they could be alone, and he told you how to do things, and that was the kind of a manager I was going to be. Oh yes, standing in the middle of Dutch Schnell's living room not many feet from his coffin I thought of my self as taking his place. As manager. Not in the coffin. These are called fantasies, dreams while awake, according to Hilary's phsychiatrist. You may ask your own if you don't believe hers. I imagined I was now the manager of the ball club, and I saw my self with my hands in my pockets. Suddenly I knew why a manager keeps his hands in his pockets. While you are playing ball you have either got a glove or a bat in your hand, but when you are managing you have got neither. Once you stop playing you are idle, you are nothing, you got nothing to do, you roam around feeling useless, you got nothing left to do but put your hands in your ass pockets and look alive if you can.

Ball players and their wives were there, including some from the 1950s I never recognized. Perry Simpson was 1 of them. He remembered me but I did not remember him and I made no bones about it, either, it's no sin if you can't remember every body you ever met. He was the first black player with the Mammoths, we played together in Queen City and then again New York, he become a 10 year man in till he drifted out of baseball and out of the news. He was a blessing to a pitcher. He fielded balls back hand on the other side of second base and threw out his runner going the opposite way. He was power and speed, he hit long, he hit short, he hit straight away or he pulled, he stole bases, he now had diabetes, heart trouble, arthritis, he was blind in 1 eye at the age of 40 and deaf in the other, and the time was here that he could not possibly rise from his chair without groaning.

"It is not your fault that you do not recognize me," he said. "No body do. You will see. It will happen to your self. You and I will meet at funerals and Old Timers Games and throwing out the first ball here after."

"*You* 2," some body else said, "will also meet in the Hall of Fame." But we never met again. The next funeral I went to was his 1 year later in Detroit.

In the car to the cemetery we sat with Suicide Alexander. "Are you a millionaire?" Suicide asked me.

"That is a comical question," I replied. "A person's financial state is my own business."

"Not at all," said Suicide. "Here, you may read my bank book," whipping it out of his pocket. It was the little bank book he showed every body, his World Series bank book, where he deposited $500,000 he earned when his old ball club won the World Series and never touched it for 20 years. It was nothing but numbers and I looked at it and give it back.

"I did not know you and Dutch were friends," I said.

"The other day," he said, "was the closest we ever come. We had a good talk covering a range of things. Your name come up."

"In what connection?" I inquired.

"Because I am always trying to find out what is what and who is who among people," he replied.

"What did you find out about me?" I inquired.

"That he advised your club against engaging you as manager," he replied.

So I am riding to the cemetery to bury a man I worked for for many years, I am sad that he is dead, and I am angry that in the last hour of his life he run me down before others. "I was of the opinion he was fond of me," I said.

"He was *fond* of you," said Suicide, "but not as a prospect for manager. You are too rich. You lack the *motivation*. You were not even interested in my bank book when I showed it to you. You did not even offer it to your wife or your child. When I showed it to him he looked at it with great interest. Soon afterward he was feeling around in his breast. I thought he was looking for a pencil in his pocket to write down the score. I said, 'What are you looking for?' and he replied, 'I do not know' and sat down on the ground, and when that position did not seem to be comfortable enough he stretched out his legs and crossed 1 ankle over the other like he was going to sleep."

"Yes," I said, "I seen him stretch out like that a 1,000,000 times. Back in railroad train days we were always delayed some where or other, and Dutch always laid down on a bench like that, 1 ankle over the other, saying, 'Wake me when they are ready to move it.'"

"You played a long time," said Suicide.

"2 in the minors and 19 in the biggies," said I.

"Now they are over," he said.

"Not to *my* knowledge," said I.

"You will see," said he.

"I wish we had rode in 1 of the other cars," said I to Holly.

It was cold at the grave and Hilary wrapped her self under my over coat like a kangaroo in her father's pocket. So she said. "Would you rather be a kangaroo or a tomb stone?" she inquired. Beside us stood Dutch's son, a man of 50 years or so. I never met him before. He lived in Florida where he run a business of some sort. He had no taste for baseball. I said to him,

"Your father was in many ways like a father to me," and his reply was 1 of the saddest sentences I ever heard a man speak. I am glancing at it in my notebook. "He was a father to many young men but never to me," said the son of Dutch Schnell.

The Commissioner spoke, and Patricia spoke. There is a very good chapter about Patricia in the book in title *Baseball Wives,* which my wife wrote, and another very good chapter about Millie Schnell. "We will not stay here long," said Patricia, "due to the cold blasts of winter. I know that with Dutch's passing away we have came to the end of an era. He was the last of your old rough and tumble managers. God put such fine material in such men He run out of it before too long, and so we have none left these days. The era is also passing when ball clubs were run by gentle men, some of who are with us here today, and of course I am thinking of my own father as well. The baseball family is no more. For my part, however, I am going to continue to conduct our club like the family it always was and the family it will always be, saying to my self, 'Make your slogan *family.*'"

A few of us returned to the house. In the car we sat with Ev McTaggart. Ev caught for us for several years. He was not the best catcher in the world but he had a good head and I liked him well enough. It was Ev recommended Hilary's phsyciatrist. He retired as a player and become a coach for us and been so for several years. He had a bad habit of never giving you an answer to a question, giving you instead a wink and a smile like you and him knew some thing no body else knew. I said, "Well, Ev, what now since Dutch is dead? I suppose you will wait and see how things shake down," and he give me a wink and a smile like him and I knew some thing no body else knew, which he did but I didn't.

I thought I would be the manager. I thought Patricia might mention some thing along those lines in the house after the funeral, but she did not. We were only family there if you consider Ev McTaggart family. I suppose so. Beansy Binz was there. You would consider him a very *new* member of the family. He

was a very fine young left hand pitcher who signed for
$400,000. He was going to be very good some day, but for the
time being his money was more sensational than any pitching he
done, and he was modest about it. I my self signed with the
Mammoths in 1949 for $4,000 and a reasonably new automo-
bile. "So you must be 100 times the pitcher I ever was," said I to
Beansy.

"No," he replied, "that is what you call inflation." He took
the whole idea of "family" very serious. He was extremely
courteous to Patricia, and it occurred to me now and again that
she might of took him to bed with her. Why not? He was only
30 years younger than her, and the older I grew the more I
become aware of things that would of formerly surprised me.

We sat in a circle in the living room where the coffin been a
few hours before. We ate, we drank, and I built a fire in the fire
place, thinking all the while I might manage a few private words
with Patricia, but she kept drifting away from me, and out of
the house all together. The last I seen of her she was walking
rather fast to a car which was waiting for her, and her coat was
flying out behind her. She moved quick. She had always moved
quick. She never had time to button her coat or say "Good by"
even to her "family." Holly wrote a very interesting chapter
about Patricia in her book in title *Baseball Wives* although
Patricia was never any body's wife for long.

"Speaking of wives," said Millie Schnell, "if only Dutch
lived in till June we would of been married 57 years like Heinz
57 varieties of ketchup on the bottle. We were married on a
Sunday afternoon in St. Joe after the ball game. The main reason
we got married was the land lady said we must either get married or 1 of us move out. Every body in the boarding house
attended the wedding out of curiosity to see just which young
lady Dutch had chose. You see, he been engaged in goings on
with more than only me to my surprise. You can imagine this
become a very great part of my education in the ways of life.
How ever, once we were married he was faith full ever after."

She looked at me, inquiring, "Were you about to say some thing, Henry?"

My face stood froze. Nothing at all.

"Henry," she continued, "why not borrow those golf clubs?"

I was *wondering* what she planned on doing with them. I like golf. I play golf with ladies. I like the privacy of the golf course. We took them back to the hotel and sorted them out. Some of them were good and some of them weren't. A ½ of them I kept and a ½ of them I give to the bell boy, but what neither me nor the bell boy knew was that the clubs belonged to Suicide Alexander, not Dutch, and I and Hilary went up the Gate Way Arch.

I was extremely angry about being at the top of the Gate Way Arch with Hilary and trying to control my self and hide my anger from her. I asked my self, "Just exactly who are you angry at?" and if I could figure out just exactly who I was angry at I could ask my self the next question in line, "Just why are you angry at who you are angry at?" I begun thinking I was angry at "the 630 foot high Gate Way Arch of stainless rainbow steel" because it was "the tallest man made monument in the nation." "Now who else could make a monument but men?" I asked Hilary. "Ants did not build it nor elephants build it nor kangaroos."

"Not even horses," said Hilary, who was at that time moving in to her horse stage.

I was angry at Hilary for causing me to be at the top of the Gate Way Arch, which was the last place I cared to be, along with the Statue of Liberty and the Empire State Building and the Washington Monument or any museum, zoo, canyon, geyser, or roller coaster any where in the United States of America. But none of that was poor Hilary's fault. She was only a child wishing to go all the places her sisters been before her. From the top of the Gate Way Arch we seen the ball park. A ball park is always a lonely place in winter. Hilary had now saw every ball park except the ball parks of California, although she never actually been *in* any yet. She never cared to go in till she heard I was finished. She cared only to see them from the out side, planning on moving in gradually during the years to follow. "I once hit a home run in that ball park," said I to Hilary, "and I once hit a home run in the *old* St. Louis ball park before they tore it down and put up this."

"You were quite a home run hitter," said Hilary.

"Those were the only 2 home runs I ever hit," said I.

"Why are you angry?" Hilary inquired.

"I am not angry," I replied. Maybe I was angry at Holly for sending me all alone up the Gate Way Arch with Hilary. Some time before Holly said, "I am handing you here with my temporary resignation as Hilary's mother. When the situation improves I will consider being recalled." Where was Holly now? She was *resting* in the hotel, or drinking a glass of wine with her feet on the bed, or dining, or shopping, or reading, or taking a walk around the block or calling up old friends on the telephone. Maybe she was having a love affair with a fellow guest in the next room running back and forth between the doors.

"You look angry," said Hilary.

"Telling you the truth," said I, "I am angry, but not at you and not at mother."

"I hope it is no body in the family," she said, "such as my sisters, although there is no telling what mischief they might be up to this very minute. I hope you are not angry at a horse."

Family. Jesus, that was it. Patricia Moors with all her talk about *family.* The more she talked the more she lied. There was no *family* any more. Was there ever any family? Oh yes, they made me feel like family, for I was important to them and brung the customers in, but things were different now and I might not be so much family any more once my stock went down. Dutch advised the club against me. Suicide Alexander heard him. You always think it is a family in till the day they throw you out.

Sitting on the door step in the cold makes your brain work faster than before, and you wonder why you never saw it from the in side.

"I got to get to a telephone," said I to Hilary. "Do not fall off the Gate Way Arch." I telephoned Patricia in New York. I was frantic and my hands sweat all over the phone. I trembled. I was in rage, my mouth was dry, my blood pressure went up, my heart pumped. I was a health hazard.

She was not in. In the old days when I telephoned the office of the New York Mammoths they put me right through to any body I asked for, no matter who, and very promptly, Patricia, her father, quicker than you could bat an eye. They said, "Hello, Author, what can we do for you, do you need show tickets, do you need restaurant reservations, travel accommodations, fresh money, we will dig up the North Pole and plant it down south if you wish, no bother, no trouble, you say it and we will do it and visa versa," but all I was told on the present occasion was that she was not yet back from the funeral in St. Louis and no body knew when she would. She would call me. I give them numbers. "Merry Christmas." "Merry Christmas."

She never did. She did not call me in the hotel in St. Louis. In the morning we left. It was snowing again. The only sun we seen all day was up above the snow. I spent many hot days of my life in St. Louis, but this was not 1 of them, in and out, in and out, in the old park in the old days and in the new park later, in and out for 19 years. Good by, Dutch, old friend. She did not call me in the car between JFK airport and Perkinsville, and she did not call me at home.

I went out before dinner and took the shovel out of the snow where I planted it 2 days before, and I begun shoveling down the drive way when Holly opened the window and I knew it was some thing bad by the way she spoke my name. "Henry?" she said, and I replied, "What?"

"Ev McTaggart been named manager," she said.

I was rather stunned. Ev manager? How could I play for Ev

when I should of been manager my self? I was 21 years with the organization. Ev was a new comer. I seen my self receiving orders from Ev. Replying to his orders I booted him in the ass and his hands were in his ass pockets and now what you were looking at was the first no handed manager.

"Another thing," said Holly.

"What was that?" I inquired.

"You been released," she said.

2

Now, ladies and gentle men, you have got to bear in mind that after Holly told me the news she closed the window, it is winter, I am wearing a wool cap to some extent pulled down over my ears, and through all this I hear the most blood curling scream I ever heard in my life.

I rushed in to the house, and when I arrived Holly was running from the kitchen up stairs, and out of 3 different bed rooms come 3 of my daughters, and from up stairs, down stairs, and in the cellar come 3 different servants while on the stair way Hilary is looking satisfied at the crowd she has attracted with her screaming. She screamed again. Where she got the breath I do not know. It was not as loud as her first scream, but it was louder than most of the screams she performed during the past year or more, and when she stopped I said, "Now that you have attracted our attention please deliver your message."

"I have never saw you play baseball," she said, "and now I will never see you at all," and she screamed again for quite some time while her sisters and her mother and the servants returned to their various activities. I sat on the steps with Hilary. I removed my coat and gloves and hat. "My dear girl," said I, "you are disgusting and unreasonable. Every ball player arrives some time at his last pitch, and I have arrived at mine."

"Every body else seen you," she said, "because they are older than me."

"We can not all be born at the same time," I said. It was some thing I had said before, too, you may be sure.

Again she screamed.

"Stop!" yelled I.

She stopped.

"Down stairs in the cellar," said I, "I have a whole room made of fire proof walls which is filled to the brim with medals, papers, plaques, certificates and 2 shelfs of moving picture film showing me playing baseball year in and year out. There is no reason why we can not take down that shelf and watch me playing baseball until we are sick and tired of the sight for ever."

Hilary thought this over and immediately begun screaming again.

"Stop!"

She stopped. "I do not wish to see you on film," she said. "I wish to see you in person. Mother seen you in person and Michele Roberta Wiggen seen you in person and Rosemary Lenore Wiggen seen you in person and Millicent Rebecca Wiggen seen you in person and 1,000's and 1,000's of strangers in St. Louis and all over the country and over seas seen you in person in till the only person that never seen you in person is your very own daughter Hilary Margaret Wiggen."

"Recently," said I, "you were not screaming so much and the thought was coming in my mind to buy the horse you often mentioned."

"Many and many a time mother went to the baseball game and seen you play. She seen you play before you were married and after. I never went. I never seen you. Michele and Rosemary and Millicent seen you in the summer time. I have saw ball parks in the lonesome winter time from the Gate Way Arch. They sat in ball parks and ate ice cream and Coca Cola and cold drinks and peanuts and hot dogs. I ate nothing on the top of the Gate Way Arch. They seen you hit home runs."

"They never seen me hit home runs," I said, "because I hit only 2 home runs and 1 of the parks I hit 1 in is tore down."

"What horse?" she inquired.

Well all right. Some day you are going to be released. I was angry. I thought they could of told me first before telling the radio and what not. Later I said to Patricia, "It seems like you could of told me first," and she replied, "I thought some body told you. I told some body tell you." I believed her. I long since give up trying to get a message through an organization. If I have some thing to tell some body I tell them my self. I pick up the phone and *talk in it my self.* I do not tell an office assistant to tell some body some thing. I make sure I see the letter I write. I get letters "dictated but not read" or "signed in So and So's absence." I remember 1 time a certain letter like that irritated me more than many others and I sent the fellow a blank piece of paper saying "read but not wrote."

Soon I was no longer angry. Now I suddenly knew what every body was talking about. But certain questions slowly rose in my mind. Why was I released? Was I released because of the fact that I could no longer play ball? Or was I released for the convenience of the New York Mammoths Baseball Club, Inc.? Should I listen to them? If I believed I was able to play further what could I do about it? Did they have a right to disappoint my daughter, Hilary? Did the New York Mammoths feel that they had many strong young fellows coming along? Is that why they released me? If so, were there not other clubs I might join which did not feel so confident of them self? Was the fact that I was no longer in the plans of the Mammoths the same as me not being in *any* body's plans? Instead of allowing them to release me from baseball should I not make that decision my self? Did they know me better than I knew my self? Were they the only fish in the sea?

"However," said Holly, "although you may not consider your self retired you must ask your self who then are you *with*."

For several days I taught physical education at Mrs. Wiggen's School for Privileged Children, Perkinsville, N. Y. This school is not what it sounds like. My wife, who is Mrs. Wiggen, believes that any child who is well is privileged. Her school also accepts handy capped students. It is a very good school and we make a lot of money at it, but after several days I resigned.

I had several immediate offers to play ball. A fellow dropped over from the Perkinsville No Pitch League guaranteeing me I could sign up any time I wished, even if I went past the dead line. It was a local league where they threw the ball easy. I said I would think over his generous offer and I done so. Maybe Hilary would think it was the big leagues.

"Oh, no," said Holly, "she would know," and the girls all said the same. Hilary knows every thing, and what she does not know she looks up in the Encyclopedia Britannica or she telephones the reference desk of the library. You can hear her now, "I am just phoning to ask you certain baseball facts. Is Perkinsville in the big leagues?" Not hardly.

Another fellow dropped over from the Mayor's office asking if I would accept the position of Commissioner of Parks and Recreation for the Town and City of Perkinsville and I said I would not. I said it very nicely. You have got to be very careful how you say "No" to people or they become angry at you and say all sorts of nasty things about you all over town which you rather not hear.

Judge Kendall Phillips and City Attorney Myron Smallman dropped over the house and asked me if I would care to run for Commissioner of Real Estate for the Town and City of Perkinsville. They felt that they could guarantee me the endorsement of the major political parties as well as the independent party. I said I would not. They said they would put me on the ballot any how. I said I would vote against my self. "Then you will capture all votes but 1," said Judge Phillips. The Judge was

in my high school class. He is in the very front row of the
photograph petting the school mascot, a dog name of Bozo. "It
is rather shocking," said I, "to think that some body my own age
is a Judge all ready."

"You and I were the success stories of our class," said the
Judge.

"What about Bozo?" I inquired.

"All joking aside," said the Judge, "you have got to become
Commissioner of Real Estate so that we can protect our
property."

"Who is threatening our property?" Holly inquired.

"People will use it for the wrong things," said the City
Attorney.

"We have got to keep the people out," said the Judge.

"Who then will we let in?" Holly inquired.

"Well," said the City Attorney, "this been 1 of your more
pleasant discussions and we must go."

I received a telephone call from a man named Mr. Clubb of
the American Embassy in Tokyo informing me that the Oyasumi
Cobras would be honored to offer me a contract to play ball with
them in the Japanese big leagues. This interested Holly a good
deal, but she could not find Oyasumi on the map and we called
him back. "You will put it on the map," said he.

It also sounded good for Hilary, who would now have the
opportunity of seeing me play big league ball. Big leagues was
big leagues whether American or Japanese, was it not? Hilary
looked at maps and come up with the opinion that Japan was a
big enough country to be considered big leagues and she
adopted the name "Fumiko" for her self.

Japan always been very good to me. Over the years I played
there several times on exhibition tours. It looked like such a
solid place I begun very early in the game placing money in such
stocks as Toyota, Datsun, Sony, Sanyo, Mitsubishi and Suzuki.
These stocks grew so big they begun depressing my American

stocks in till the money I made in Japan I lost in America and visa versa.

As a token of their sincerity Mr. Clubb mailed us air plane tickets to Tokyo to go and take a look at Oyasumi and surroundings and meet the people and make up our mind. "In Japan," said he, "expansion is the name of the game, you will make money, you will have fun, you will melt away to your heart's content in the hot springs of Oyasumi sheltered in doors from the winter, every thing that ever ailed you will be cured, and your playing days will be extended by 3 or 4 years." I and Holly knew all about the hot springs of Japan in doors and out as it was in a hot springs that we conceived of Hilary.

Mr. Clubb mentioned several American ball players then playing in Japan and I and Holly tacked up the air plane tickets on the bulletin for further consideration.

A publicity man from the Mammoths drove up 1 day to talk things over and tell me how to live. He mentioned a number of possibilities for me to pursue. He invited me to play in the Old Timers Game in June. I declined, saying I did not feel like an Old Timer, I was still thinking I might play ball. "Author," said he, "of course you do not have to come and play in the Old Timers, you know, except you will wish to think of such a spectacle as $1,000,000 worth of national advertising for your self putting you back in people's mind."

"I can not believe," I said, "that by June I will have fell out of people's mind after 19 years at the top."

"Do not bank on it," he said. "Get your self seen. Appear. Get in line for the Hall of Fame. You have got to talk your self up. Print your life time career on post cards and drop them in the mail where ever you go. Keep vibrating in the public mind. Get your picture in the paper when ever you can. Sell Christmas trees for charity year in and year out. Coach brats. Talk on TV. Give out opinions. The Hall of Fame is worth another $1,000,000 right there, but very few people ever get elected to it that leave them self submerge from sight. I will put you down for Old Timers in June, no questions asked, forwarding you details as the time draws nigh. Give out the information that some body wants you. No body wants you in till some body else wants you. Once you got your bags unpacked you become instantly hated. Give your self a tribute banquet. I can arrange 1 before or after the old shits game whereby 1,000's of people will attend and sing your praises. I handled a tribute banquet recently for Phil Resek and cleared him $40,000."

I received a telephone call from Suicide Alexander. I thought it might be some thing but it was nothing. "I understand you took a bag of golf clubs home from St. Louis," he said. "They were mine."

"I took home ½ a bag," said I. "I give ½ the bag away. I thought they were Dutch's."

"Give them to me when you see me," he said.

"I would love to see you," said I, "and talk about playing ball for you."

"I am open to that idea," said he, "but I suppose you would wish a lot of money."

"I am not too interested in the money," said I. "It is a family matter. I wish to have my little girl see me play."

"Talk to Jack," he said. "He lives near you, does he not?"

"A wonderful idea," said I, "for Jack and I are friends from way back."

That particular call come to me from Suicide Alexander in his apartment in Newhall, California, from 1 of 4 telephones on his bed all rigged up to tape recorders. With so many telephones on his bed I do not know where he slept. He had a type writer on a rolling table in the bath room. To use the bath room it was necessary to wheel the table out before using the facilities. Maybe it was more of an office than apartment.

I telephoned Jack Sprat, the manager of California, at his home in Tozerbury. He was not at home. I spoke to his wife,

Marva, who is not in Holly's book in title *Baseball Wives* but
ought to been, for she is a rare character. She said Jack was in
California visiting Mr. Alexander. Since I just got off the phone
with Mr. Alexander I wondered why he said nothing along that
line.

Tozerbury is 50 miles north of Perkinsville. I played baseball
there against Tozerbury High nearly 30 years ago now. We were
suppose to hate 1 another. Marva and I talked about this and
that. I mentioned horses. She mentioned a certain horse lady
owning barns and stables and what not in Tozerbury, and I
wrote her name down.

I was interested in seeing Marva again, for I remembered her
as an unusually beautiful woman when I seen her last. Some
place we met. Maybe some winter banquet. Maybe a ball park.
"It must of been 5 or 6 years ago at least," said I.

"If 5 or 6 years ago," said she, "it must of been some other
unusually beautiful woman since I have not strayed out of the
house in 9. That was the All Star Game in Washington because
Jack was playing in it."

"I played in that game," said I.

"Yes," said she, "but it was not you I went to see, it was my
own Jack."

"Are you perfectly well?" I inquired.

"You are 1 of those unusual persons that dare to ask," said
Marva. "Most people think that if I stood in the house all these
years I must be either in a chair or out of my head. I might be
out of my head but look at the rest of you."

Holly and I and Hilary drove to Tozerbury on the Sunday
after New Year's Day. I could not remember the last time I
been there. Those old high school bus rides seemed very long,
but now the drive was short, and while we drove Hilary give us a
great deal of information regarding horses which I forgot right
away. She also asked many questions about horses and was surprised that we could not answer them although I told her time

and again I knew nothing about horses out side the fact that they were longer than cats and taller than dogs and did not give milk like cows. "Horses give milk," said Hilary.

"Not to me," said I.

"To baby horses," Holly said.

"Correct," said Hilary. "Would you rather be a Palomino or a Tennessee Walking Horse?"

"A Tennessee Walking Horse," I replied.

"Why?"

"Because Tennessee is close to Kentucky," said I.

"Very good," said Hilary.

Just as long as you give *some* answer or other she left you alone. Many people found Hilary difficult during this period of her life, including Mrs. Wiggen's School for Privileged Children. Hilary was not now attending that school or any other. The person she soon got along best with in all the world was the horse lady of Tozerbury, which was rather a mystery to me in till I realized how simple the answer was. "She gets along very well with the horse lady of Tozerbury," said Dr. Schiff, "because there are horses present." Hilary learned horse riding in 1 minute, leaping on the back of the first horse she seen and riding around and around in the corral in side the stable, and after they had rode about 7,000 miles she brushed them and combed them and cleaned up their stalls like no pleasure on earth could equal cleaning up after a horse.

The horse lady her self was an extremely attractive person. She had a slight foreign accent, maybe Italian, and she was dark skinned and wore these tight fitting horse riding pants and high boots above her ankles. She never cared how deep she stepped in the horse manure contributed by the horses during periods Hilary was not there to shovel it up. When we went to her house afterwards she wore her boots at all times. It seemed rather odd to me that such a beautiful woman would wear such filthy, dirty, smelling boots right in their own house. I am sorry that I can not remember her name.

Our first visit was only an introduction. We did not buy a horse on that visit but bought horses from her in the future, and that very summer I took up riding for the first time and went galloping with Hilary through the fields and roads around Perkinsville like the midnight ride of Paul Revere.

Suzanne Winograd telephoned from some place warm. "South," she said, maybe South America, South Africa, or the South of France, making a lot of money playing tennis, "keeping the tip of my nose barely out of the water," she said, and I believed her and was eager to help her if I could. She been stole blind by agents and managers and husbands and hustlers at every level. "So you quit," she said.

"No," said I, "I been released. They never give me a chance to quit."

"They were in too much of a hurry," she said, "they grind their own ax first, never mind you and me that the people pay to see, we make them rich and they throw us on the junk, we are nothing, we are the dirt under foot."

"I am O. K.," I said. "Dutch Schnell died. They had to move fast."

"Oh, come on," said Suzanne. "He was long over due. Stop making your self feel better. They had their move planned for a long time. You were fucked and you know it."

"It was nothing as nice as all that," said I.

"You understand what I mean," she said.

"No body ever speaks plainer than you," said I.

"Very well then," said she, "speaking plainly on the subject of quick money, how would you like to take a Celebrity Tour with me? We will see baseball and tennis spots all over the world. Golf maybe. What ever we get the customers for. These will be very rich fans paying for every sight they see, and the most expensive sight they will see is you and me. Privileges are extra, and you and I are privileges. For example, a meal in a restaurant might cost $7.50 but if they sit at the table with you and me it cost them $25. If no body eats with us we eat alone. A bus ticket will cost extra if they sit on the same seat with you and me, like wise steam ship or air plane. Dinner on a steam ship will cost them 3 *times* as much at our table, no paper work to do, it is all did by the travel agent, no money counting to bog you down, no selling, no speech making."

"What baseball sights would we be taking a steam ship to?" I inquired.

"We will find out when we get there," she said. "Tennis and golf are every where. In the States we will cover big ball parks, the Astrodome, the Hall of Fame, visit a few birth places and graves, finally connect up with the Little League finals in Pennsylvania and get lost in the crowd and go home. I hate it, but I am desperate and it is money."

"You would not be so desperate if you would not think of counting your own money as bogging you down," said I. "When are you planning to learn some thing?"

"You sound cool to my proposal," she said. "What about becoming Honorary Co Chair Person of the President's Committee Focusing on Aging? We begin and end by making a very short film in Washington. It is a god dam fraud on the public."

"I dislike the President," I said, "and he dislikes me."

"You are so boyish," she said. "He cares nothing for likes and dislikes, it is money, 1 day's work and out."

"Speaking plainly," I inquired, "about how much money?"

"For you a lot," she said, "for me less because I need it more. That is what they do to you."

"Suzanne," said I, "I will do the 1 day job as opposed to the world tour because I am hoping to spend more time now with my family. Regarding money, speak to my lawyer." I give her her number.

"How is Hilary?" she inquired.

"She is progressing," I replied. I was planning to ask for her daughter, too. We all first met in Dr. Schiff's waiting room. I hoped it would not sound like I was asking for hers simply because she asked for mine. "And how is Bertilia?" I inquired.

"Coping," she said.

"Of course you know that the problem is not Bertilia but her mother," I suggested.

"Now on to things of a more long term nature," she said. "I and Jerry Divine have got a big idea going that will make us all a lot of money once we can attract your interest."

"Announcing," I said.

"You guessed it."

"I do not think I would like it," I said, "sitting in a booth through hundreds of ball games with Jerry, though I like him well enough. I can not stand watching ball games."

"I will also be in the booth," she said, "so please do not make up your mind in till I present all this to you in person. I am putting down this telephone and flying out of here. What is today? I will see you Thursday if you will be home there. What is the name of your town again?"

"It is a city by now," said I. "I will be here Thursday if you will. There is no body in the world I rather see than you. We can hit some golf balls on the range if we get any weather."

However, instead of Suzanne flying in from the south of where ever she was it was Jerry Divine drove up from New York. He was a poor substitute for her, and I was disappointed. "We are all 1 team," said Jerry. "We work as a unit. When she said she was coming she meant me."

Jerry limped a little bit. He played ball awhile for us and others in till his career was ruined on a street corner in Cleveland. "In 2 seconds my life turned around," he said. He stepped off the curb and was clipped. He had a good face and a good voice and he knew the game and people liked him. I had a good memory of him from 2 or 3 times he interviewed me. He asked intelligent questions and he listened while you answered. He never tried to back you off in some corner where you'd blame your problems on some body else, stirring up a fight for the amusement of people more interested in gossip than in the game. He was relaxed. He was different than the others. When he announced a game he was very low key and he did not fill your head with 10,000 statistics per minute. Most announcers I turn down the sound.

He never stood with 1 program long. He was in and out of net works. He bounced around. "However," said Jerry in the kitchen of my house that winter day, "I can tell you that we are at the cutting edge of a new revolution in announcing ball games and you are the key to it. I only want 5 words from you. When you say to me, 'Jerry, just count me in,' I pick up the telephone and the funding is raised. If you can not spare 5 words make it 4, lop off the word 'Jerry' no questions asked."

"Henry will love being in the crowded booth with Suzanne Winograd," said Holly.

"I was thinking so my self," said I, "but I am not ready for a booth just now no matter who is in it through hundreds of ball games per year."

"I am glad you raised that objection," Jerry said. "You can dismiss it from your mind. The beauty of the proposition is that we are not talking about day after day and night after night, being away from home month after month. We are talking about only 1 or 2 days of work a week through an idea thought up by a genius based on surveys, called "Friday Night Baseball." Think about that."

All this was in the kitchen. I don't know why. When Jerry arrived we just settled in the kitchen and never moved out all day. We forgot to eat lunch. We ate lunch about 4 o'clock in the after noon and we were not ready for dinner. We sat in the kitchen while my family come and went through dinner and 1 of my daughters dropped cranberry sauce on Jerry. It slid off a platter in his lap and he scooped it up with 2 hands and placed it back on her platter with out hardly skipping a word. "Only 1 night," said Jerry with enthusiasm, "and the name of the night is Friday. What will happen? We will be low key, I agree with you, we will not stir up fights, we will relax, we will not bury the public in statistics or laugh at each other's jokes like they are funny. No. Who are we? We are just Jerry who is Mr. No Body Knows and Suzanne and Henry. Suzanne is a famous and average woman just sitting around with her 2 friends and chatting while watching and talking about 1 thing and another. The key to the audience is women. That is what the survey shows."

"I do not need all these guarantees," said I. "Make an offer in writing to my lawyer. I am just becoming worried that the hour is growing late and you got that long drive back."

"I love the long drive back," he said. "I want you to know the sure thing that you are getting in to. I want you to remember that all the former surveys show that Friday night is down town night. People stay down town for such things as theaters and shows and restaurants rather than go home and come all the way back Saturday night."

"It is not my impression that people stay down town Friday or Saturday," said Holly, "as there is no more down town in most places. Henry and I go in the city on week day mornings."

"Friday night is the coming night for TV," said Jerry. "You have heard of the Catholics and the Jews. The Catholics eat fish on Friday and do not have the strength to go running around town Friday night. Fish leave you weak."

"You do not say so?" Holly asked.

"It is what the survey shows," Jerry said. He could tell that Holly was against it. Now that I was home she thought I should do certain things I always promised to do. "And there is more. You know that the Jews go to the synagogue on Friday night. If there was a ball game on TV they would rather stay home and watch it. I know that Holly is going to laugh in my face, but I am only telling you what the survey shows."

"I believe the survey showed what they wished it to show," Holly said. "I bet it would of come out different if they asked it in the synagogue."

"The Jews will pour out of the synagogue for Friday Night Baseball," said Jerry.

"The Catholics will pour out of the butcher shop," said Holly.

"We will beat all the opposition," Jerry said. "Friday Night Baseball will be the thing."

"We wrapped up in our coats and walked down the drive way with him. He limped worse than he limped in the morning, for he tired as the day wore on. Later in the summer he begun carrying a cane. "I hope you will say, 'Jerry, just count me in,' because this is our 1 and only big chance. You know," he said, "I got no pension. I was not up there long enough. Leave me ask you 1 question that been killing me with curiosity, Author. How much money did you put away?"

"Do you require the exact figure?" I asked.

He stopped walking and looked at me. He really expected me to answer him in numbers. "Just a ball park figure will do," he replied. "We work as a unit and can not have secrets from each other."

It is a question I am often asked and avoid answering. "How much money did you put away?" "How do you throw a curve ball?" "What time is it?" He drove off, and Holly and I walked very slowly back up the drive way again enjoying the cold. I enjoy becoming very cold and popping in the house and sitting around with a glass of brandy. "A man that shoveled all this snow has still got a certain pep," said I.

"To what?" she asked.

"To play ball some more," I replied.

"Well, there is pep and there is pep," she said. "Shoveling snow pep is not the same as baseball playing pep."

"What am I going to do with the rest of my life?" I inquired.

"Now is our chance to do a 1,000,000 things," she replied. "We will flower my garden in case there is still a garden there under the snow, or we can buy a vineyard in Spain or California as discussed, or we can move to some other climate that is better for the aches and pains we some times feel. We can try Paris or Europe."

"Right at the moment," said I, "how about Tokyo?"

"I can be ready on short notice," Holly said. "What about Hilary?"

Yes, there was always Hilary. "Hilary will scream if we do not take her," I said.

"I will not go if Hilary goes," said Holly.

I and Hilary drove down in the city to talk to Dr. Schiff regarding Tokyo. We told her we could not take her, but she did not scream. She had now went with out screaming since the day I was released. Why was this? She would not say. She only smiled and read her book and talked on the telephone and asked me questions all fairly much at the same time. Would I rather be a pencil or a crayon? Would I rather be run over by a truck or a steam roller? "Since you have stopped screaming maybe we do not need to visit Dr. Schiff," said I. But this put her once more on the edge of screaming, for she enjoyed visiting Dr. Schiff or any how enjoyed driving down with me and eating in McDonald's and staying over in the apartment and all the other goodies that went with it. "Now that you are home at last," said Dr. Schiff, "she plans on making a father out of you. Where were you all her life while she was growing up?"

Her and Hilary visited. I waited in the waiting room in till they called me in. In the waiting room several interesting posters are hung on the wall. They looked to me like they were drew by school children in the lower grades, but Dr. Schiff had actually drew them her self. They said such things as *Feel Free* showing some flowers feeling free, I suppose.

Men, Women, and Children First

I liked that 1, while over her door hung the following.

How Do You Do? Come On In and Meet Your Self

Make Love Not War

Never Break a Promise to a Child

War Is Unhealthy for Children and Other Living Things

In the waiting room I some times met interesting people, such as Suzanne and Bertilia and the wife of a Latin American soccer player and daughter and the wife of a well known hockey player and her 2 *twin* daughters and several others. I never met another man there. I was the only man I ever saw, although I know that Ev McTaggart went to Dr. Schiff since he recommended her in the first place.

"We been asking our self," said Dr. Schiff, "what Hilary is trying to tell you by not screaming."

"I am thanking him for the horse he is going to buy me when he returns from Tokyo," said Hilary.

"She is merely being a good girl for the moment," said Dr. Schiff, "and then she will start screaming for some thing else once she got you saddled with the horse."

"I did not say that," said Hilary.

"That is what it sounds like to me," said Dr. Schiff. "I would certainly go about it that way if I were you."

"That is not very *nice*," said Hilary.

"What do I care about being nice?" said Dr. Schiff. "I want what I want when I want it. I do not care to take 'No' for an answer."

"You have got to learn to take 'No' for an answer some times in this life," said Hilary. Her sisters told her so.

"I am getting sort of interested in horses my self," I said.

"A whole new world is opening up to you now that you stopped playing ball," said Dr. Schiff. "Many athletes begin discovering life once they retire."

"He is not retired," said Hilary. "He is continuing. That is why I am permitting him to go to Tokyo."

"Then I see that we are not yet done with the screaming," Dr. Schiff said.

"Leave us go to McDonald's," said Hilary.

"I am dying for Coca Cola," said Dr. Schiff, although she was drinking 1 that very moment. We always walked around to McDonald's and Dr. Schiff always bought 1 more Coca Cola than there were persons. "Talking all day makes me dry," she said, but she drunk Coca Cola steadily whether she was dry or not, winter and summer, night and day. It was almost all I ever seen her consume except once I remember she ate a Filet O Fish and another time a small side dish of onion rings. She stood very lovely and slim. She would be expensive to dress and cheap to feed.

Hilary on the other hand went more for the Hot Caramel Sunday followed by a Big Mac 1 day or a Quarter Pounder the next sprinkled in with French fries and shakes with plenty of mustard and ketchup. It was a mess. I touched nothing. I kept regular adult food in the apartment. Hilary never finished far beyond the Hot Caramel Sunday and we packed it all in a dog bone bag and took it to the apartment. She stood in the shower an hour or more and come out and nibbled a bit out of the dog bone bag and went back in the shower another hour.

It was a very large old fashion shower complete with marble benches. We had it built in some years ago when I was very young and cared less for my privacy. I loaned the apartment out to young baseball players who brung their lady friends there for showering as a group and there by saving New York City tons of water. All that was before Hilary's time. She loved staying at the apartment with me because no body told her "Do not use up all the water, remember that you got 3 sisters to share things with," or "Eat over the table." She did not even eat *at* the table. She settled down in bed with the Encyclopedia Britannica and the third and fourth bite of her Big Mac or her Quarter Pounder well covered with ketchup and mustard and the sheets and the pillow cases, too. The bed smelled like onions. She hated going to sleep, though when she got there she slept sound enough.

"I can not believe she is finally asleep," said Dr. Schiff.

"Will you change off from Coca Cola to wine?" I inquired.

"More Coca Cola," said she.

"Among the many things depressing me in recent years about young ball players," said I, "was all the Coca Cola they drunk and all the bad food they ate."

She tip toed in and looked at Hilary and tip toed back. "When I was a little girl," said she, "a great part of my education come from listening to the grown ups talk when they thought I was asleep. We did not have 1 bed room per child like you."

"What did you learn?" I inquired.

"The facts of life. I could hardly believe the swearing and the filth. Grown ups were different people when they thought you were asleep."

"A great part of my education come from playing ball," said I.

"I will go to Japan and watch you play," said Dr. Schiff.

"However," I replied, "I will be accompanied by my family if I do."

"If Holly will not go if Hilary goes," said Dr. Schiff, "you should take Hilary alone and I will accompany you as medical care for Hilary."

"This is very good wine you are missing," said I. I believe it was Cabernet Sauvignon from Napa Valley. I always brung wine from California.

"Coca Cola does the trick for me," said Dr. Schiff. "Why do you hate the young people for drinking so much Coca Cola? They are in title to their bad habits."

"And eating such bad food," said I. "I am sure I do not hate them. None of the young ball players seem to be enjoying them self."

"They are too tense," she said. "They are still struggling. Is it so long ago that you have forgot how it was? It is very easy to tell other people 'relax and enjoy your self' once you your self have got it made."

"It is like telling a young fellow he must not focus all his efforts on getting laid," said I, "for when his ambition is accomplished he still got many problems waiting ahead of him."

"Why do you hate Hilary?" Dr. Schiff inquired.

"I beg your pardon." We were sitting with our feet on the radiator watching the lights switching off and on in the Waldorf Astoria. Just when you thought things were quieting down over there a new party started up.

"Because you neglected her," she said. "You promised you would come home and be a father to her, but you can not face it. The easiest thing is running off and playing ball some more if you can, and tell your self it is Hilary making you do it."

"She did scream," said I. "It was not my imagination."

"She will scream at this and that and eventually stop," said the doctor.

"Then why am I bringing her to you?" I inquired.

"You are like many men," she said. "You realized at last that the actual work you done was more fun than the fun you thought you had. You now wish to enjoy the work you forgot to enjoy when you were at the height of your skill and power."

"I am at the height," I said, "but I have not got the fast ball."

"Or if you are not doing it for Hilary you are doing it to prove that Patricia Moors is wrong, or Ev McTaggart is wrong. You had yours. You had *more* than yours. Now step aside and leave the young fellows enjoy them self. You should abandon your wife and marry me."

"I see," said I.

"You and I should go to Tokyo and leave Hilary home," she said.

"Hilary was conceived of in Japan," said I, "in the hot springs of Beppu."

"It is no wonder you are afraid of taking her back to the scene of the crime. I am sure that you and your wife will once again be laying around in the hot springs."

"Certainly not in the *cold* springs," said I, thinking I was being the least bit comical, but Dr. Schiff was in no mood for comedy.

"I certainly hate you," she said. "I regret that I must go home as soon as I finish 1 more Coca Cola. Why are we here? A rich man like you can afford a baby sitter. Why are you afraid to leave your child alone? I got a beautiful apartment with no children or other interferences." She begun stomping around the apartment. And yet she done so quietly on tip toe, and all though she begun screaming at me she screamed in a *whisper* if you can imagine it. "This is the safest apartment house in the world with 29 doors to get past with a key for every door and a man in a uniform guarding every key hole and a second man guarding the first man. Or you could of left her in Perkinsville in the first place."

"How can I take my child to the phsychiatrist with out bringing her along?" I inquired.

"Just send me an X ray of her brain," said Dr. Schiff. "I would like to drop an atomic bomb on this apartment all though I am a peacenik just like you." She begun destroying my apartment with out actually hurting any thing much. She turned all the water on full force in the marble shower. She poured my wine bottle down the sink. She put Coca Cola cans in side McDonald's paper bags and flung them across the kitchen. She snapped up the window shades and kicked the radiator and said, "Are you afraid Super Man is going to fly over here from the Waldorf and kid nap your child? Do you wish to know the truth about Hilary? She is *over protected*. Well, this is not the end, for I am filled with admiration for you when I do not hate you. You got self control."

"I am famous for my control," said I.

"The number 1 sign that a person is growing up," said she, "is their ability to put off in till tomorrow what they use to require right away."

"In many ways I have mastered that ability," I said.

"I wish I had it," she replied. We said "Good night." I walked her down the hall and give her a small kiss by the elevator and she give me in return her Coca Cola can.

3

The scene shifts to Tokyo. On the air plane out of San Francisco I read the following story in 1 of those magazines. It was the only story I read concerning my so called retirement and I borrowed the magazine from the air lines and placed it in my file marked "retirement" and there it laid for several years. The item says I was 40 years of age. I was not 40 until July, 6 months later.

RETIRED. Henry Wiggen, 40, released by the New York Mammoths after 19 years of singular toil; 27th winningest pitcher in baseball history (tied at 247 victories with Joseph J. "Iron Man" McGinnity and John Powell) whose southpaw career spanned Korea and Vietnam and whose popularity fluctuated with the popularity of the wars he opposed; he refused to tour for the entertainment of American troops abroad; he asked General Hugh Weiskopf at a public ceremony in 1969, "Why do you like to kill young boys?" But nobody ever detested him so much as enemy batsmen, past whom he threw a wide assortment of well-controlled pitches. Sometime author of autobiographical volumes (*A Ticket for a Seamstitch, etc.*) he stimulated interest in baseball among readers who had never suspected its human dimension; one of his rules of writing: "If you do not know how to spell a word make your very best guess at it." Shrewd, venturesome, instinctual, he was once characterized by baseball's intellectual Red Traphagen as having "the instincts of a crayfish"; Author Wiggen boasted that he never threw to the wrong base or invested a bad dollar; to his home in Perkinsville, N. Y.

At the air port in Tokyo we were met by Mr. Ishibashi and Mr. Ishima, representing the Oyasumi Cobras. They both talked very good English when they were talking to us but very bad English when they talked to each other. I said they should feel free and talk Japanese to each other, but they said that would be impolite. "You would think we are putting some thing over on you," said Mr. Ishibashi. Holly said, "I already think you are putting 1 over on me since you seem to be unable to tell me where the city of Oyasumi is that I can not find on any map."

"Think of Japan as a dog sitting down with her tail stretched out behind her," said Mr. Ishima, "and Oyasumi is the tip of the tail. It has hot springs and water falls and sandy beaches and has some times been called 'The Sahara of Western Honshu.'"

We met in an American restaurant with Mr. Clubb. "Oyasumi might not be much of a city yet," he said, "but when you get down there and meet the people and size things up you will be charmed off your feet. Do not worry about being forced to eat raw fish. The Japanese baseball industry rest assures me that no American baseball players will be forced to eat raw fish against their will. You will be provided with American food from first to last and you will be provided with long sleeping berths on the trains."

"I been here several times," said I. "I ate raw fish and slept fine on the trains."

"Do not worry about it," said Mr. Clubb, "it will never happen again. The guys and gals of Oyasumi will take the very best care of you. The money is going to be very good. If you insist on a great deal of it being paid under the table you will not need to pay taxes on it to the government of Japan or Uncle Sam. From a tax point of view it is the next best thing to being a waiter in a restaurant." Mr. Clubb told us he had a promising career in baseball and would of made it his line of work if he had not of been so interested in foreign events. If all the people who ever had promising careers in baseball went in to it the leagues would expand to 7,000 cities. He said to Mr. Ishibashi and Mr.

Ishima, "He has thought it over and he will play for you."

Soon 3 American ladies entered the restaurant and presented Holly with a fan with Japanese writing all over it. However, when Holly opened the fan it turned out that the Japanese writing was English after all, and what it said was *Duplicate Bridge.* She was promised a place in the bridge club. She could play bridge night and day while I was on the road with the Oyasumi Cobras. "How ever," said Holly, "I will not be living in Tokyo but in Oyasumi."

"Where is that?" asked 1 of the ladies.

"It is a city in the west," said Mr. Clubb.

"I never heard of it," the lady said.

"You never been out of Tokyo," said Mr. Clubb. "The Wiggenses are on their way to it right now by train."

"Why do they not fly?" the lady asked.

"It has no jet air port," said Mr. Clubb, "although I under stand that 1 is in the process of being built and will be completed any day."

Traveling across Japan 1 of the most frightening things begun happening. In the middle of the night in the inn in Nagoya I arose with the idea of urinating, but when I arrived in the bathroom I was unable to proceed with my plans. I returned to bed. However, the pressure on my bladder continued, and I tried the bath room again, standing for a long time in 1 place while 3 or 4 drops of urine dribbled forth and the pressure on my bladder increased in pain. I felt like God was punishing me for I knew not what. What ever I done He was banging the old gavel and crying out, "3,000 years in Hell or prostrate trouble, take your pick," and I like a fool took the prostrate trouble, for that was what it was.

I decided I would stand there until obtaining some decent results, which by the look of it was libel to be some time. I took a book which Holly was reading, full of pretty pictures of

Japanese people and places and flowers and glass jars and what not and stood for a long time looking at pictures and waiting for some thing to happen. Maybe it was the jet lag. But I rode many 1,000,000's of miles of jet over the years and never stopped urinating. Now and then a drop or 2 appeared and I thought, "Watch out now, folks, here comes the down pour," followed by the most intense pain in my bladder, followed by nothing. You may laugh. But when it happens to you it is some thing else again. Now I suddenly knew what every body was talking about.

Holly called out, "Henry, is some thing the matter?" I did not answer her. "Henry, answer me." I reached around and locked the door. "Henry, that is against the rules," she said, for in our house we got a rule no body locks a bath room door, but I knew of no rule covering Japanese inns and I stood there indefinitely looking at the pictures in the book until at last an actual small *stream* occurred and I cheered like young fellows cheer on a bad ball club if they win 2 in a row.

"Are you having trouble?" called Holly through the door. "Maybe it was the raw fish."

"Go to bed," said I, "you do not piss fish."

"I can not go to bed when you are ill," she said. "Only tell me what the trouble is and I will do every thing I can."

"It is too embarrassing," said I.

"Nothing is too embarrassing," she said. "The older you grow the more embarrassing every thing gets. I am a little worried about some thing my *self*."

"Such as what?" I inquired, opening the bath room door.

"I am just a little bit worried," said she, "because I am wondering if it can be possible that you have a certain amount of blood in your seminal fluid."

"What time is it in New York?" I inquired. I thought I would telephone the doctor.

"Do not panic," said Holly. "There may be medical advice available in Oyasumi." Medical advice in Oyasumi! It makes me laugh when I think of it now. There were slot machines, cards and crap and roulette, liquor, drugs, prostitutes, TV sets, telephones of every color, hot springs, strip teasers of all sexes, dog races, automobile races, motor cycle races, golf tournaments, tennis matches, and the world's most unusual baseball park, but no such a thing as medical advice in Oyasumi. We sat on the side of the bed deciding if we should go back home. In the morning we still couldn't decide and we crossed over from the west bound side of the train station to the east bound side and sat on our suit cases trying to decide some more when simultaneous trains begun arriving from both directions. We crossed back over to the west bound side and continued on to Oyasumi.

Suddenly I was happy again. I don't know why. It was a beautiful day to be gliding through beautiful country and we did not yet have any idea the miserable location we were heading in to. My bladder felt rather well as long as I was sitting down. When I stood up the pressure made me dance. I would rush to the lavatory of the train, where the rail road kept 1 little white rose in a vase hanging from the wall to remind you while you were standing in this stinking little room that some where in the world pretty things grew. Finally I had a little success. Maybe the train shaking helped, and I went back to my seat again in till my bladder felt full again, though it never was. In Oyasumi I felt wonderful. It was the hot springs curing every thing for the moment.

In the Montana Inn in Oyasumi I received a cable from Ben Crowder, the manager of Washington, reading, "Come and play for me if you are serious." I sent him a cable in return reading, "I am always serious and I will drop down and see you as soon as I am back." Ben was never 1 for mixing words. I never knew him very well and the little I knew him I never liked. Later he said he never received my cable. I have a copy of it in front of me, and his to me on the stationery of the Montana Inn showing Japanese girls in towels holding up the globe while flying through the air on a gray hound. When I asked 1 of those very girls why the inn was named for Montana she replied, "It is only because Montana is the most important state."

Nobody wants you in till they hear that some body else wants you. Once I went to Japan people started getting stirred up in the United States. They begun thinking they might of missed something. They begun busting their ass getting a hold of me in western Japan when they could of picked up the telephone and called me in Perkinsville.

I received a cable from Patricia Moors reading, "Henry dear, please phone me when you can," which I stuck in the air plane magazine with the cables. I played ball for her and her father for 21 years in their organization and often had reason to believe they would give me a crack at managing. I thought I would be very good at it. I still think so. I thought it was all in the family. But when the day come to fill the promise the last I seen of her she was sneaking rather fast down the late Dutch Schnell's drive way to her car with her coat flying out behind her, and for that reason I did not plunge madly for the telephone to answer her.

I had fantasies of her, however. I was pitching for Ben Crowder in Washington. It was the September stretch. We were neck and neck with the Mammoths all the way. We are up against the Mammoths in New York. It is do or die and every body I ever knew is watching. I am pitching against the Mammoths and I beat them and Patricia strangles her self with a diamond necklace which I seen an actress name of Lisa Mayflower do in a movie in title *Lonesome*. I remember the movie only because she was a friend of mine. Lisa now sells real estate around Los Angeles. Estimating 8 months in the baseball year, estimating ½ that time on the road, estimating 1 movie a week on the road, I saw more than 300 movies and can not name 6 beyond *Lonesome*.

A few hours after we reached Oyasumi I and Holly were floating like angels in the hot springs when in comes a Japanese inn girl all wrapped in a towel announcing a telephone call. "Will you take your phone in the water?" she inquired, and I said I would, and she come splashing through the water with my telephone.

It was Jerry Divine and Suzanne Winograd. He was in New York and she was in a foreign country. "Do I hear you saying, 'Jerry, just count me in'?" Jerry asked, "because I will be heart broke if you play ball over there instead of announcing with us. Here is the latest, Author. It is an inspiration. Remember that we are 3 blokes in the living room, but we never say more than 1 sentence at a time and we go by turns. Now is the time to get in practice."

"I speak and then you speak," said Suzanne.

Silence. It was my turn to say some thing but I had not yet got the hang of it. I was suppose to say some thing whether I had any thing to say or not. More silence. More more silence. "This is valuable air time," said Suzanne, "so you better say something."

"Suzanne," said Jerry, "you are talking out of turn."

"Maybe this idea will never work," said I.

"That is the boy, Author," said Jerry, "you are catching on."

"Do not play Japanese baseball," said Suzanne.

"You caught me in the hot springs," said I. "What time is it there?"

"Author," said Jerry, "say only 1 sentence at a time."

"Do not sign any thing until you speak again with us," Suzanne said.

"I am speaking with you now," said I.

"Just 5 little words from you and we are signing the biggest 3 way deal in sports casting," said Jerry.

"I spoke to your lawyer about making the old age film in Washington," said Suzanne.

"I hope it works out," said I. "I am curious how much my pay will be for this sports casting."

"Speak only 1 sentence at a time," said Jerry.

"I can see that he will catch on," said Suzanne.

"Just give me a ball park figure," I said.

"It will be upwards of $400,000 for 26 Friday nights," said Jerry.

"And that is a lot of fish," said Suzanne.

"Do I really care to sit through 26 games where I am not even playing?" I inquired. "Is the $400,000 for me or split 3 ways?"

"Author, you got 2 sentences going there," said Jerry. "Please speak only 1 sentence per speech."

"We under stand that Japanese baseball is expanding like mad," said Suzanne.

"Is the $400,000 for me or split 3 ways?" I inquired.

"Good economic times are ahead for all of us," said Jerry.

"So please deliver Jerry those 5 little words," said Suzanne.

"Is the $400,000 for me or split 3 ways?" I inquired.

"Author Wiggen is really asking a probing question there," said Jerry.

"Through out your career you had a reputation for asking probing questions, Author," said Suzanne.

"Do I really care to sit through 26 baseball games?" I inquired.

"Of course you do," said Jerry.

"Why should you not?" asked Suzanne.

"Because I rather play," I said.

"This is Jerry and Suzanne signing off," said Jerry. They rung off.

On the following morning in the hot springs a Japanese inn girl come churning and thrashing and splashing through the water after me announcing that a gentle man was telephoning me from the lobby. "Do you wish a telephone?" she inquired. I did, and she brung it, and it was Mr. Clubb from the American Embassy in Tokyo. "Ha ha," said I, "I thought she said you were here in the inn, it is that old communication problem."

"Ha ha *ha*," he replied, "I *am* here." Mr. Ishibashi and Mr.

Ishima were also there. They had flew from Tokyo. "I thought you said there was no air port here," I said.

"No *jet* air port," said Mr. Clubb. "We flew on a small propellor."

"How has your health been while you have been here?" Mr. Ishibashi inquired.

"It has been fine," I replied, "but I had some difficulty urinating on the way." I was asking every body I knew their advice regarding my problem, and people I got to know slightly better I asked about blood in your seminal fluid.

It was a beautiful, clear, cool day. Not a cloud was in the sky and I was anxious to see the ball park. Mr. Clubb and Mr. Ishibashi and Mr. Ishima were dressed in their finest suits and their shiniest shoes, and in front of the inn a highly polished Lincoln Continental drove up. Behind the wheel was an American ball player name of Henry Cobb, a black fellow living in Oyasumi and doubling as the Cobras' representative in the winter. Him and Mr. Clubb never agreed on a thing. Mr. Clubb said it never got either too hot or too cold in Oyasumi, but Henry Cobb said it got *extremely* hot in the summer and extremely *sandy* in the winter. "Those suits you Tokyo men are wearing," said Henry, "are going to be filled with sand in your pockets in 2 hours."

Cobb was an infielder. He told me where and when he played and I since looked him up in the *Baseball Encyclopedia* and he told me mainly the truth. I do not care so much for a fellow's record, but I look him up for his character. If he tells me the truth in 1 matter he might tell me in an other. "I hit against you a couple times," he said. "I hit a soft fly ball to center field. You changed up on me."

"I do that," said I.

"Well," said Mr. Clubb, "if this is not all the races of the world in 1 car."

"Not all the races," said Holly, "but all the sexes." I seen that she did not like what she was seeing out the window.

Henry Cobb was a great Big 10 school athlete, the Univer-

sity of Purdue. Then some body sold him bad advice, he give up
school, accepted a bonus, rushed in to the professional life and
very soon saw that he was not about to make it big. "They
guaranteed me I was a sure thing," he said, "which as you can
see, if you can pardon the expression, was a sample of bull shit."

"From what you tell me," said I, "I believe I wasted the
change up on you. I could of blew the fast 1 past you."

He laughed. "You are as right as rain," he said. "I could of
hit the fast ball if you threw it down the middle but I would of
been standing waiting yet for that, would I not?" He was now
driving us along a wide street with nothing much on it. "Yet
this," he said, "is Main Street."

"Oh no," said Mr. Clubb, "this is not Main Street."

"Then show me where Main Street is," said Henry Cobb.
"This is as main as any other. I been here 2 years and can not find
Main Street though I looked."

"Cobb," said Mr. Clubb, "you talk too much."

"You have got to break the news to them some time,"
Henry Cobb replied.

"We can see what we are seeing," said Holly.

We talked about the difficulty of urination in till Mr. Clubb
said, "I am wondering if that is the subject we come to discuss."

"When you have got such difficulties," I replied, "it gets in
the way of your earlier plans."

"Please show us where your hospital is," Holly requested.

"There is a large and beautiful map in the inn," said Mr.
Ishibashi, "showing the location of the hospital."

"Yet now that we are up and around," said Holly, "we might
as well see the hospital as the map."

"The map was completed before the hospital," said Mr.
Ishibashi.

"What he is trying to tell you," said Henry Cobb, "is that the
hospital is some time in the future."

"I my self would be interested in seeing your residential
section of town," I said.

"There is residential and then again residential," said Henry

Cobb, driving along. "Every thing you are passing every minute is residential."

It looked like pure desert to me.

"You under stand," said Henry Cobb, "by residential I am speaking of the residences of field mice, desert rats, and snakes small and large."

"There are no snakes in Japan," said Mr. Clubb.

"There are mighty big worms," said Henry Cobb.

"I do not think Hilary would recognize this as a big league city," said I to Holly.

"Does the city support the ball club?" Holly asked.

"What city?" asked Henry Cobb.

"The city of Oyasumi," she replied.

"There is no city of Oyasumi," Cobb replied, "only mice, rats, and snakes."

"You see," said Mr. Ishima, "we are an expansion club like your American expansion clubs."

"To expand," said I, "you have got to have a city to expand *in to.*"

"You see," said Mr. Ishima, "the big money we are making we are making on the road."

"But the *very* big money we are making we are making from TV," said Mr. Clubb, "and when you play ball for us you will be making very big money, too. You always drew crowds in Japan and now you will draw them more than ever on TV due to your stand on Vietnam. I am told that no body drew crowds like you since Lefty O'Doul. Give us time to build up the city."

"Oyasumi was not built in a day," said Holly.

"Almost," said Mr. Clubb. "This place went up so fast there is no telling what they forgot."

"I do not know about that," said Holly, "as I can name a few things they forgot such as schools, parks, play grounds, medical advice, trees, shrubs, bushes, post office, grocery stores, animal hospitals, bicycle shops, banks, churches, places to buy roller skate keys, places to have your ice skates sharpened, street signs, shoe makers, and main streets."

My stomach sunk deeper and deeper to think about spending any time there. You could not live there unless you lived all your life in the inn. The more we rode around the more anxious I become to leave Oyasumi behind.

And then, in a twinkling of your eye, the whole scene changed. I mean the ball park. We come over a hill and there it was, a dream, a fantastic ball park, splendid and beautiful. I am always thrilled to see a ball park, but this was special yet, a fine old fashion ball park with here and there a Japanese touch, a line, a shape you would not see in America, and Mr. Clubb looked at me and smiled and said, "Now you can see what the shouting been about." We entered. Mr. Clubb led us, walking backwards, facing us, like he was a band leader and we were the marching band. The grass was artificial, but the best I ever saw, quite up to date, and Henry Cobb said to me, "You will not only make a lot of money here but have a ball besides. You will win many games, over hand fast balling these small fellows to death."

"I won only 3 games in America last year," said I, gazing around the ball park. There was some thing wrong with the park, beautiful as it was.

"You will win 13 here," he said. "I am a 200 hitter in America. I hit 290 here last year. From the point of view of the Japanese hitter your fast ball will be coming down on them out of the second story window."

"It is no place to bring a child," said Holly.

"I might come by my self," I said.

"I know you might," said Holly, for she knew I was fond of the hot springs and all the young ladies dashing through the steam. "And do not forget to bring your catheter."

"You and I can have a lot of fun here," said Henry Cobb to me.

Now I seen what was wrong. We were standing near the pitching hill. Every thing was where it ought to been except that there were no seats. No, there were 500 seats behind home plate, but that was all. "Do you play in silence?" I inquired.

"You get use to it," said Henry Cobb, "like you get use to being black."

"They run a sound track on the TV," said Mr. Clubb.

"Fabulous," said I. Holly was smiling, looking at me. She knew I could not go for this.

"Fabulous is the word all right," said Mr. Clubb. "It is marvelous beyond words what they can do with their sound track. They can switch on cheers, they can switch on clapping, they can switch on stamping or chanting or singing or what ever the situation calls for. They can switch on the sound of a fan calling out an insult or a blessing in a Tokyo accent or an Osaka accent or a Hiroshima accent. I tell you that you will be living in the land of geniuses. When I am watching the Cobra games on TV you would never know that they are playing in an empty stadium. They got 7,000 ways of making 500 people look like 75,000. You would think you were in an actual place. Name it and they can do it. Can you wonder why I am enthusiastic about these people?"

"It would be a new thing to me," said I, "no noise, no children hanging over the rail waving a piece of paper in your face, though I suppose they could pipe in the smell of hot franks and cigars."

"I am returning to my inn," said Holly. "Henry, please drive me back." Henry Cobb she meant, but Henry Wiggen went along, too, and Mr. Clubb and Mr. Ishibashi and Mr. Ishima, and we all drunk some excellent Japanese wine with a fine dinner and lots of laughs, and Mr. Clubb from the Embassy said, "I did not think you would."

I telephoned home. I noticed that all my daughters sounded the same except Hilary. "Hilary did not scream once since you were gone," some body said to me.

"I will never scream again," said Hilary.

"Father is not too well," said Holly. "He has a problem in his urinary track. We are wondering if it might be his prostrate."

"I am wondering if the girls really require so much technical information," said I to Holly.

"I think it does no harm giving them all the technical information on every subject," she said. "We always did."

"Then you have forgot to discuss the seminal fluid," said I in a some what sarcastic tone of voice.

"If you wish to talk to each *other*," said 1 of my daughters, "why not hang up the phones and talk and call back when you are free?"

"Are you in the same room?" some body inquired.

"Spell the name of the disease you are having," said Hilary, "and I will read about it in the Encyclopedia Britannica."

"I think of you all the time," said I to my daughters.

"What good does it *do* me that you think of me all the time?" Hilary inquired. "I have many facts about Japan if you would care to hear some although I can not find Oyasumi on any map."

"Telling you the truth, sweet heart," said I in my stupidity, "1 of the things wrong with Oyasumi is that it is not yet actually a place. It is no wonder they have not put it on the map."

"Are you telling me that you do not plan to play in the big leagues in Japan?" inquired Hilary.

"I am afraid that that is what I am telling you," said I.

A silence followed while my words flew ½ way around the world and registered on Hilary's brain, and when they did she begun screaming. She screamed for 5 minutes. Holly hung up her telephone and laid on the bed with a pillow over her head. "You *must* call home. Why? Why did she need to know your plans *now*? Hang it up."

"I can not hang it up while she is screaming," I said, and I my self begun screaming across the Pacific Ocean, "Michele! Rosemary! Millicent! Some body! Any body! Can not any body do any thing?"

"*You* can not do any thing when *you* are here," replied 1 of my daughters, "why do you expect 1 of us to do some thing?"

"Tell her it is not true," another of my daughters cried out to me across the ocean. "Tell her a lie! Lie to her for once! Tell her it was a slip of your tongue. You *are* going to play ball, you are, you are."

"Hilary," I called, "I am going to play ball again. I forgot to tell you. I have just changed my mind. I received a cable from a man in Washington, D. C., and I am going to play there for him, Ben Crowder."

"That is better," said Holly.

"I hate to lie," said I.

"Hate to lie?" said Holly. "Since when do you hate to lie? Tell her a few lies and save wear and tear on our nerves. You lie to me, you lie to the doctor, you lie to the Internal Revenue Service and the State of New York so why not lie to Hilary?"

"I never tell a lie of importance," said I. *"Never break a promise to a child.* It is 1 of the posters of Dr. Schiff."

"Oh, yes, Dr. *Schiff*," said Holly, "if you can not tell a lie tell me how many times you fucked Miss Cunt Off the Street the mental physician."

I felt that I was now engaged in a small argument with ladies of my family on 2 sides of the ocean. Where should I turn first? "Hilary," said I.

"Mental physician to the world of sports," said Holly.

Hilary gradually calmed down and soon stopped screaming. "Is it final?" she inquired.

"I am afraid that it definitely is," I said. "I could lie to you and tell you other wise but you know that I would never do that."

"I mean is Washington final?" she inquired.

"I am going to finalize it as soon as I am home," said I, although I did not have any guarantee of any thing.

According to her sisters Hilary never screamed between the time Holly and I left Oyasumi and the time we returned home. It was early on a Sunday morning when we drove in to Perkinsville, feeling like 8 at night. "My body is on Japanese time," I said.

"Then your body is snapping back slower than it use to," said Holly, "for you and your body use to arrive home at the same time. It is also clear to me that your body is less romantic than it use to be, for in the past, if you recall, we made love many times in the hot springs of Japan."

"I recall," said I, "but never before were the bottom of the hot springs littered with beer bottles and other types of beverage cans. The older I grow the more I go in for the old fashion bed."

In front of the house was new snow. It froze hard and the handle of my snow shovel was barely sticking out above the drift. Some child or other hung a blue wool hat like a flag on the handle of the shovel, and I jumped from the car and run up the snow drift and grabbed the hat with out losing a step, and down the other side. "Only a man in the very best shape could run up and down like that," said I to Holly.

"I am sure you are in the very best shape," said she, "barring certain urinary difficulties and related factors."

"There are no related factors," said I. "I am at the top. I am going to get on with Washington and win games for him down there. You are as young as you feel."

"No," said Holly, "you are as young as Nature says."

"I am talking back to Nature," said I.

"But will Nature listen?" she inquired.

Hilary was asleep. Her room was still full of books open at Japan, and on her bulletin board was a photo in title *Japanese Cherry Trees in Bloom*. After awhile she woke up, but she remained in her room a long time. "How come?" I inquired, for in the past she rushed out to see what I brang her.

"It will only be some thing from Japan," she said, "and I am too heart broke to think about Japan," and now and then through out the day she cried, which was better than screaming.

"You matured a great deal in the short time we were away," said I.

"I believe I am honestly trying," she said.

"You know," said I, "many thoughts been passing through my mind on the way home. For 1 thing, you do not need to go to

Japan to see Japanese cherry trees blossoming, since I have saw them over the years in Washington. Time and again, coming north with the ball club in the spring, we seen Japanese cherry trees passing through. I can tell you there is no more beautiful sight in creation."

"You use to say the most beautiful sight in creation was the sight of a hitter swinging and missing," said Hilary.

"Cherry trees rank right up there with that," I replied.

"There is no such a thing as a substitute for ancient Japan," she said.

"I am not so sure Oyasumi was *ancient* Japan," said I. "It is no place for children. You might as well live in Las Vegas."

"I am available at any time for Washington, D. C.," she said.

"I assume you are not yet back in school," I said.

"I do not seem to be wanted there," she said. "Many people consider me a mischief and trouble maker."

"Many people consider me a mischief and trouble maker, too," said I.

"I never been up the Washington Monument," said Hilary. "Michele, Rosemary, and Millicent all been up the Washington Monument at least once, Rosemary twice, and Michele at least twice, but I never been up it."

"I am going to try and work things out and get back to you," said I. "We will go down soon and look it over 1 way or the other. By the way," I continued, "I am wondering what you might of mentioned to mother about Dr. Schiff. Did you say that she stood the night in the apartment?"

"Yes," said Hilary, "because I could smell her in the morning."

"I can smell *onions* in the morning in that apartment," I said, "but that does not mean that the onions are still there. In fact, the onions are gone. They are down your stomach."

"You are being perfectly logical," said Hilary.

"Well then," said I, "please do so your self here after when reviewing the day's events with mother."

* * *

For 21 years if I had the slightest ache or pain the New York Mammoths Baseball Club become immediately concerned. Some body made sure I was saw by the doctor. In those days you could get a message right through the organization. No body said to me, "I thought some body told you" or "I told some body tell you" or "It was very busy around the office that day." Oh no, they checked me through in those days and did not rest in till they had the doctor's report back in their hand.

Lately the doctor I been seeing was Frank Pointer, for the club thought high of him and his location was convenient to my apartment. I would enter his waiting room, his nurse run and got him, he would come forward from his examining room, he shook my hand, he said in a loud voice through out the waiting room, "Henry Wiggen is here for his health."

Now, however, when he come forward from his examining room he shook my hand and said in a low voice to me, "Author, you know that you are now off the Christmas list."

"It is hardly a secret," I said.

"You under stand what I am driving at," he said. "Nothing personal is meant."

"I under stand every thing," said I.

"Well," said he, "some people take it hard."

"I am taking it hard," I said, "but I still under stand it."

"All right," said he, raising his voice again. "Nurse, Henry Wiggen is here for his health. He is off the Christmas list and is therefore a new patient. How do you do, Mr. Wiggen."

I filled out various forms and papers for his nurse, and also for the nurse of his brother, Dr. Howard Pointer, dentist. They shared the same office and they were jolly fellows chattering and laughing a lot. I liked them. If I went to see Frank his brother always popped his head in and said "Hello" and visa versa. We went back in his examining room and he asked me why I was there. I told him of my urinary experiences in Japan. I also told him the difficulties *went away* in the hot springs, and he shook his head like he under stood it perfectly while at the same time he kept pulling on these big rubber gloves because no matter how well he under stood it he was also planning to *feel* it and *see* it and what not.

"Is that the whole story?" he inquired.

"Pretty much," said I.

"What little interesting details have you left out?" Dr. Frank Pointer inquired.

"Did you ever hear of any body with blood in their seminal fluid?" I inquired.

"Certainly," said he. "Dracula."

"My wife says I lie to you," I said.

"I have caught you in several," he said. "Do you find your self getting up nights to urinate?"

"Some times," I truthfully replied. I guess the point was to cure it and not lie about it.

"I could of told you that," he said, "so continue telling me the truth. How is the force of your stream? Would you say it is like it always was or down some what or down a great deal?"

"Down some what," I replied.

"I am guessing that you have got a some what in large pros-trate gland which might or might not some day require surgery. This is very normal in younger older men like your self."

"Younger older," said I. "Well, now that you know what it is you can put away those gloves since there is no need to go up there."

"You are incorrect," he said, pulling on his rubber gloves tighter than ever and chatting away about this and that, asking all sorts of questions with out expecting any answer, while I am meanwhile bent over head above heels with my ass in the air and it was very pain full. "Now I am exploring the area," he said.

"I never could of guessed," said I.

"Done," he said. "My guess was correct, I am sure. What you have got there is a certain amount of over population in Prostrate City. This causes a traffic jam through the canal where the Precious Golden Cleansing Fluid is being carried down from Old Bladdersville to Genital Corners and out."

"As a father of 4," said I, "you could just call the parts by their names."

"Yes," said he, "you are a big boy now. I remember when you were a father of no body and never dreamed about prostrate trouble."

"What about the blood in the seminal fluid?" I inquired.

"It is undoubtably caused by some sort of an infection resulting from the over population in Prostrate City," Dr. Pointer replied. "It will clear up with some nice little pills I will give you."

"How will I know if it does?" I asked.

"Inquire among your friends," he replied.

"What brings on prostrate trouble?" I inquired.

"Time," he said. "I have saw it happen sooner in the case of a person sitting too long in 1 place."

"I sat 47 hours talking in the radio when my daughter was high jack," said I.

"I remember that," he said. "You had some thrilling experiences in your life and now it is over. The high jack, the girl with the weapon system, the war, the general and all that and a lot of exciting baseball games. The way it is now you should not experience any loss of activity. You will learn to adjust your system to it. From time to time you will become impatient with the long time it takes you to urinate, which from what you tell me all ready been the case. Stand right up to it and think good thoughts. Keep a little handy dandy reading on the tank of the bath room fixture."

"*Bath room fixture*," said I.

"Right," he said. "I forgot. You are the fellow that got 4 daughters and calls things by their name. Toilet. Keep a cassette in the bath room and switch it on to your favorite music. Play tapes of old ball games that appeal to you, such as some of your own victories close to your memory. Do not read pornographic literature as it causes excitement without gratification, which is bad for the prostrate gland. My goodness but it is complicated. I tell you, you got more systems in you than Bell Telephone. Infection can be caused by the bowels as well. Explain to me why God in His wisdom placed the jewelry so close to the Out Basket."

"What does the prostrate gland do," I inquired, "besides slow traffic between the bladder and the penis?"

"I am glad my nurse did not hear you speak like that," said he. "Why, I am happy to explain it to you between gentle men. God made the prostrate gland to store the sperm. He probably realized it would get in the way of the shipments of the Precious Golden Cleansing Fluid coming down the ways, but He had so many god dam things to pack in there He was frantic all ready and worried about catching His air plane. What He could not fit in just right he shoved down and slammed the lid. This causes 1 thing you might some time notice, and that is that urination is easier directly after a sexual experience, due to the emptying of sperm from the prostrate gland. Unfortunately it is not practical to enjoy a sexual experience prior to every urination. Now, a very clever thing He done was He made these sexual experiences *fun* if possible. While the average person is having *fun* the net result is the increasing population, which He wants because without increasing population business goes to hell, doctors and dentists got no patients and baseball players got no fans to watch them play. So you have got to take care of your prostrate gland in order to reproduce the race. However, if God put it to you in those words, saying, 'Take care of the prostrate gland to keep the race increasing' no body would pay any attention to Him. They would have the trouble some prostrate gland took out the minute it caused trouble, like their wisdom tooth or their appendix. They would say, 'What do I care about the reproduction of the race, leave George do it,' whereas as long as it is *fun* they are not going to be all that quick to have it took out. You have *fun,* God gets His *numbers,* the waiting room is full, the ball park is full, children got parents and parents got children and every body is happy."

"I am certainly relieved in my mind that it is nothing more serious," said I, "and I thank you for every thing."

"What are you going to do with your self now?" Dr. Pointer inquired.

"I am planning to join another ball club," I said.

"Join who?"

"Leave us wait for the official announcement," I said. "I been requested to handle it that way."

"Perfectly under stood," he said. "I know that you all ways loved the game and were all ways a credit to it. I am not sur-, prised that you will be remaining close to baseball. I will be scanning the news for further details."

"Do you think I can do it?" I inquired.

"Of *course* you can," he replied. "I am surprised to think that you have any question about your old confidence. In what capacity?"

"To play," said I.

"Oh," said he, "to *play*. No, I do not think you can do it."

4

Here is a sentence you can say 2 ways. Numbers of parents with difficult children asked me over the years how I first got in touch with Dr. Schiff. Numbers of difficult parents asked me over the years how I first got in touch with Dr. Schiff. They often ask for her telephone number, which I am pleased to give out on request.

I first heard about her from Ev McTaggart, who become manager of the New York Mammoths after the death of Dutch Schnell and been so ever since. Ev caught for us for several years and probably could of played longer but preferred becoming coach, and so he coached for us for several years, and then Dutch died. Ev's career was baseball. Some of us go on to other things and some of us can not and I do not know which is best.

My last year with the ball club Hilary was at the height of her fits of screaming. She had took it up in a big way, believe me. Holly and I thought it would pass like every thing else, all our daughters went in fits in 1 direction or another, they done bad or stupid things from time to time, they got over it and never done them again. I become an expert on the time tables of young girls. If I heard a fellow say, "Holy Jesus, we sent our daughter to a school, she stole the chocolate supply and run away," I replied, "It sounds to me like your daughter is 13 and 3/8 years old and is 7½ pounds over weight. Leave a light in the window and she will return home at age 13 and ½."

However, Hilary's fits of screaming did not pass away like every thing else. The opposite. They grew more frequent, longer, and louder. In the beginning she screamed or cried or stamped her foot like any ordinary child, refusing to take "No" for an answer. Of course we are all that way now and then and we out grow it. Dogs and cats have got to be trained, but human beings grow out of it and become reasonable, and so did Hilary grow reasonable from her own point of view, saying to her self, "If I wish to watch TV until 3 o'clock in the morning there is 1 reasonable way to get my wish." By screaming. She could make your skin crawl with her screaming, she could rip you down the spine, plus which she had fabulous *endurance,* she could scream for 10 or 15 minutes and enjoy herself and get her way besides. It go so I just as soon give her the world as hear her go on. I emptied my pockets. I give her my car to drive back and forth in the drive way at age 9. I give her a telephone credit card so she could call her friend in Hawaii and the Petrotones in Los Angeles and the editors of the Encyclopedia Britannica in Chicago, London, and Toronto. (I see where they now got a ball club in Toronto.)

She begun to look worse and worse compared to her sisters. Michele was extremely selfish in till at a certain age she grew out of it and become the world of co operation, and Rosemary painted obscene words on the cellar walls and grew out of it, and Millicent sulked and refused to smile at man, woman, child, beast, or teachers in till 1 Sunday after noon at 2 o'clock sharp she begun smiling a little and soon give every sign of becoming a reasonable person.

Hilary, however, made no forward progress prior to the year 1971. She went backward, continuing backward at a rapid rate. This was on my mind 1 day near the end of summer when I fell in to conversation with Ev McTaggart, who was coaching then, and he give me a wink and a smile like him and I knew some thing no body else knew. "You know, Ev," said I, "I do not mean to be rude, but you always give me this wink and smile

like you know some thing. Now, do you know some thing or not
which will be help full to my family?"

I forget where this was. I remember that we sat down on a
couple chairs in a hotel lobby, but I forget the city. "Here was
our experience," he said. "We got 4 or 5 like you."

"4," said I.

"Our number 4 is a girl."

He told me her name but I do not remember it. I got no
memory for the name of other people's children, although I am
quite fond of them when I meet them.

"So 1 day I come home off the road and the wife comes
rushing out the house at me screaming to the effect that Number 4 was *forced* by a certain neighbor child to swallow 9 pennies,
so of course we rush Number 4 to the hospital while the wife is
crying and ringing her hands. The X ray shows nothing. Nothing shows nothing. The doctor says, 'Are you sure this kid is not
some kind of a crack brained liar since she been here before on
these false alarms if you will remember?' O. K., I decided I
would check in to it. You know me, I am a man that looks
before I leap. I tell Number 4 tell me again the name of the
neighbor child that forced her to swallow them pennies, but
there was no such neighbor child with in 1,000 miles and the 9
pennies in question were still on the table in the breakfast room
where they been sitting for days and days waiting for another 1
to join them and make them a dime. The wife cried and was
extremely depressed. Here was a child that lied and lied and lied
and got us all in to all sorts of trouble. At least 5 times in the
past we fell out with neighbors due to the lies of Number 4. A
certain party recommended us to Dr. Schiff and she said, 'Bring
that dirty mouth lying brat in and we will get to the bottom of
it.' I wondered about that way of talking, but some body said oh
no, that is how she does, she is a whizard with children, she
solved ours and she will solve yours unless it is clear cut *brain
damage*."

"If she cured Number 4 of lying she might cure Hilary of
screaming," said I.

"She is also expensive," said Ev, giving me a wink and a smile, but she wasn't all that expensive, either. 1 man's expensive is another man's bargain. I will admit she looked expensive, which a great many people in New York look, until when you get to know them they prove to be expensive in 1 department and cheap in another. I give her a call. "You," she said, "I thought you were the soul of health."

"It is not me, it is my daughter," said I.

"I doubt that," she said. "It is more likely you. Send me a copy of your books and come in the office in 2 weeks with your wife and your daughter and we will get to the bottom of all this hysterical madness as quick as we can."

"*If* she can," said Holly. She would not go. "I do not believe she can tell me any thing I do not know, and I do not believe she can tell you any thing either. I think the reason you are going is because Ev McTaggart told you she was an expensive woman."

"She cured Ev's kid," said I.

"Maybe she cured *Ev*," said Holly.

As a result I went on our first visit alone, sitting in the waiting room with various little girls and their mothers, or in 1 or 2 cases their personal maids or tooters since their mothers and their fathers were too busy to take them, or playing tournaments far away. I never saw a father there, and Ev never saw 1 either, never saw a *man* there you might as well say, never an uncle or a brother or a friend. The first day I was there I met Suzanne Winograd in the waiting room. Suzanne's personal situation was similar to mine but reversed. She had several years of good competition in her, but she hated the game and every body in it, she was trapped. She had financial problems, romantic problems, marital problems, and parental problems, to hear her tell it. Her daughter Bertilia sat beside her giving me a look as if to say, "I have heard all this before and you too will soon be tired of it." However, I never become tired of Suzanne. We were very good friends. We played tennis together and golf together and in the years since we have passed little jobs to each other in film work and TV and such.

"I can not quit the god dam game because I am the sole support of 15 people," said Suzanne, "and 3 of them is this child's father."

The child looked at me to see how I took it. "Explain your self a little," said I to Suzanne.

"This is the waiting room," said Bertilia. "Explain nothing. The *doctor's* office is in side."

"I am *ruled* by this child," said Suzanne. "I could scream."

"You often do," said Bertilia.

"Do not bring up screaming," said I. "That is my very own problem."

"Your wife screams?" Suzanne inquired. "I do not blame her with you gone on the road many months of the year. If I was her I would strap you to the clothes line and keep you there and take you in at night."

"I believe he means his child screams," said Bertilia. "Probably a daughter if I under stand the scene."

"He knows what he means," said Suzanne, speaking very angrily to her daughter. Then suddenly she grabbed a hold of her daughter and called her "my little chipmunk" and kissed her. "You do not know how deeply I love my daughter," she said.

"When she thinks about it," said Bertilia.

"Get back in line," said Suzanne to Bertilia.

"Get back in line your self," said Bertilia.

By this they meant that the mother should behave like the mother and the daughter should behave like the daughter. This was what they ended with after months with Dr. Schiff. It was their poster on the wall in the doctor's office.

Get Back in Line

"When they first come to me," said Dr. Schiff, "Suzanne wore shorts and pig tails, Bertilia wore a dress. I argued the pig tails off the mother back on to the child. They were ready to fall off the edge when they walked in that door, but you can see now that they are almost sane. I am making Suzanne stand up to the world like a grown woman. All her life she took orders from agents and managers and husbands past and present, but now at last she is talking back to them and getting her fair share of things. In your case you are ahead of the game. Your daughter screams. I am not worried when the child screams as long as the adult does not simply scream back."

"We are back in line," said I.

"Then why did you come here? What makes you think you need me? Have you tried smashing her in the mouth? This time of day I am up to my chin with children and especially with their parents who are the cause of it all. It sounds to me like your wife is the smart 1 of the family."

"If you are at the jagged end of the day," said I, "how about we go and have a drink?"

"A wonderful idea," said she. "Talking all day makes a person dry," and up she got from her chair and dropped from sight for a moment, returning with 2 cans of Coca Cola. This was her idea of going and having a drink. "Tell me all about baseball," she said.

"I know too much about the subject to tell you in an hour," said I.

"I understand that you have played baseball for a long time and are not very good at it any more," said she.

"I would not state it exactly that way," said I. "I can still get people out. I pitch here and there. It is an odd thing, but for 2 innings at a time nobody can score on me much at all. I can do every thing I ever did but I can only do it for $2/9$ of the time."

"You are talking about baseball and not about fucking," she said.

I was quite surprised by those words. "My goodness," said I, "but you have certainly got the knack of speeding up a discussion in a hurry."

"It is the Coca Cola," she said. "If I shocked you I apologize. The reason you are being such a brute to Hilary and making her scream all the time is because she is not a boy. You are taking it out on her for not being a son."

"No such a thing," said I. "If I did not have such good recommends on you I would think you were slightly goofy your self."

"I *am*," she said. "You have got to be 1 to see through them. You wished to have a son to carry on the tradition of playing baseball in your family like your father before you."

"Wrong," said I.

"Probably so," she said. "I took my information out of your book in title *The Southpaw*."

"It sounds to me like you barely read beyond the first chapter," said I.

"Right," she said. "I launch in to Chapter 2 tonight. What are you doing tonight?"

"I am playing baseball tonight," I replied.

"Maybe I will watch you," she said, "if you will really *play*. You have not played in 2 weeks. I have hardly even saw you throw a ball. You run around in the outfield catching flies before hand then you sat down all evening on the bench smiling and laughing with the manager."

"We are old friends," I said. "I played ball for him for 19 years. I will tell you what I will do. Tonight I will throw in the bull pen and give you a chance to see me throw. How would you like that?"

"Then I will be seeing you at your work," she said.

"Not really," I said. "You will be seeing me warming up for the work I use to do but do not do too often any more."

"Maybe he will rush you in to the game at the last minute to save the day," said she.

"Save the night," said I.

"I will," said she, "for you. Where will we meet?"

"I will put a pass in the pass gate for you," said I.

"Do you mind if I look at you through my opera glasses?" she inquired. "Can you imagine my poor mother give me those glasses to go to the opera with to see wonderful singers and instead I am looking at ball players."

"Dress up warm," I said.

To keep warm she wore a fur coat and drunk plenty of ice cold Coca Cola. Shortly after the game begun I went down in the bull pen and begun throwing a little. I believe that at that point I had hardly threw a ball in a week and had no special desire to, nothing was happening, the ball club was no where, and I was really sunk in spirits. I don't know why. It was a cold, damp night, foggy and misty and very quiet. The seats were empty. It was the end of the season.

This kid Beansy Binz was in the bull pen throwing some soreness out of his $400,000 arm. He was extremely courteous to me, but never the less I felt this terrific feeling of anger towards him which I kept under perfect control. Him and another young pitcher were tugging and pulling at each other and laughing and bragging, and when I walked in the gate they straightened up and squared away like 2 kids in school. They had all this energy. They would be back next year, no question of that, nothing was behind, every thing was ahead, they were healthier than baboons, quick on their feet, quick with their hands, quick with their eyes, and full of respect for me to my face. "You are a stranger out here," said Beansy Binz.

"I just thought I might throw a little," I said, and I begun throwing. I felt extremely foolish. Why was I doing this? When I sat down he asked the same question, "Why are you throwing?" like I had some intelligent reason in mind. He was a very smart young fellow.

"I told a friend I would," I said.

"I see," he said, looking around in the seats like he might see who I was throwing for. He said to the other young pitcher, "He just told a friend he would," and they shook their heads together. I am sure they thought some very distinguished person was in the stands. They would not think I was throwing for some young woman. They would think I was throwing for the Chief Justice of the Supreme Court or the Archbishop of Babylonia. Young fellows nod their head and believe every word I say with out under standing it. They know that I must be right, and they even tell me so, but they then go on doing every thing their own way. I do not believe there is any point in trying to make them do different until they learn for them self, which is why I believe I was never made a manager. I could never teach any body any thing by *telling*, I could only say, "Watch me and suit it to your self."

Right at this point Beansy made a suggestion to me that would be very important up ahead. I can not imagine why I never thought it up my self. "You know," said Beansy, "if you do not mind me being personal, I would think you could go on playing ball for years and years. You are in tip top physical. You are a team man. You got the winning spirit. You got a wide variety of pitches left besides the fast ball. Sure, some thing has been took off the fast ball, but you got plenty yet to mix up. Now here is the main idea. If I am being too personal just stop me. Why not pitch relief? Why do pitchers think it is a step down in life to go from starting to relief? I am just a young fellow and I know I am not suppose to know any thing, and I can hardly believe I am talking to you as free as all this, but you as a relief pitcher will save many games per year and *probably win a pennant*."

"Yes," I said, "I been turning it over in my mind my self." I should not of said that. I should of thanked him. I got up and begun throwing some more to a young catcher there. Catchers always enjoyed catching me. No surprises. They put up their glove and I threw the ball in it and that was that. I threw off and on for 5 or 6 innings and right about then the telephone rung and it was Dutch and he asked for me and he said in the phone, "Why are you standing up this time of the night?"

"Keeping warm on a cool night," said I.

"Come in and pitch if you feel loose," he said, and the next inning I went in and pitched. This woke the ball park up a little. It was a bonus. During the year I pitched several Sundays, I was announced ahead, and I brung out a crowd. When a ball club is not winning people will pay for 2 things. They will come out for free prizes, Jacket Night, Jacket Day, Batting Glove Day, Camera Day, Hat Night, all those awful events, or they will come out and see a famous celebrity, especially if they think you are on your last legs. When you are on the way out they love you. When you are just breaking in with a big promise they love you. But during the many years you are merely doing a fine job at your work they hate you. I hate the fans. I really do. I never made any bones about it.

It was the seventh inning and the score was tied 4–4 or 5–5, it felt like that, and I never really felt better in my life than I felt that night, which was a night in the middle of the week in the middle of September in a cold ball park in front of maybe 9,000 people including my new friend in her fur coat keeping warm with Coca Cola. I never enjoyed pitching more. I never felt it was ever more worth the while, it was perfect, it was wonderful, it made more sense to me than it ever made before in all the years. I enjoyed every pitch of it while I was doing it, knowing what I was doing and why. It was a dream like feeling.

The ball done what I told it. The only thing it could not do was go fast. My fast ball come up nothing, like when you change your mind at the last second. If I got a strike on the hitter I knew I could get him out. It was like a game. True, it was only a 2 inning game and I could still mix in 1 fast ball in a 2 inning game, and that helped. I could soon get the second strike, too, because when they had 1 strike they begun going after curve balls if that was all I was going to throw them, no sense waiting for the fast ball. I kept throwing further out, or I threw it lower or higher than he really wished, cutting the corners very fine. The benefit of the doubt was on my side, and they swung at bad pitches.

I got 5 men out. They were convinced I would throw nothing but curves. Up come a big chap that was going to hit curve balls then if that was all I planned on throwing. He fouled several off. I then threw a fast ball unexpected and he swung late and shook his head and run off. I learned I could get away with 1 fast ball unexpected every 2 innings.

We scored 2 runs in the bottom of the eighth inning. A kid hit for me. When the name of the kid was announced the crowd booed and he looked back in the dugout like the whole bottom fell out of every thing he ever knew or under stood about life. Then he under stood they were not booing him but booing Dutch for taking me out of the ball game. I sat down beside Dutch, and he punched me on the thigh and he said, "I seen you sucked in your breath," meaning I knew I might of made a bad mistake throwing the fast ball at that final boy.

"Yes," I said, "a person got to be careful when they got no fast pitch."

"Count your stars," said Dutch. "Most pitchers live their whole life that way," and after a bit I got up and went back and got dressed. It was my third victory of the season, it was the last baseball game I ever played for the New York Mammoths Baseball Club, Inc., and the last conversation I ever held with Dutch Schnell.

5

Every January I go to New York and see my lawyer and we discuss many interesting matters, beginning with money. The main subject was usually the income tax, but 1 year we drew up a will and another year we set up trust funds for the girls and so forth. This particular year we discussed ways and means of living with out a definite salary as well as ways and means of living without a husband, for her husband recently died.

"So you have retired," she said.

"I was released," said I.

"Either way you are no longer receiving a salary," she said, "and so you are starting a second life and so am I."

"I am hoping to get back on salary again," I said. "I am hoping to catch on with another ball club."

"Who?" she inquired.

"Maybe Washington," I replied. "Maybe California."

"Doing what?" she inquired.

"Playing," I replied.

"I under stand," she said, and I know that she did. She under stood every thing very well for as long as I knew her, which was 20 years now. A fellow recommended her to me when I barely broke in, saying "You are going to need a lawyer for the complicated life you are going to lead," and I went to her, saying "I need a lawyer." "For what?" she inquired, but I had no particular case in mind, and she laughed so hard she leaned against me to keep her self from falling down, or so I thought, for I was much younger in those days. She owned a $15,000 piano which impressed me.

"Over the years," she said, "I been gathering thoughts for this very occasion. I wish you would not think about playing, since every dollar in salary you earn is more trouble than it is worth. You should of retired 3 years ago when you could at least got a few pennies out of a dollar. Every 3 months the Government rips you off for what ever little scrapings might be left in your account."

"But I still got some playing in me," I said.

"What about a baseball *school?*" Barbara inquired. "A person suggested such an idea to me. It sounds very perfect to me since it can always be a financial loss to you. You can travel around meeting people, coming and going at home and abroad in search of students. By losing sufficient money you can square your account with the Government and have more fun doing it than by simply paying them direct."

"I been thinking about a winery," I said, for that was when I first thought about a winery. "A winery takes several years before you begin making money."

"How so?" she inquired. "Does not wine age very fast?"

"Not if you have not yet grew the trees," I explained.

"And you have not yet bought the land to grow the trees on," she said. "How marvelous. You and I might go prospecting for land in California."

"You and I and Holly," I said. "It is her idea to buy a vineyard in California or Spain."

"Well, we will discuss it," she said in a business like way. She had many pages of material in front of her on 1 subject or another and she begun considering the pages 1 by 1. Some years there were more than others. "Here is a party that would like your body," she said.

"Would you repeat the question?" I inquired.

It was a scientific hospital. They would pay me a certain sum now if I left them my body in my will. "They appear to believe that medical science will profit by studying such a well controlled and efficient body as your own," said Barbara.

"How do they know I will not take the money and disappear?" I inquired.

They tattooed your foot. I was not fond of that idea or many others which come to her in the mail over the year, such as opportunities in film making, announcing, bowling alleys, horse raising, and running for office. "Now here is 1 which will amuse you," said Barbara, "since it comes with a pretty picture of a girl." She sounded unhappy saying *girl,* for she her self was no longer a girl. She was 10 or 15 years older than me, and I was no longer a boy. I took the picture.

It was a photo of a young woman in West Des Moines, Iowa, representing a company known as Life After. You paid her a certain sum now and she put you in a freezer scientifically drugged, and you woke up in 125 years. "Just exactly who remembers to wake you?" I asked Barbara.

"Well, we are not interested in hokus pokus," she replied. "Speaking of your interesting body, leave us go and feed it."

After our annual conference we always went and ate together. In the early days we went to lunch, but later it become dinner, for my business grew. When I arrived in her office she took my coat, but when we were leaving I helped her on with hers. When I entered her office every year she held the door open for me and swung it closed behind, but when we were leaving I held the door for her. I pushed the elevator button. I took my hat off in the elevator. I whistled for the cab. I helped her in. I give the door man a buck for watching me whistle. In the early years she decided what restaurant to go to, but as the years passed it looked like I knew more restaurants than she knew, and I decided. In the early years she bought and paid for our lunch, but as the years passed I bought and paid for hers, which now become not lunch but dinner, and in this particular year when we entered the taxi cab I suddenly seized a hold of her and give her a tremendous kiss because suddenly we were the same age.

In the restaurant we discussed Henry W. Wiggen Mini Park. In the year 1959 the Town and City of Perkinsville give me 3,150 square feet of property across from the railroad station. This property was formerly known at Depot Park and any body over a certain age still calls it that. It is officially known as Henry W. Wiggen Mini Park because I was there the day they changed the name with many speeches to go with it by the leading politicians of Perkinsville. They were caught up in a fit of enthusiasm. It been a big year for me. If it been as big a year for the rail road as it been for me they would of kept it for them self, but the rail road was failing and every body had the idea that the town was growing in the other direction. They give me not only the park tax free but a large scroll in memory of the occasion. Luckily I put the scroll in the cellar in my room with fire proof walls and piled things on top of it for 12 years in till Barbara dug it out.

It was only a little ½ assed park. However, if it was going to have my name on it I was going to keep it looking good, which I did. I hired gardeners and lawn mowers. As time went by I brang home seats and benches from baseball parks tore down for 1 reason or other. In Henry W. Wiggen Mini Park you got seats and benches from Brooklyn, New York, Boston, Washington, St. Louis, Pittsburgh, Philadelphia, and San Francisco. Children climb and jump on the seats and old men sit on them. In the winter the old men go some where, I do not know where, and papers blow through the park. The park is 75 feet long and 42 feet wide and now has a fence around it 1 foot high constructed by Ed Lewis of Tozerbury. This fence is an "improvement" dreamed up by Barbara. As long as we dream up such improvements they can not take the park back. To arrive at this situation we were 6 years in the courts.

At the time of our first discussion, I am sorry to say, the

Town and City were taxing me for the park at so much and so much per square foot *plus* so much and so much per square foot per year going back to the year they loved me so much they give me the park in the first place, *plus* charges and interest and costs and what ever else they thought up at the time.

"Why, them bastards," Barbara said. She always started out taking my side whether I was right or wrong or not. She asked me many further questions, writing down thoughts on little scraps of paper. In her office she kept these little memorandums in a very large wine glass on her desk, but I can not remember that once she put the memorandum in I ever seen her take it out.

After our annual dinner I always dropped her at her apartment and drove home. This year, however, she invited me to join her in a small glass of Lochan Ora, which was a favorite liqueur of her husband before he died. "He would wish us to enjoy it," I said, although I hardly knew him, and we done so, drinking several small glasses. It was many years since I was there. Her windows looked out on the East River. "I remember when I was here," I said, "and all the ladies were awfully sweet to me and admired me and felt my arm, but once they seen me they seen me if you know what I mean."

"They went off in the night on the arm of old men," she said.

"It give me a fit," said I. "All evening the old men talked to them self and I talked to the women. The old men stood aside. They had that god dam confidence. They knew the women would go off with them instead of me, although I might of been on the front of the paper that very day."

"They were in the back of the paper," said Barbara, "on the financial page."

When I first come it looked like for ever, I was confident, I was strong, I had enthusiasm, I had motivation, I drank nothing, I smoked nothing, and I could throw a baseball harder than almost any body. The rivers flow and the bridges stand while the people come and go.

"You have never saw my Henry Wiggen shelf," said Barbara.

"I never knew you had 1," said I.

"Would you care to see it?" she inquired, but she already kicked off her shoes and climbed on a chair and begun bringing things down from the shelf. I never seen her with out her shoes before. I was simply bowled over and no mistake. I never knew she thought about me from January to January, yet here she kept a special shelf full of articles and photographs. In some photographs I barely recognized my self. My hair was very short and my face was very smooth and I was always saying I was going to do this or that in the future. Every thing was out ahead of me and every thing was possible. Some of the things I did and some I didn't. I was not exactly certain which things mattered and which didn't. The less certain I was the louder I sounded.

"Oh, that big future," said I. "I should of enjoyed it more while I was doing it. Instead, I was always looking ahead, and now the future is past."

"By no means," said my lawyer. "You are now in a new stage of later existence. Many pleasures of the past are gone, but many new pleasures come to replace them. Every thing is solid. Nothing can break. Your marriage is made and can not break, your fortune is made and can not disappear. Now at last you have arrived where you formerly thought you wished to be. It is up to you what you do with who you now are."

"I wish to play more baseball," said I.

"You can not go back," she said. "You can not do again what you all ready once done. Tell me what you think of my Henry Wiggen shelf."

"I notice pictures of me standing beside boys I can not even remember their name," I said.

"You take a picture," she said, "you walk away, you drop out of each other's sight forever. Here and there, however, 1 face in every so many remain famous."

"You watched me very close," I said.

"Many a girl kept a special shelf in her house for you," said Barbara.

"Not as many as you think," I said.

"More than you know," she replied.

She said the word *girl* again. I remember that. "It occurs to me," I said, staring down on those old papers, "that in my new stage of later existence I might never again be on the front of the paper."

"Often," she said, "that is when a man begins to be interesting."

"Of course," said I, "we can look on the brighter side. I will make the front page on the day I die."

"Surely in New York," she said, "barring a new war or stock market crash or some goon shoots 15 people out a window."

Did she truly think that the older you grew the more interesting you might be? You must remember that when people are talking about some body else they are really talking about them self. Did she think she was more interesting now than before? Maybe she was. "I noticed some excellent champagne in your refrigerator," I suggested.

"Locate the bar towel," she said, collecting all the papers again and tying them up like she had them before. "The space you get when you die," she said, "probably depends on how long the time was from what you did. I would suggest to you that you do not sit and bury your self in memories of when you were famous. For God sake do not lift a single finger to keep your self in the spot light."

"Was I famous?" I inquired. "I never *felt* famous."

"With your well controlled and efficient body you have years of pleasure and enjoyment ahead of you," she advised me. "You must of been, for people wrote me all the time asking this or that. People followed your career. People hung pictures of you on their wall. Children slept with you under their pillow. You were in people's dreams."

"And then there was the girl with the weapon system," said I.

"Not every body loved you *beautifully*," Barbara said.

"She is still locked up," I said.

"No, she been released, but you are in no danger from her any more. It was you being so famous brought out her hatred. Retire to your house and no body will hate you."

"I never felt famous in my house," I said. "After the early years ball playing was my job whereas being father and husband was some thing else again. I was the chauffeur going and coming to school and I was a member of the P. T. A. pushing a basket around the super market. Up and down the streets of Perkinsville people were use to me."

"You were 1 man in the winter and another in the summer," said Barbara.

I popped the champagne open. Yes, in the winter I was like many another man, now I was home and now I was gone. "Where is your husband?" "Oh, he is out of town on business." "So is mine. Ain't that nice?" "Well, it is a relief, we eat scramble eggs for dinner." I never thought of my self as famous. Once in the winter I was laying in the side of the road fixing a flat and I said to my self, "Is this such a famous man fixing a flat in the road like any body else? If you are so *famous* why did you forget to renew your AAA?" The famous man went to the bank, to the shoemaker, to the drug store for drugs and wiped my daughters' nose when they took cold. I went to the hard ware store for nails, I went to the pet store for the needs of our dogs and cats and birds and hamsters and white mice which from time to time took up residence in my residence, I changed the bulbs when they blew, I washed finger prints off the windows, I shoveled snow, I put chains on the wheels, I paid bills by mail, I bought postage at the post office, I fell down on the ice, I caught cold, I went to dinner at the houses of many people in and around the Town and City of Perkinsville, N. Y., who were not the least bit famous for any thing and never would.

I was famous. I knew that. Some where in the back of my mind I always knew that people were keeping silvernears of me. That was good. Only I tried to think about it as little as possible and keep it from my daughters as much as possible, for I did not wish them to think that they were no body unless they were famous. I wished them to see that fame was luck, a famous man was a slob like every body else's father down the street, he blew up from time to time, he picked his nose, he needed a shave, he left a ring around the bath tub, he farted in the dark, he belched, he burped, he threw the newspaper across the room, he studied him self in the mirror for the gray hairs, his car wouldn't start, his fuses over charged, his fire place smoked, his TV tube blew like any body else.

"I believe that is along the line of my own thought," Barbara said.

"Even so," said I, "I am going to go down to Washington and talk to Ben Crowder about pitching for him."

"Here is to Ben," said Barbara, and we toasted Ben and filled up our glasses once more and toasted Suicide Alexander, the owner of California, just in case things didn't work out with Ben. We drank them down. "Shall we have another?" Barbara inquired.

"Say when," I replied.

"When ever you wish," said she.

Up I went again. Pretty soon I lost count how many times I drove down and up between Perkinsville and New York that winter. JFK, La Guardia, St. Louis, Japan, Washington, lawyer and phsychiatrist, "monkey business," Holly called it. She thought I was engaged in a love affair with Dr. Schiff.

Driving was a drag. It become boring to me. In the past I rather drove a car than almost any thing else, but now I begun to dislike them and become afraid of them. I suddenly realized that I did not know how they worked. "By exploding gasoline," some body told me. All right, then, what kept the exploding gasoline in its place? Why didn't the whole god dam machine explode from front to back? Nothing exciting ever happened on the road. I don't know what I expected. I always expected the most beautiful girl in the world hitch hiking by the side of the road, but it only happened once. The kind of women I now liked were never hitch hikers any more.

The only time I ever picked up the most beautiful girl in the world by the side of the road I was driving to Florida 1 time with a fellow name of Raney Nelson. He was also called "The Hat," for he always put on his hat the minute he stepped out of the shower. He played right field for us for 2 or 3 years late in the 1950's. His arm was powerful, he picked balls off the walls and fired to third base with never a glance. He was a comfort and friend to a pitcher and he lived in Queens and this girl was waiting for us on the Jersey Turn Pike. She was headed for Hickory, North Carolina, and we took her there, stopping first for the night at a motel some place between 2 places, God knows where.

I rented 2 rooms. It was not yet clear what the arrangement was. We ate dinner in the motel restaurant and I paid for the dinner like I paid for the rooms because Nelson had no money and never would. He did not care to fight for his job. When he quit he simply quit, drifting from the scene with out a word. After I paid for the dinner I went back and put a tip on the table for the waitress, but Nelson and the girl were gone, 1 of the room keys were gone as well, and I seen them next at breakfast. "Author," said Raney to me, "all is fair in love and sex, I will purchase the breakfast." It was a story he liked to tell, and he told it time and again over the year. He told me once he would never marry, it cost too much, and I replied, "A man that buys dinner, transportation from Queens to Florida, and spends the night with a beautiful girl all for the price of 3 orange juice has got to be a mighty fine money manager." I got no idea where he now is.

In the very same January following my release I was driving home up the Taconic when a police car ordered me over to the side. I couldn't imagine what I done, but I seen his eye in the mirror and I knew he meant business. I got out and he got out. The ground was hard and the wind blew and spring was a long way off. He was a young fellow. It looked to me like they were making police men out of children. "Sir," he inquired, "may I ask you why you were driving so slow?"

"Officer," I replied, "I did not know I was driving slow. I must of been thinking deep thoughts."

He walked around the car, examining it in full. "Deep thoughts and safety do not go together," he said. "Are you tired? Are you intoxicated? If by driving slow you hope to avoid being noticed you ended by doing the opposite. Give me your license." He took it with out looking at it and held it in his hand and said, "I know by your face who you are but I can not place your name. Are you associated with sports?"

"Yes," said I, "1 down, 19 to go."

"Are you playing at present?"

"No."

"You formerly played?"

"Yes."

"With the Mammoths," he inquired, "because I notice the parking sticker?"

"Yes, " I replied.

"What was your name?" he asked.

"Henry Wiggen," I said.

"Correct," he said, "how many did I guess it in?" He studied my license and handed it back to me. "Of course I would never give you a ticket, but you must not drive so slow any more. Pick it up."

"I use to drive a lot faster," I said, "but then I use to do a lot of things faster."

"I am just wondering," he said, "if that is a real telephone you got there."

"I am a little old for toy telephones," I said. "Make a call and see."

"How do I work it?" he inquired.

"You work it like a telephone," I replied.

He telephoned Yonkers and spoke to a child. "You will never believe me," said he to the child, "but I am telephoning you out of a telephone in Henry Wiggen's car." Then soon he hung up.

"What did the child say?" I inquired, but he did not wish to tell me. "Come on and tell me," I said, "because I am interested in the things children say, having 4 daughters of my own."

"I know you have," he said. "You must understand, sir, that this is my daughter's honest opinion and none of my own."

"Which is?" I inquired.

"Which is," he said, "that she would be interested in the telephone in Beansy Binz's car but not in yours. All due respect to you, sir, my daughter believes you are a has been."

Very soon there after I and Holly and Hilary drove down again to the air port on the way to Washington. From the air port in Washington I telephoned Ben Crowder, and I said, "Ben, how in the world are you and how would you like a lead on a promising older pitcher?"

"How older?" Ben inquired.

"About my age," I said.

"Shit," he said.

"Welcome to Washington," I said, "capital of the nation."

"What are you doing down here?" Ben inquired.

"I received your cable in Japan," I said, "saying come and play for you."

"I never said *play*," said Ben.

"I got it right here in front of me, Ben," I said.

"You will never stop arguing," he said. "What are you doing down here?"

"I come to see *you*," I said. "I believe she fired me too soon. I really and truly believe I got a number of games to play. I really and truly believe I am going to be a big help to some body yet."

"Not to me," he said, "Because I need a pitcher *coach* and not a pitcher."

"Let us get together and talk about it," I said. He didn't say "Yes" and he didn't say "No." I didn't even know if he was still on the line. He was that way. "Should we get together, Ben? Ben? Benjamin? Benjamin, old pal, are you still there?"

"Now?" he inquired.

"That is why I am here," I replied.

"Where?" he asked.

"In Washington," I replied.

"Are you driving?" he inquired. "If you are driving drive on out." It was my telephone he was interested in seeing, not me, and he give me directions to the suburb where he lived. I never heard of it. He was insulted that I never heard of it.

When Hilary heard that we were going to see Ben Crowder prior to the Washington Monument she begun screaming screams the equal of any former screams. Crowds of people come running from every corner of the air port. "You insane fool," I screamed in reply, "the very reason we are here is because you wish me to line up a job in the big leagues."

She only continued screaming. Holly walked away very quickly in 1 direction and I walked away in the other and Hilary sat on our bags in front of the Hertz desk screaming. Soon I returned, but Holly did not return. She went on to the hotel. "Ha ha," said Hilary, "she got no clothes with her."

"She rather run around naked than be in your presence," I said to Hilary, "and I do not blame her."

The lady behind the Hertz desk said, "A neighbor back home had 1 of those."

"How did they finally make her stop?" I inquired.

"They sent him to a special school," said the Hertz lady. "A *jail* was the way I heard it."

"No school will take me," said Hilary. "Even my very own mother's school."

"Where is the mother?" the Hertz lady inquired.

"She is running around the hotel naked," Hilary replied.

"I can begin to see where this is a complicated problem," said the Hertz lady, looking at me with a question in her eye, but

I didn't say "Yes" and I didn't say "No," simply taking the key from her and driving off.

Ben Crowder lived in a very big house and he come to the door in his stocking feet with holes in them. He was not the kind of a man that manicured their toe nails. He give Hilary a look and said, "There are many grand children up stairs." That was all he ever said to her, and up she raced. Maybe he would of been a better father for her than me. He did not smile and he did not shake hands and he did not offer me any thing to eat or drink as long as I was there. He did not introduce me to a single member of his family.

"I was excited to receive your cable in Japan," I said.

"You were not so excited you answered it," he said.

"Ben," said I, "I certainly answered it."

"The first word out of you is a dispute. I wonder if you and I can ever get along," he said.

"We have not yet give it much of a try," said I.

"I suppose you have got the cable in your pocket," he said.

"Yes," said I, "I happen to."

"Keep it there," he said. "I do not need a pitcher. I need a pitcher coach. I got a No Name pitcher staff with plenty of pitchers needing professional instruction."

"You got a No Name pitching staff and I got a name," said I.

"You got a name all right," said he, "but no fast ball. All my pitchers have got fast balls more or less if only they knew where to throw them. They need the development of their mind."

Ben's office was in the cellar. The furnace went on and off, making a terrible racket. We shouted when it was on and forgot to stop shouting when it was off. When I left his house my throat was hoarse. On a black board standing beside the furnace he had wrote the names of all his pitchers with a word or 2 beside each, such as

Jones   medical question
Brown   narrow ass

Smith   possible lush
Green   ask Black about.

"Do you not think it would look swell to have the name 'Wiggen' up there?" I inquired, picking up a piece of chalk and writing

Wiggen   experienced veteran.

Ben picked up his black board eraser and erased my writing and said, "I need a pitcher coach."

"I never been a pitcher coach," I said. I don't know why I said it.

"You never been 40 neither," said he. "Why do you give me those smart ass remarks? I wonder if you and I can ever get along. It is not surprising to me that she does not want you over there."

"Did she say so?" I inquired. "Did you speak to her?"

"No," he replied (lying), "I have not spoke to her in 15 years."

"I thought she would make me her manager," I said.

"I never thought for 1 minute she would make you manager," said Ben, "because you ain't a sufficient prick. I could of told you 2 years ago Ev would be the manager. Ev will stamp their head to a pulp when necessary whereas you are not a head stamper. Between you and I we could wipe up the universe. These god dam black board kids will win because of fear, for while I am turning the switch in the electric chair you are giving them permission and encouragement to where they are jumping out of the chair in shock and frightened 1/2 to death and doing their job for fear of being sat down again. They are hustling. Their ass is scorched with electricity."

"I wish to pitch," I said. "I got several good games left in me."

"I know you wish to pitch," he said, "and I know you got several good games left in you, but I do not need several games,

I need dozens and dozens of games from boys with fast balls. I am a developing club going no place for the present while going into paradise on earth in the near future. I wish you would be my pitcher coach."

"Is there any way of turning this furnace off?" I asked.

"No," replied Ben, "it can never be turned off."

"Is there any way of us going up stairs and talking?" I asked.

"Later," replied Ben. "Or we can turn the furnace off."

I wrote my name on the board again.

Wiggen pitcher *and* pitcher coach

He erased it again, saying, "I got no room for such a luxury. These kids have got to *play*. You are not only too old, you are *much* too old."

"I am 38," said I, rounding it off a little.

"You are a fucking 38 year old liar," said he, "because you are 40."

"I am 39," I said.

"Why in hell are you arguing about numbers all ready up in the sky?" he inquired. "What kind of physical condition are you in? You were always a clean liver."

"Perfect," I said. "I went to the doctor the other day, he looked me over in side out and said I got the body of a younger child."

"You wear contacts in your eye," he said.

"Who said?" I inquired.

"Some body told me," he said.

"The only thing wrong with me is I am developing busted ear drums from your furnace," I said.

He turned the furnace off. It was very quiet there. "I also hear you got the prostrate glands," he said. He saw by my face that he probably struck close to the mark, and he switched on a small electric heater glowing all red. "Leave us talk man to man," he said, "for we are grown ups now. If you wish to show her that she made a mistake making Ev the manager the way to show her is not by pitching against her. You are not a *soldier* any more. You are a *general* in the ranks. You are a pitcher coach sending boys out there to kill them. A general in the ranks does not go out there and kill them by him self. *He sends boys.*"

This made some sense to me and I inquired, "How much money does a coach receive?"

"I am not talking about any ordinary coach," said Ben, "I am talking about you. You name it and I will get it for you. The more you ask the greater they will think you are and I will back you up to the hilt."

"Can you think of *any* body," I inquired, "that might care for simply several games?"

"You are talking about some body that is planning on winning this year," said Ben. "Try Chicago. Pittsburgh. Considering what you got in mind I would think you would of went to them in the first place. Try Jack Sprat in California. Ain't he your neighbor right up the river there?"

Some body up stairs rung a bell and we walked up the cellar stairs to the dining room. No body was there. When we were in the cellar they were on the first floor, but now that we were on the first floor they all went up to the second, and I suppose when he went up stairs to bed they all went up and laid on the roof. I would of done the same my self. It was a big table set for 1 person, and Ben sat at the head and begun eating his soup in till he discovered he still had a piece of black board chalk in his hand. He threw it through the kitchen door. After he ate his soup he ate a plate of fried ham and greens keeping warm on an interesting little dish with a flame under it. I asked him where he bought such an interesting little dish and he replied, "What in the hell is interesting about it?" and when he was finished with his ham and greens he turned to the air beside him like some body was standing there and said, "Coffee." However, since no body was actually there he got up and got it him self and come back and spoke once more to the air, saying, "I also wish a piece of pie," and he turned around and went in the kitchen and brought back a piece of pie and ate it. This also was interesting, to watch a fellow do this and never offer me a thing. I couldn't of done it my self and I doubt that you could of done it, either, but Ben done it without any difficulty what ever.

We chewed the fat. We talked about various people. Where was this 1 and where was that 1? He asked me who all was at Dutch's funeral, and he said, "I am now the oldest manager in baseball." He was tired hearing about funerals. Some years before he become tired *going* to them. "You can not tell 1 from an other any more," he said. "In the old days you knew whose it was by the style, if he was a noisy fellow it was a noisy funeral, if he was a drunk you all drank your way through, whereas now a days they took the life out of it."

"Well," said I finally, "I am off to the Washington Monument."

"I never been up the fucking thing," said Ben.

"I been up it any number of times," I said.

"I am a tax payer," said Ben, "I always left the schools take them up it and take them and see the Congress and the statues and the Smithonia and what ever they cared to see I had no use for."

"I am wondering when the Japanese cherry trees will blossom this year," I said. It was a mistake to said it.

Ben squeezed his eyes shut like I insulted him. He was in pain. For a moment I thought he might be having a heart attack. "I was right in the first place," he said. "You and I can never get along. I need a pitcher coach and you would be an angel on the job. Is that not what you come here for, looking for a job? Instead you are asking me the time table of the Japanese cherry trees. More than ½ the time when I ask you a question you answer with a question. What kind of an example would that be in front of young ball players? I want you but I could never have you. No way in the world am I going to answer your smart ass questions about Japanese trees."

"It was not intended as a smart ass question," I said.

"Do you still have your telephone in your car?" inquired Ben.

"I would not be with out it," I said. "How else could I make telephone calls while driving?"

"Do you see what I mean?" he inquired. "You answered my question with a question."

It begun growing very cold in the house. His wife called down from up stairs, saying, "Ben, you must of turned off the furnace." He replied that she was losing her mind. Never the less he rose up from the table and went around the wall in his stocking feet and turned the furnace on again, and I went up stairs for Hilary, meeting Ben's wife and daughters and their children, and Hilary come skipping along like the sweetest child in the world. "What a darling girl," said Mrs. Crowder, "she is a saint and no mistake. She tells me you are going to play ball some more."

"Not for me," said Ben, "I need a pitcher *coach* and I know where to get 1." (He all ready *got* 1.) He put on his shoes. Soon we were standing beside the Hertz car. I thought he become very polite all of a sudden, walking out to the car with us like that. "Where is it?" he inquired.

"Where is what?" I replied, answering a question with a question.

"The telephone in your car," said he.

"This is not my car," I said. "This is only a Hertz."

"That is too bad," he said. "I was looking forward to it." He turned around and walked back in the house with never a word of "Good by."

Suzanne Winograd is the only person I know sun burned all over all year around. When we arrived in the hotel she was visiting with Holly. Her daughter Bertilia was also there. Suzanne chose the name "Bertilia" so the child could call her self "Bert" and be a girl or a boy, which ever she preferred. "I did not get the job," said I to Holly.

"I do not get a lot of jobs," Suzanne said, "and the job I got I hate." She was playing tennis all over the world.

"All he was offered was coach," said Hilary. "I wish to see him play. I do not wish to see him coach."

"Hilary was a perfect doll," said I to Holly. "She did not scream once since the air port."

"She better not scream in front of the President," Suzanne said. She rotated her shoulders, staying loose. It was her trade mark. For some reason or an other Suzanne Winograd rotating her shoulders fired up excitement through out the male world when the film appeared. I could never under stand it. "You are certainly looking well," said she to me.

"I thank you," said I, "and I am feeling as well as I look."

"He got prostrate trouble," Hilary said.

"I got weight trouble," Suzanne said. "I been on a diet in till after we make this film, but I am below my weight which hurts my game."

"You look far better than when I seen you last," I said.

"It is because we are much less insane than ever before," she replied, hugging and kissing Bertilia and referring to her as "my little chipmunk."

"Why are you hoarse?" my wife inquired.

"From shouting over Ben Crowder's furnace," I replied.

"I got a gargle right here," said Holly, "if you would care for it," and I said I would and took it in the bath room and begun gargling. Suzanne followed me in the bath room.

"How do you do?" I said. "Come on in and meet your self."

"Never mind humor," said she. "You and I are being *screwed*. How much are they paying you for this film on focusing on aging? I suppose you are doing it for per diem and a 1 time honorarium, which I am. We are fools. They are using and abusing us and I am tired of it all my life."

"I just as soon not do it," I said, "if you feel that strongly."

"Go on with your gargling," she said. "I am trying to think.

They will be here any minute. Exactly how much are they paying you?"

"That may be where the problem is," I said. "Maybe they are not paying us the same thing, which is why you are feeling used and abused and I am not."

"How much?" she inquired again.

"$10,000," I said, although it was actually more than that. I thought she would be getting the same sum, but I was wrong.

She sunk down on the edge of the tub. "I am weak with anger," she said. "I am ashamed to tell you I am getting $2,500 for the day's work."

"I am sorry to hear it," I said. "What can I do? I will back out if you wish."

"They will just get some body else," she said. She sat on the tub looking forward. *Staring* you might say. She had 50 projects going and none of them paying very much. Her managers and husbands ate her up. "I am the goose that laid the golden egg," she told me 1 time, "and after I laid it my managers and husbands stripped the skin off every inch of my body." She was now playing tennis matches all over the world paying off advances on contracts her husbands and managers all ready collected. "We should of thought about all this when we were young," she said on the side of the tub.

When Suzanne walked in the bath room I was enjoying a fantasy of Ben Crowder. I was pitching for Jack Sprat in California and knocking Ben out of the pennant, which was all the worse for Ben since *it was his last year,* he would never again have another chance, every thing fell in on him, his furnace set fire to his house, and so forth, but when Suzanne begun telling me her troubles my fantasies switched. Some times I think about being single again. I can not help what I think about. I think of all the wonderful women I would rescue from their troubles. I thought about rescuing Suzanne from her troubles. We would do Friday Night Baseball together, her and I and

Jerry Divine, clear up all her debts and marry. She had a lively body. She jumped around when she talked, she went up on her toes, she threw out her leg, first 1 and then the other, she rotated her shoulders around and around, staying loose. But how many women could I go to bed with any more, and why would I wish to, and why would I go through all the trouble of rescuing them when I discovered some years before that all you needed to do was *ask* them and they went? And why not? I could of said it to 500 women over the years and seldom heard "No" for an answer. I once did say it to a young woman after a ball game in a restaurant in Chicago. I was over come by her on sight. I also had a drink in me. I probably also come off a good ball game and was confident and high. It was a noisy place and we were standing up when introduced and instead of saying "How do you do?" or "How pleased I am to meet you" I said "Leave us go to bed right away and see what it feels like," and she replied, "How about we eat first?" and we did. I can not remember her name or where we later went or any of the people we ate with. I ate in a lot of restaurants with a lot of people.

But I had nothing in me now besides gargle, and I was older than ever before, and I knew that Suzanne would be a great deal more trouble than I cared to under take, although I begun to hate all the men that fucked up her life for her, and I wished to help her, and I was fond of Bertilia, too. Suddenly I seen my self back in the head lines again.

Stars Wed

Then what? Why, I suppose I am then up the Washington Monument with Bertilia saying, "Leave us try walking down like I walked when I was here with Hilary." It was 898 steps down, according to Hilary, and we enjoyed being up there, for the view was spectacular and I loved high places to begin with, such as the Gate Way Arch in St. Louis and the Eiffel Tower in Paris. I was fond of low places, too, such as tunnels, caves, and under water observation in glass hemispheres. Every where we went we took the girls up things or down things or across things such as bridges and straights.

"I will tell you what we will do," said Suzanne, jumping up from the side of the tub.

"Tell me and I will do it," I said.

"Stop gargling," she said. "Here is what. We will revolt in the presence of the President in the morning. Say nothing today. I will deliver such hell to him straight to his face it will cause a national scandal. He would probably not be crazy about a national scandal. Who is going to benefit the most from the President's Committee Focusing on Aging?"

"Me," said I.

"You are only a drop in the bucket," said Suzanne. "The people who will benefit the most are the people who make the film and the whole office staff and a number of people in politics that attach them self to the whole project such as Deck Roberts."

"Who is he?" I inquired.

"He is a crook," said Suzanne, "who give me several jobs over the years. If I could afford honesty I would report him to the police." We strolled out of the bath room. "Are we not a couple of perfect specimens for the President's Committee Focusing on Aging? I have weight problems while he has prostrate trouble and we run to the shrink with our loony children."

"Tell me more about my husband at the phsychiatrist," Holly said.

"He is trying to cure her of tobacco and Coca Cola," said Suzanne.

"In the beginning I did not even know she was a woman," said Holly.

"She is a woman all right," Suzanne replied. "He is locked in there with her for hours."

"My mother is stirring up trouble again," said Bertilia.

"It is no secret he is horny," said Suzanne. "All athletes are horny."

"School teachers are horny," said Holly.

"Athletes are hornier than all the rest," said Suzanne.

"Every body thinks their own group is the horniest," my wife argued, "because every body knows their own horniness with in."

"With in the class of athletes," said Suzanne, "tennis players are the horniest, and with in the class of tennis players the women are hornier than the men."

In come Deck Roberts, the Presidential Assistant, and his *own* assistant, a woman whose name I never caught. Probably he never *threw* it is why I never *caught* it. He was the kind of a fellow I do not generally like, and when I give Holly a glance I could see that she did not like him, either. He looked at his watch when he walked in and seen that he was an hour late. But never a word of apology. "Suzanne," he said, "you look marvelous. You been carrying on the noble fight against weight. Americans are too fat. I am an athlete my self," he said, looking at me side ways. I made no objection and he added on, "I played a bit of big league ball my self."

"I was sure that you did," I said.

"I had a rather promising career at 1 time but went over in government service instead."

"For how long?" I inquired.

"15 years," he replied, not looking in my direction.

"15 years in *baseball*," I exclaimed. "Then I must know you."

"15 years in the government," he said, "but only very briefly in baseball."

Actually I do not find his name any where in the *Baseball Encyclopedia*, although the all time register leaves no body out no matter how brief. It is sad and amazing the very short lives you see there. Some times I just flip open a page any where. Let us look at page 178. Robert Gamble, a pitcher, born in Hazleton,

Pennsylvania, in 1867, *played 1 game* for Philadelphia in 1888 and lost. His life time record was no victories and 1 defeat. Robert Mitchell Garber played 2 games for Pittsburgh in 1956, no decision either time, life time record no victories, no defeats. He was born on September 10, 1928, in Hunkers, Pennsylvania. Alexander Garbowski, bats right, throws right, played 2 games in 1952 for Detroit. Life time batting average .000. Ramon Garcia Garcia, born March 5, 1924, La Esperanza, Cuba, bats right, throws right, pitched for Washington in 4 games in 1948, no decisions, life time record 0–0.

"How briefly?" I inquired.

"Notice how thin the President remains," Deck Roberts said. "He wishes us all to be healthy and defeat our enemies. Henry, you look in the peak of condition. The President told me personally he feels lucky to be getting you for the President's Committee Focusing on Aging. It is a mouth full but we say the whole thing every time. Glance over the scripts my assistant has gave you. Leave us try reading it out loud. Do not read the material in capital letters."

I read my part out loud as follows. I had a little trouble due to my sore throat. Hilary run down in the lobby and bought me some drops.

Henry Wiggen Wearing Baseball Cap and Baseball Glove on Right Hand. Looks at Red Light and Smiles.

HENRY WIGGEN: Good morning, Mr. President. Some people say that time flies.

No.

Time stands still. *We* fly. We all grow older.

Hi, there, my name is Henry Wiggen and I was a baseball pitcher for 19 years for the New York Mammoths. You have heard it said that the man in the grandstand grows one year older every year. But the player on the field remains the same age. That is poetry. But poetry is not truth.

I have grown older.

I have hung up my glove.

Removes Glove and Throws Glove Aside. Continues to Smile.
HENRY WIGGEN: You will never see me play baseball again.

While I was continuing to smile Hilary returned from the lobby
with my throat drops. When I read off the line, "You will never
see me play baseball again," she begun to scream. It was not a
high power scream. It was only a warning blast. She heard the
line I my self did not hear, all though it was I that was reading it.
"She is correct," I said to the Presidential Assistant, "I have not
quit baseball all that flat. I am still looking for a place to land.
Only this morning I met with Ben Crowder."

"We can not change any thing now," he said, "since it is all
wrote up on the Teleprompter."

"It is not too late to change the Teleprompter," his assistant
said.

"It is much too late and complicated," Deck Roberts replied.

"It is less late and complicated to change the Teleprompter,"
said I, "than for me to change my whole plans for my career."

"You all ready had your career," he said. "You can not continue with your career just because some kid screams. You can
not be playing baseball and aging at the same time. This is why
we are paying you good money to be Honorary Co Chair Person."

"The money you are paying him is more than honorary,"
Suzanne said. "I am the 1 being treated honorary. I am going to
revolt in the presence of the President."

"Oh, Suzanne," said Deck Roberts, "you are always going to
revolt and never doing it."

"This is really quite crazy," I said. "All I have to do is leave
out the part I object to."

"You can not leave any thing out," said Deck Roberts. "That
is what the President approved."

"The President never even seen it," said Deck Roberts's assistant.

Roberts sat down on a chair with his legs stuck straight out.

His legs were long. He was bony and thin and tired. "No matter what you do every body gives you an argument," he said. "If only I was an ordinary citizen instead of the direct representative of the President I would tell you what I think. Why can you not read a simple piece of paper instead of arguing?"

"Another thing," I said, "which might not be a big point, but I been trying to think back in my mind and I can not honestly and truly ever remember seeing a glove *hung up*."

"What about glove hung up?" Deck Roberts asked.

"In the script," I said.

He read the line in the script, "I have hung up my glove."

"We can change it," his assistant said.

"No, we can not," he said, "because it is already on the Teleprompter. I hung up many a glove."

"Where?" I inquired.

"Oh, all over," he replied.

"I seen gloves threw down on the ground or down on benches or lockers or on the floor," I said, "but never hung up."

"It says 'throws glove aside' so you are not hanging it up any way," said Holly.

"Right," said Deck Roberts, "your husband is an arguer."

"I seen gloves on beds, in bags and baggage, I seen gloves laying on pianos, but I never seen a glove hung up," I said.

"Little girl," said Deck Roberts to Hilary, "if I had a father like that I would scream my self." He begun putting on his over coat, hat, and gloves when several platters of food arrived, and he removed his gloves and ate a couple pieces of fried chicken still wearing over coat and hat. "What ever you do, be on time for the President in the morning. The President is never late. Remember that he is the President of the United States, not some Uranian ass hole." He completed his chicken and wiped his hands thoroughly. The reason he was tired, he said, was because he was up all night writing the script.

"I wrote the script," his assistant said.

"Tomorrow will be a triumph," Deck Roberts said. "Jesus

Christ, folks, play the game, take the money and there will be more where that come from in the good old U. S. treasury if people remain healthy and well and young. I will send the limo to your door in the morning."

In the morning 2 limousines come to the hotel from the White House, 1 for the Winograds and 1 for the Wiggenses. My throat was very sore and I carried my gargle with me. We stood in the freezing cold between the limousines with our hands stuck out in front of us while Hilary recited rhymes I had not give a thought to in years. We recited these rhymes when choosing up sides for games in Perkinsville and her sisters before her.

> Engine, engine, number 9,
> Going down Chicago line,
> If the train should jump the track
> Do you want your money back?
> Yes.
> No.
> Maybe so.

While she recited she counted off our hands, and where ever she stopped was o–u–t if you know what I mean, and when your both hands were o–u–t you went in the limousine Hilary told you.

> Bubble gum, bubble gum,
> In a dish,
> How many pieces
> Do you wish?
> 1.
> 2.
> 3 or 4.

Some how it come out that I and Holly and Suzanne went in 1 limousine and Hilary and Bertilia in the other, and we glided away to the filming.

"Believe me I appreciate your promptness," Deck Roberts said. "The President is always late so we will have plenty of time to get ready."

"Get ready for what?" Suzanne inquired. "I am refusing. I intend to revolt in the President's face."

"Suzanne," said Deck Roberts, "you are such a child."

"Our phsychiatrist is correcting that," said Suzanne.

"Well, he will not have it corrected by the time the President arrives," Deck Roberts said. "Here, put this on for size," and Suzanne slipped in to a white leisure time sweater bearing certain words across her left bosom. I never noticed what the words were, but 100,000,000 men and many women lost their eye sight trying to read them at night and never succeeding. Good as she looked she smelled bad, for she begun to sweat, planning her revolt in the presence of the President, and my own voice was hoarse from shouting over Ben Crowder's furnace. It struck me that this was going to be 1 of your major failures as a film. However, there was some thing about it that made it sensational instead. I do not under stand it to this day, though I have saw it many times, it keeps popping up, I am watching TV when all of a sudden there we are, her with her racket and I with my baseball glove advertising the President's Committee Focusing on Aging, which never done 1 thing for any body old or young. I hear my music, I say my lines, I remove glove and throw glove aside. Then the show really begins. I have met people that hardly even know that I am *in* that film. By the end of 60 seconds they have forgot the first 30 if you can believe me. No sooner do I toss my glove aside than we see Suzanne rotating her shoulders like she does. She been doing it for years. She rolls her shoulders out of habit, "keeping loose," she says, "staying warm," prior to serving a tennis ball or driving a golf ball or diving in the water, her breast rising up with her swinging until you seen that some thing was wrote across her beautiful white sweater but you did not know what. People by the 1,000's tried to guess what it was, guessing all sorts of simple things such as "I love you" and all sorts of peculiar things such as "It is a racket," and all sorts of vulgar things and all sorts of secret government messages. Many people said to me, "Tell us what is wrote across that girl's sweater, for you were on the spot when they shot the picture." When I said I did not know they become rather angry, and later when I knew they did not believe me. Her sweater only said *Friday Night Baseball*. But people have the feeling she is a secret and mysterious person who if only they could read the writing on her bosom they would know the answer to their problem. As a matter of fact she is not secret or mysterious but a simple lady with many problems such as weight, money, men, and caring for Bertilia.

"I am once more being humiliated," she said, turning her self around in front of a full size mirror in her new sweater.

"Do as you are told," Deck Roberts said. "Stay or go."

"You did not change a single word on the Teleprompter," I complained.

"I did not have time," Deck Roberts said.

"You had all night," said Suzanne.

"Say it or not," Deck Roberts said. "Who cares? No body will pay any attention 1 way or the other."

"I will talk off the cuff," I said.

"No body talks off the cuff in front of the President," Deck Roberts said.

"You got a second guess coming," said Suzanne, "for what you got ahead of you now is a grand revolt in the presence of the President."

"Remember that you have not yet received your honorarium *or* your per diem," said he.

"Why are you worth so much more than me?" Suzanne asked me.

"I am not worth more than you," I said. "It is what my lawyer negotiated."

"Give me the name of your lawyer," she said, which I done, and Suzanne was grateful to me for that.

"Holy Christ," called Deck Roberts, "every body straighten

up, here he comes, look your best," straightening up him self and checking his neck tie and buttoning his coat. I could see how pitifully thin he was, while across the room the President come, stepping over the wires and shaking hands with every body and showing me how to twist my wrist when throwing a curve ball.

His eye stopped on Suzanne. She was rotating her shoulders, and I think she had not decided even then whether she planned to revolt in the presence of the President or go along with the film, and she looked at me and said, "Go ahead, do what we are told, it is the President," and I begun reading off the Teleprompter soon there after, "Good morning, Mr. President," about like it was wrote.

6

I and Hilary stopped off in New York on the way home from Washington. Arriving in the apartment was a message on the machine, "Call Patricia Moors," which I done with my shoes still on, thinking, "Ah ha, they have come to their senses, they have discovered where Ev McTaggart is a fake, they see where they will require an experienced veteran for left hand relief," and so forth and so on, pipe dreams while the phone is ringing at the other end. In my fantasies I am back in a Mammoths uniform, the race is neck and neck, Washington is coming up fast, the series is crucial. I knock them out. Ben Crowder *is in his last year*, he will never have another chance again, he lays down on the grass and weeps, his furnace set fire to his house, and so forth.

I was angry at Patricia and I was as sweet as pie. "Did you by any chance receive my cable in Japan?" she inquired.

"Cable in Japan," said I, "I honestly did not. Did you send me a cable in Japan?" Of course she did, for I received it there and am staring at it now, "Henry dear, please phone me when you can." Ben Crowder handed me a basket of lies yesterday in Washington, and I passed a part of it along to Patricia in New York today. Unknown to me, she had a few of her own for me very soon. "How is every little thing going with you?" I asked.

"We are working hard," she replied, "rebuilding the wreckage you left behind."

"It is nice of you to say so," I said.

"And how about your self?" she inquired. "How is Holly and how is your lovely daughter?"

"Which lovely daughter?" I inquired. It makes me rather peeved when people leave any of my daughters out.

"The 1 at Dutch's funeral," she said.

"Difficult," I replied.

"We ladies are often difficult," Patricia said.

I wished I was there. I could hardly believe I no longer belonged to the ball club. For several weeks now I hated the organization and every body in it, but I would love them all in a minute if only some body said the right thing, like "Come back." If she asked me to come back as pitcher coach I would of took it. I don't know why and neither did she, for when I said some thing along those lines she said to me, "I am a little bit puzzled whether you are serious or not. It is not as if you were 1 of those fellows on the edge of a pension that 1 more year could carry over the top. It is not even as if you got along with every body specially well these past few years, for you did not."

"It was hard watching how things were did," I said. "How is Ev doing?"

"He will do it," she said. "Leave me tell you why I am calling."

"Why not?" I inquired.

She give a small laugh. For 21 years I heard that little laugh. She had a quick ear and she always laughed ahead of every body else. "It is not even as if you were not good humored and quick witted," she said. "I did not know you would care. You got a lot of other irons in the fire."

"On to your business," I said. "It is all in the past."

"We are making plans for Opening Day," she said. "We are going to have a little ceremony and all that, observing 1 minute of silence for Dutch, where every body will stand with their head bowed."

"When did he ever observe 1 minute of silence?" I inquired. "I can see him now. While every body in the ball park is observing 1 minute of silence he is moving in behind some ball player his mind been on and talking a blue streak in their ear."

"You could always hear 1 voice above the others," she said. "However, coming to the important part, during the 1 minute of silence you been standing bowing your head in the company seats with all the various dignitaries, and as soon as the 1 minute is over you throw out the first ball."

I seen myself throwing the ball out from the seats. Who would know who was throwing it? Who would see me? "I will throw it out from the pitcher's box," I said, "but not from the seats, company seats or any other."

"Therefore I can put you down as doing it," she said.

"For a certain sum of money," I said.

"Really?" she said. "I had not thought about money."

"I am part of the attraction," I said. "Who knows how many people will come to the ball game to see me throw 1 last pitch?"

"Leave us name a sum of money," she said.

"The best thing is give my lawyer a ring," I said.

"Your same lawyer?" she inquired. "The same old person?"

"She is not old."

"She is older than me," said Patricia, "and I am older than you. She is no *chicken*."

"Leaving a loop hole," said I, "whereby I will not be there that day in case I join another ball club. I might be throwing *against* you. Did you ever think I might be knocking us out of the pennant 1 of these days?"

"You might join who?" she inquired.

"Probably Washington," I said. "Also, Jack Sprat seems after me from California."

"Washington," she said. She sounded surprised when I thought back over it. Washington my ass. She closed a deal 2 days before with Washington, conversing with Ben Crowder, who told me the following day he had not spoke to her in 15 years. She traded Andy Whedon to Washington as pitcher and pitcher coach in exchange for 4 young fellows off Ben Crowder's black board. The news was not yet public. When I was released it was public in 2 seconds. For Andy Whedon and 4 young fellows on the black board the news was held back until they were informed first. "Then if you do not go with Washington," she said, "you will throw 1 last pitch for us on Opening Day."

"Or with California," I said. "There is no telling how many people might be coming at me as the spring time advances."

"Another thing," she said. "You heard about the Old Timers Game."

"I been informed," I said. "Your man drove up 1 day."

"It will be combined with Flag Day," she said.

"An inspired idea," said I, "and you might as well speak to my lawyer regarding the fee for that, too, while you are on the line."

"Of course," she said. "I am sorry about every thing."

"I am sorry, too," said I, "and Hilary is sorriest of all." Hilary was in the apartment with me at the moment.

"Who is Hilary?" Patricia inquired.

"My lovely daughter," I replied.

"Which lovely daughter?"

"The 1 you met at Dutch's funeral. Hilary wishes to see me in regular action."

"Show her movies," Patricia said.

On the following morning at breakfast in McDonald's Hilary said to me, "I see where Ben Crowder got his new pitcher coach after all." Patricia knew it all day yesterday and Ben knew it all day the day before while I was making a fool of my self. "Well any how," said Hilary, "we got to go up the Monument and in the White House."

"He knew I sent him that cable back from Japan," I said, "and he knew what he said in his own cable to me."

"You knew you received a cable in Japan from Patricia Moors," said Hilary.

"He said he never spoke to her in 15 years," I said, "but he spoke to her the day before."

"Maybe he forgot," said Hilary.

"For screaming blue murder at the Washington air port and 1 short blast later in the day," said Dr. Schiff to Hilary, "you got the Washington Monument and the White House and your own private limousine. Keep up the good work. You are a genius, the more you scream the more you get. I notice you did not *dare* scream in front of Ben Crowder or the President."

"I am rather shocked by all the lies they told me," I said.

"If you played in Washington I would move my office there," said Dr. Schiff. "From what I hear about that town I imagine that many children are a wreck down there. Why did you decide against playing in Japan after Hilary give you full permission to go there in the first place? No wonder she screamed across the International Time Zone, I would of screamed my self and got what I wanted. That is a very good trick, get your father on the telephone on the long distance rates and keep him there in till he gives you what you want."

"That is not what I did," said Hilary.

"Probably not," said Dr. Schiff, "because *you* never think about the rates." Dr. Schiff's idea of breakfast was Coca Cola and orange juice. "Japan, Washington, promise after promise broke."

"It was not exactly promises," said Hilary. "He done the best he could. You can not make a ball club take you when they simply do not have the room."

"Perfect bull shit," said Dr. Schiff. "There is always room for 1 more."

"There is a limit," said Hilary.

"Bust the limits," said Dr. Schiff. "You went to the trouble of collecting all your Japan facts, and after that you went to the trouble of collecting all your Washington, D. C. facts. Where is the end to this torture chamber? You must be getting rather good by now at taking 'No' for an answer. I never take 'No' for an answer."

"You must take 'No' for an answer some time," said Hilary.
"You can not have every thing you want when you want it. The
world is not made like that. My mother is of the opinion that
some body that drinks so many Coca Cola is them self some
what childish."

"Did your mother graduate from medical school?" Dr. Schiff
inquired.

"Hilary is sounding so reasonable to me I can not imagine
that she will ever scream again," I said.

"She screamed 2 days ago in Washington," said Dr. Schiff,
"so I am taking no bets. I am a very good doctor but I do not
know if I am that good."

"When I am with you I feel reasonable," said Hilary to Dr.
Schiff.

"But when you are in the presence of your father you let go.
He is very strong, which is why he can leave him self look
weak."

She mentioned doctors. It made me think of Dr. Frank
Pointer, who must of told Patricia about my prostrate glands.
How else would Ben Crowder of knew? He also knew about my
contacts. "What do you think about a doctor violating confidences?" I inquired.

"They will do it," said she. "Who violated what to who? He
needs her more than he needs you. He probably been violating
confidences on the condition of ball players for years and years. I
am some what surprised that you are so hurt by all this. You are
a big boy now. Of course, the trouble is that you lived all your
life on your talents. You had what you had and every body could
see it out there in the wide open air, whereas the talents of other
people are not so clear and they must wheel and deal and fight
and scramble for the buck. You know about Tarzan and Jane, I
am sure, you seen Johnny Weismuller and others in the old
movies swinging around from tree to tree in their jock. Tarzan
lived in a cave with Jane. He went off to work in the morning.
He run down the lanes between the trees and was attacked by
snakes and vipers and poison spiders. He crossed the river on a

log and was snapped at by the various alligators, crocodiles, sharks and screaming eagles. In the office, when he finally got there, he was hounded to death by wolves and bears and tigers and lions, every body wanting their piece of the pie. Finally come quitting time and he started home through the 5 o'clock rush. Wild horses kicked him and wolverines snarled at him and leopards bit him and elephants charged him plenty in till finally he crossed that last river and dashed up that lane to the cave containing his beautiful Jane, and she opened the door, greeting him there in her coolest lounging apparel and offering him a martini in a frosted glass. He took the glass and sat back with a great heave of relaxation in his favorite easy chair, saying to Jane, 'You know, Jane, it is a fucking jungle out there.'"

"We are planning on buying a horse," said Hilary.

"What!" said Dr. Schiff. "You are *planning* on buying a horse. I thought he was suppose to buy you a horse when he returned from Japan."

"We were introduced to the horses," said Hilary.

"What good is introduced to a horse? Your ace in the hole is actually getting the horse. A horse in the hand is worth 2 in the bush."

"We are going up to Tozerbury tomorrow," I said.

"To buy a horse for a child that no body will take in school," said Dr. Schiff.

"Also to get back in baseball," I said.

"With who now?" asked Dr. Schiff.

"Jack Sprat in Tozerbury," I said.

"Is Tozerbury in baseball?" Dr. Schiff inquired. She really did not know for certain, and I and Hilary laughed.

We got a late start out of Perkinsville on the following morning due to a telephone call from the railroad station from a young woman from West Des Moines, Iowa, representing a company known as Life After. Said she, "I am here."

"Honey," I inquired, "who is where?"

"I am the girl from Life After," she said. "I wish to see you."

"I wish to see you, too," said I, "but my daughter and I are off on a business trip. Let us set up a date."

"Today," she said.

"Too short notice," I said.

"Do you really wish to see me?" she inquired. "Are you really interested in Life After?"

"Is it a flash light battery?" I inquired.

"I wrote you a letter," she said.

I knew it was cold at the railroad station and smelled bad and she sounded timid and scared and I flashed on 1 of my own daughters some day, out in the world trying to sell some thing or other. "I will come down and have a cup of coffee with you," I said, "and see you off again on the 9:55 back to New York."

"Fair enough," she said.

More than fair, I thought. It was on just such a sub freezing day in 1963 I received a telephone call from a young woman name of Willa W. Huffaker informing me, to begin with, that her initials were the same as mine backwards, plus which we were born under the same sign. "Honey," said I, "I thank you for this information. I am off on a business trip to the South." Spring training, so it was around February 20, not January, as at present.

"I have got to meet with you," she said, giving me the address of the restaurant in a hospital in New York.

"For what reason?" I inquired.

"For no reason," she said.

"That is not a good enough reason," I replied. "Can you write me a letter? Is it a photo or an autograph you wish?" No, she had 100's of photos of me including photos of me with my eyes poked out with her hole making machine from the office and photos of me pasted on top of photos of various people on the obituary page of the paper.

"No," said she, "for my business is very confidential. "I will meet you in the restaurant in the hospital in Aqua Clara, Florida."

"Then you are on the move," said I, "you are not confined to a hospital."

"Will you send me the money to go to Aqua Clara?" she asked.

"Actually, no," I replied.

Could she write a letter to my lawyer or representative?

I give her Barbara's name and address, which turned out to be 1 of the luckiest strokes of fate of my life, for she went and seen Barbara.

When I arrived in Aqua Clara a message was there from Barbara marked "urgent." I telephoned her immediately. "Do not under any circumstances go and meet that girl with your initials backwards," said Barbara, "for she is insane and dangerous and armed. Call the police. Hire a body guard."

"That seems some what Hollywood," I said.

"Henry," said she, *do what I tell you*," which I done, especially since she under lined it like that. The idea calling the police went against my grain. Here was a girl quite fond of me traveling all the way to Florida for a sight of me and I am putting the police on her instead. What kind of a gentle man is that? Give a girl a break. Where is the harm in it? It is all in fun. A touch and a peck on the cheek or where ever could not hurt 2 grown up people.

When Willa W. Huffaker telephoned me the second time a police man took the call instead, agreeing to meet her in the restaurant of the Aqua Clara Hospital. When he done so she had in her possession 1 knife, 1 gun, 1 bomb, 1 bottle of acid, and 1 bottle of poison pills which she planned on washing down with a glass of Tampa Citrus just before falling across yours truly where I was laying as comfortable as could be except only stabbed, shot, and blew apart.

Due to this experience I usually hesitated when a stranger on the telephone said she wished to see me, but in the case of the woman from West Des Moines I went. With the train coming I could keep the visit to a limit. We crossed the street. I showed her Henry W. Wiggen Mini Park, and she said, "Never in my life was I ever in a park with the person it was named for." She admired the various seats and benches and we went in the diner for coffee. She was the *whitest* girl I ever seen, and thin, and she wore a cloth coat that did not look very warm to me. This is comical when you think about it, for what she was selling me was *ice* from her *Iceoleum* in West Des Moines.

She had a plan for putting me on ice for 125 years. After 125 years some body would wake me up. "When you awake," she said, "you will be in the wonderful world of the future. Disney World will be nothing compared to the vision your eyes will meet. All the problems of the present world will be solved and all your present enemies will be dead. Every body will be as happy as they can be. You are on record against the wars. All the wars will be over and no new wars started then or after. You are a man that is famous for playing games. Life will all be games for every body. You are a friend of all the races and colors. All the races and colors will be kissing and dancing. Every thing will be did by computers."

"This is a bad day to be selling me ice," I said.

"You will feel nothing because you will be sleeping comfortably from being injected with a wonder drug timed for 125 years."

"Only 1 thing worries me," I said. "Who will wake me?"

"It is in the contract," she said, showing me the contract. "The people at Life After will wake you. That is what we are for. Now that you are through using your body you are setting out in that part of life when a man seeks peace for the soul, which you are never libel to find on this earth up against life in its present form. There will be no peace on earth for 125 years. I know what you are going to ask," she said.

"Then you ask it," I said.

"How much is this unheard of opportunity going to cost me?"

"Well, all right, that is as good a question to ask as any other."

"The prices vary," said the freezer girl. "The price for a

single man resting alone is $5,000 including every thing, no strings attached."

"But when I wake up where will my family be?" I inquired.

I do not think she had give this much thought, having no family of her own, but she come up with family rates in no time at all, $4,000 for Holly, $2,500 for each child, and $1,000 a piece for pets. "We all ready signed up Lassie the TV dog," she said. "We got plenty of space still left."

"I will bet," I said. "I got still another question. How do we know that these people from Life After that you mention in the contract are really going to be there and wake me up when the time comes?"

"I guarantee you," she said. "It is all planned out. Life After never fails."

"Honey," I inquired, "do you not recognize that you are talking nothing but a bunch of words? It never fails because it never yet been tried. You are making promises you do not know if you can keep and I am hearing too many of these these past few weeks and feeling double crossed. I worked for a lady 21 years and she double crossed me. A medical doctor double crossed me, giving away secrets."

"Are you sick?" she inquired. "In 125 years the cure will be found for every bad disease going. You will wake up in a world of healthy people."

"No, I am not sick," I said, "and feeling lucky to say so. I got a slightly in large prostrate. Finish your breakfast so as to be ready for your train."

"A slightly in large what?" she inquired. She wrote it down. Some months later I seen why.

"From what I know about life it is hard for me to trust ahead for 125 years," I said. "This lady I worked for become filled with emotion at a certain funeral and we were all 1 big *family* and what not. So she said. A few days later she released me. I heard it on the radio because she could not get the word direct to me, it was a busy day at the office. I am paying you $19,000 for my

self and wife and 4 children plus a number of cats and dogs yet
to be decided on and you are going to make a little note saying
'$19,000 received from Wiggen party, wake them in 125 years,'
and the note is going to sink farther and farther down in the pile
on your desk in till you your self may have took to the ice and
some body wraps up your papers and stores them away. Mean
while what is happening? What is happening is my family and I
are over sleeping."

"It is a money back guarantee," she said.

"I know a nice lady signed contracts to play tennis and was
suppose to receive a certain amount of money. Every body
received the money except her. Mean while what is happening
again? She is playing tennis around the world whereas her managers and husbands fled to the 4 corners of the earth."

"Your money back guarantee will be in the inside pocket of
your coat," she said.

I think she was thinking it up as she went along.

"Ladies will carry their purses with them," the freezer girl
continued, "and their money back guarantee will be in their
purses."

"Here comes your train," I said.

"How do you know?" she asked, looking out of the diner
window through a small spot cleared of ice.

"Because that man with the stick," I said, "is coming to
knock the ice out of the guard rails so they will come down
automatically when the train hits the signal up the track."

"Nothing but unbelievable inventions 1 after another," she
said, "and the top of them all is Life After with its incredible
Iceoleum in Iowa."

"You could write a song," I said. We walked back across the
street through my park and in to the depot. "Tell me," I inquired, "did you actually ever sell 1 of these things to any
body?"

"I sold quite a number," she said.

"I am astonished," I said.

"I sold them but no body bought them," she said. She meant that certain people agreed to buy them but did not yet pay for them. She mentioned several people. I remember Elvis Presley and Muhammed Ali.

"I only wish," said I, "that I had enough where with all to eat breakfast every morning with all the young ladies that look to me like they need food and heat."

"Why not save time and just *give* me the $19,000?" she asked, climbing up on the train.

The very night after I seen Ben Crowder in Washington I telephoned Jack Sprat in Tozerbury saying, "Jack, how in the world are you and how would you like a lead on a promising older pitcher?"

"How older?" Jack inquired.

"About my age," I said.

"Author," he said, "to tell you the gosh God truth this is my luckiest day. I been waiting for your call for weeks. I was in the room when you spoke to Suicide Alexander. He said, 'Wait in till he telephones direct and we can see how deep his *motivation* goes.'"

"My motivation goes to the deepest depths," I said.

"What you got to do," he said, "is hop in the car and come down and we will carry on some exploratory conversation which I know will turn in to the happiest day of our life. Marva will throw another steak on the fire."

My whole mood changed. Driving along with Hilary I was singing and whistling and drumming my fingers on the wheel while Hilary sung and whistled and read about California in the Encyclopedia Britannica. Play ball! It was the coldest day of the year, 2 months to spring time for every body else, 1 month to spring time for me, off I would go to the South again, never mind the big freeze in 125 years, give me a ball field in southern California now, there was Jack Sprat my manager, there was me, his most experienced hand, a young club with tons of energy and spirit, I seen Ben Crowder drooling, I seen Patricia crying her eyes out watching California sail past, 3 games ahead by the end of May, 6 games by the end of June, 9 by the end of July, 12 games by the end of August, followed by a spurt in the stretch where we put the pressure on and won the pennant by some sort of a record, what ever the record was.

"So you see, my girl," said I to Hilary, "how things are looking up at last for us. I am back in the picture again. I got an extremely strong hunch that Jack Sprat is going to give me a job playing ball and my very own daughter name of Hilary Margaret Wiggen will be sitting in the stands and watching like her sisters before her."

"I hope we are going to the horses before we are going to the Sprats," said Hilary Margaret.

"No," said I, "we are catching Jack Sprat while he is hot and as soon as we are done with our business there we will scoot over to the horses." She was silent. It was the silence before screaming. "If you scream," said I, "I am going to open the door of this car and push you out with out slowing down too much if at all."

She begun screaming. While she was screaming I telephoned Holly, saying "Listen to this I am putting up with for a change. Can you hear me?"

"I thought Dr. Schiff cured her," said my wife.

"You are not helping," I said.

"I can not help a man that is doing him self in 2 ways," she said. "You are taking her to horses because she was disappointed regarding Washington, and you are seeing Jack Sprat because she was disappointed about you retiring."

"Released," I said.

"Released. She not only wants both things but she wants them both at the same time, and you are giving them to her. She wants the first prize and the consolation prize in all divisions and all classes at all weights and if she does not get them she will scream. I hear that she stopped."

"What is she saying?" Hilary asked.

"Speak to her your self," said I.

"Yes, mother," said she, listening awhile and hanging up. "Mother says we should go to the Sprats first and buy horses second," she said.

"Horses plural," I said. "We said 1 horse and 1 only."

"They need company," said Hilary.

"Only 1 horse, not 2, not 3, and not a 6 pack of horses neither."

"I am putting my self in Dr. Schiff's office," said Hilary. "Do not settle for 1 horse when you can get 2 or 3 or 6. If I hear it in her voice it sounds disgusting, but if I hear it in my own voice it sounds perfectly nice. I realize that I been extremely selfish all along. I will never scream again."

Soon we passed through Minnow, which is a small town on the road between Perkinsville and Tozerbury. Some times the school bus stopped there when we traveled back and forth for ball games, and I stopped there now for gas, stepping out of the car for a breath of air and suddenly feeling tremendous pressure on my bladder. For several moments I wondered if I could actually stand the pain. I dashed in to the filthy little men's room.

But the pain stopped. The reason it stopped was because the pressure of the Precious Golden Cleansing Fluid was temporary only, while passing through the canal. It was not like I was full. This was an important lesson to me and a great help. I learned to figure the difference between *a full bladder* and a *temporary traffic jam* through the canal. Once learning this I lived accordingly. I put a watch on it. I discovered that my bladder fills only once in 4 or 5 hours whereas the pressure might come and go several times in 4 or 5 hours. Therefore I learned to pay no attention to it and live through it and bear the pain for a few minutes and forget it. I regulated my liquid in take and acted accordingly, too much liquid in take increased the pressure sooner, go easy on the liquid in take and you know the pressure soon will pass. I do not remember any thing else I ever learned while passing through Minnow except for this.

Jack Sprat was not home when we arrived. Some thing went out of me right away. Only a little while before I been singing in the car. "Marva will throw another steak on the fire," he said. If you say your wife will throw another steak on the fire she should be throwing it on when your guest arrives.

"He did not mention you were coming," said Marva. She was watching the TV and having a hard time taking her eye off it. "These are the morning stories I am watching," she said. "They will be over in a few hours." There were 8 or 10 pieces of furniture in the living room and 6 or 8 of these were old TV sets now used as tables. You could also sit on 1 and no body complained. The only 1 she cared about was the 1 that worked at the time. It went 24 hours a day with out stopping. That night I turned it off. "Is this not a grand surprise to see you?" Marva inquired, but she did not act surprised at all and I begun to think she knew I was on the way after all. Some thing had went wrong.

"And a grand surprise for me, too," said I, "to be seeing you after all these years."

"We last met at the All Star Game 9 years ago," she said.

"Is that definite?" I asked.

"I looked it up in my little memory book," she said. She wore a house coat. I did not see her dressed all spring. She said she planned going out 1 day in the summer. She said she would go to the World Series if Jack got in it in October. "Other wise," said she, "I plan on staying around home and keeping an eye on the cock roaches."

They had winter cock roaches and 2 very big dogs that knocked every body down where ever they went, and many fine children. "Oh no," said Marva, "the fine children belong to the neighbors, we got only Robert and Stuffy."

"We can go and see the horses mean while," said Hilary. "I thought Mr. Sprat was so hot over you."

"Jack *is* hot over you," said Marva. "Trust me. The minute you were released he said 'I would bite off my own thumb to have him pitch for me.'"

"Maybe he is out biting off his thumb," I suggested.

"He simply went out for a bottle of wine," Marva said. Later she said he went out and seen a man about some fence. Still later she said some thing else again. "He will be back any minute," she said. "He must of been slightly delayed."

The very same thing was happening on 1 of the morning stories Marva was viewing on the TV. A certain man was expected back where several women and children were waiting for him. "He stepped out some time ago," said Marva. "In fact, about 6 months ago."

"The ladies are certainly patient," I said. "Where are the children?"

"We never see the children," Marva said.

"Where has he went?" I inquired.

"I do not think he is coming back ever," said Marva Sprat. "He is on another show." She switched to another channel. "There he is," she said, "and I do not think he will ever come back." She continued watching the other show, which also had children you never saw.

"I hope Jack has not went over to another show," I said.

Marva smiled. It was the first time I seen her smile, although I was there at least a ½ hour by now. "Jack is no morning story. Where ever he is he is out fighting to get you on his ball club."

"Fighting who and where in Tozerbury?" I inquired.

"Take my word for it," she said. "Jack would never lie."

"Mean while," said I, "Hilary and I will go and visit the horses."

"That is a very good plan," said Marva, "and when you are back Jack will be here I can guarantee you."

Hilary and I and Stuffy Sprat drove over to see the horse lady. "Some thing went wrong with your father," I said to Stuffy. "Is he 1 of those men that often forget appointments?"

"Maybe he had a fight with your mother," Hilary said, "and raged out of the house in a fit."

"They never fight," said Stuffy, "and he never forgets. He is a great man."

"You and your mother are agreed about that," I said.

"We believe he will win the pennant," said Stuffy.

"The last manager I saw was in a coffin," said Hilary.

"He was not so sure," Stuffy continued, "but with you on his ball club he is confident of it now. He believes you will save 25 or 30 games for him in 2 inning jobs."

"Then where is he?" I inquired. "Never mind," I added on, "do not answer," for I could see he was under instructions. "I hope this horse lady has a bath room," said I.

"You just used the bath room at our house," said Stuffy.

"He has got the prostrate problem," Hilary said.

We bought 1 horse. When we entered the stable all the horses begun urinating at once. It was a noise, I can assure you, and it increased the pressure on my bladder some thing awful. You will think that I talk too much about the urinary habits of people and horses, but when you your self have a particular difficulty in some area of your body you can not talk about very much else. You think that no blessing on earth can be greater than simply doing once again what you formerly done constantly with out thinking. During all the years I played ball I rose in the morning and urinated if I did not forget. If I forgot I urinated later, standing a minute or 2 and delivering a stream with all the force of a fire hose. Probably I urinated before the ball game if I remembered, or between the games of a double header, and before I went to bed if I remembered. How many times I heard my roomie pissing in the night with all the force of Niagara Falls in the toilet. There was no such a thing as a problem, no dribbling, no leaking, no question in my mind, "Should I or should I not go to the bath room?" I never woke up nights. I never left a bed, never left a ball game, never left a meal, never left a moving picture, never left my seat in the air plane, never knew I had a bladder, never knew I had a prostrate gland, and never knew how precious my Precious Golden Cleansing Fluid was. And of all the sounds that put the pressure on my bladder no sound was heavier than the sound of horses urinating on the wooden planks of their stalls in the stable. Other people say other things, but for me the pressure was from horses first, and after that several other types of noise, such as the humming of electric razors in the club house with electric hair dryers close behind, ball park crowds booing, or a woman whistling.

"I love them all," said Hilary, running around and greeting all the horses.

"It is too bad you can not buy them all," said the horse lady. She had an Italian accent, I believe, and her boots were covered with manure higher than ever. It looked to me like she might not of shoveled the place out since the last time Hilary been there.

"I can only buy 1 at a time," Hilary said. "Who is not sold?"

"All horses not sold please raise their hand," said the horse lady. It was her sense of humor. "Are you going to play for Jack Sprat?" she asked me.

"Well," said I, "picking up a little horse talk I can tell you that I do not intend to be turned out to pasture."

"Good for you," she said. "Jack is a wonderful man and every body in town loves him." She told me a funny story. When Tozerbury had a ball team she thought it was the big leagues. She just come from Italy and never knew a thing about baseball. "Do you know that the baseball is called a *horse* hide?" she inquired.

"Yes," said I, "and you better lower your voice, for when Hilary first heard they made horses into baseballs she screamed for 1 hour straight."

Hilary rode around and around on every horse. Some were sold and some were not. She had an extremely difficult time making up her mind. She thought it would be easier buying 4 than making up her mind. It turned out that 1 of the problems was she did not like their names. "Darling," said the horse lady, "a horse does not mind if you change their name," and this made it easier for Hilary. She bought a horse and named it "Late Manager Dutch," which was the name we needed for the various papers. "Dutch," for short, remained boarding with the horse lady in till the spring. I could of boarded my self some place cheaper.

Returning to the Sprats' house I asked Stuffy Sprat to direct me past the high school field. It sat beside the lake. I had forgot about the lake. I played ball games there against Tozerbury High in 1946, 1947, and 1948. "That was all most 25 years," I said. Stuffy whistled between his teeth. He was a very polite boy, like his father. "Did we beat you?" he inquired.

"Stuffy," I replied, "I do not wish to sound like a boaster, but you did not beat me because as a high school pitcher no body beat me. I won every game I pitched. In high school the boy with the fast ball can not be beat. It is all you need." I had no memory of the details of the games I played vs. Tozerbury High although I later looked them up in my scrap books in my cellar. I remembered, however, that I played high school ball games on *3 whole hours sleep* after chasing 17 girls in automobiles from 1 end of the county to the other and done so again on the following night and felt all the better for it and looked forward to doing it once more tomorrow.

Jack Sprat was still not home when we returned. "He had a little problem settling some thing at the telephone company," Marva said. "We will go ahead lunch and he will be along lickety split." Every body took a glass and a plate and sat in front of an old TV set and ate off the top of it while 2 big dogs jumped up and down arguing over the menu. It was not comfortable. If I had knew Jack would not be back I would of stopped at McDonald's. "Marva," said I, "I want to face right up to this thing. If Jack is sending a message in my direction I wish to go home. I am told on every side that he wishes me to play for him.

If he is receiving contrary advice from some other party they are not the first 1. Save me from wasting my time."

She was on the edge of tears. "I am in a bind," she said.

"I must be going home," I said. I telephoned home, speaking to Holly. "We are on the way home," I said. "We are leaving now."

"Do not say that," said Marva.

"What do you suggest I say?" I inquired. "Am I suppose to sit here all day just you and me and the dogs?"

"Why not?" she inquired.

"Who is that voice in the back ground?" Holly asked.

"Marva Sprat is pleading with me to stay," I said.

"Did you have a good visit with Jack?" asked my wife. "I suppose some thing went wrong or you would of told me."

"A wonderful visit with Jack," I sarcastically replied. "I have not *saw* Jack."

Marva now stood beside me at the telephone and I decided to stay. She did not touch me, but she was close and I was sorry I had spoke to her as above, saying "Am I suppose to sit here all day just you and me and the dogs?" Later, as we become friendlier and friendlier, she some times said to me, "No body here just you and me and the dogs and it is not so bad after all."

"However," said I to my wife, "I am going to give him a little more time to collect him self together."

"Tell her he been on the phone all day with Mr. Alexander," said Marva, "although I was not suppose to tell you."

Yes, he was 10 hours on the telephone with Suicide Alexander in California before the day was out. It was a long day for all of us, and interesting. Hilary went back and stood with the horses and I remained at Marva's waiting for Jack to return from the telephone company. He went there to be private, fighting for me against Suicide Alexander. I was told that Jack cried and raged and quit and was rehired all in the 1 long conversation.

The 1 thing he did not do was swear. Jack was famous for 2 things and 1 of them was not swearing. Some times he tried but he could not do it right. I heard the story that he once called an umpire an "organist" and expected to be threw out of the game. The game was held up some minutes in till every body could stop laughing. Hard as he tried, his swearing come out twisted or backwards or up side down or simply wrong. I wrote some things down, although people don't generally enjoy you writing things down. Jack did not mind. He trusted me. He trusted every body in till they were proved bad. His favorite swear word was "damgod" and another was "screwbitch," while "batsucker" was still another. "Them batsucking screwbitches," he might say, "and their damgod pig knots." What did such a thing mean? Nothing. His ball players laughed and I did not think it was a good thing for ball players to laugh and imitate their manager. On the bench I heard him say, "It is a terrible thing to call a fellow, but he is a blamey ass snotty wiper. Do not tell him I said so."

The second thing he was famous for was chewing licorice. He chewed licorice because he did not enjoy chewing tobacco, and he told me he did not really enjoy the licorice either but chewed it because people thought it was tobacco. "It makes me look tough," he said, "and brings about respect. I know I do not look tough on account of my chin recedes. No body notices it but I notice it when I look in the mirror buying a suit. I should get a chin transplant."

When Newton ("Jack") Sprat become manager of California every body said "Who?" He played 11 years and was steady. He coached for 8 more. He was a short stop and he made the plays. He was not much of a hitter but he run every thing out and got on base a lot and used his head when he got there and scored many runs. I personally found him very rest full to pitch against. I use to let him get a piece of the ball because he never hit it very far. I never tried to strike him out but he struck out any how. He hit 6 singles off me in 11 years and 1 more single in high school.

According to the record he played in 1 World Series and 1

All Star Game and from what I can guess he been faith full to 1 wife since they were sweet 16 in Tozerbury. Marva on the other hand was far from faith full to him. He was never a loser but he was simply never a winner. When Suicide Alexander chose him he chose him for his *motivation,* for that was the question Suicide asked about every body, "Where is their *motivation?*" That is what they talked about 10 hours on the telephone, "Where is Wiggen's *motivation?*" Have you got the desire? If you have got the desire, for what? Jack Sprat never made any big money and so he had it dangling before him yet to make like the carrot chasing the donkey. He was a hard working man. He was my own exact age and looked 20 years older and he thought he was now about to become a big winner at last.

About 5 o'clock in the afternoon I said, "Stuffy Sprat, you are living through a history making moment. Where is your father? He left the telephone company but has not returned here. Very shortly I am leaving for home for ever. That will be the end of my baseball career."

"He will be here," said Marva. "Before you leave you must stay for dinner."

"I all ready stood for lunch," I said. Between lunch and dinner I had no exercise and no out of doors. Marva walked around and around the living room all afternoon. It was her exercise. I would of thought some body that stood in the house all the time would of had very bad muscle tone, but that was not the case. Now and then she breathed deep out a window for fresh air.

"Many people been held in prisons much worse than this," she said. "The difference between this and them is that here the prisoner got the key." She talked 10 times on the telephone in the afternoon to people in Tozerbury she had not saw in several years. She had ½ a mind to go out and see what the telephone looked like in my car but she never quite worked up to it.

Hilary loved her. At dinner I had fantasies I was married to Marva Sprat, there we were, I was at the head of the table in Jack's place with our children name of Hilary, Stuffy, Robert, and 2 big dogs. Hilary did not think any thing was wrong with Marva at all. Between the 2 of them they believed every thing was facts. Hilary said she drunk a great deal of coffee, as many as 12 cups per day, and Marva believed her. Hilary at that time never drunk a cup of coffee in her life. Towards the end of dinner Marva said, "All right, leave us go in and sit by the fire in the fire place awhile." I did not remember any fire in the fire place. I love a fire and would of remembered and would of probably threw some wood on it because I love to watch the wood burn. When we walked out of the dining room in to the living room there not only was no fire in the fire place, *there was no fire place.* Yet her and Hilary sat around facing a wall where there was going to be a fire place 1 of these days as soon as some body built 1. They had many plans for improving their house. Hilary warmed her hands before the fire in the fire place not yet built. And yet if I or Holly seen a fire place where there was none we would of had a great deal of explaining to do.

Marva washed the dishes and I dried them and she smoked a cigarette when the children were out of sight. "Do not mention to Jack that I smoke," she said.

"Jack who?" I inquired. Once again I telephoned home. "We are on our way," said I to Holly, "and this time it is for real. We had dinner. We had lunch and bought a horse and saw the Tozerbury High ball field and watched the morning stories on TV and chewed the fat all afternoon. You missed a weirdo for your book in title *Baseball Wives.* Marva give me all sorts of cock and bull stories where Jack was, he was seeing a man about a fence, he was buying a bottle of wine, he was telephoning from the telephone company for privacy in till she finally admitted she could not imagine where he went, or why, or when he will be back, and here he comes right now, walking in the door, so I do not know *when* we will be home."

"Author," cried Jack, rushing up to me and placing his hands on my shoulders, "I owe you 10,000 apologies."

"You owe me more than that," said I.

"I will bet you are starving for dinner," he said.

"No," said I, "we ate dinner. I occupied your place at the table. I took over your duties as husband and father."

"You do not know what I been through," he said. "I will tell you more and more about it. I am drained. I am rung out like a limp dish rag."

"Probably you could use a drink," I said.

"We do not drink in this house," he said, adding on in a lower voice, "in till the children are retired for the night." Raising his voice again he introduced me to Ed Lewis. "Ed is my fence man and fire place man and Jack of every trade. He was also quite a ball player in his day for Tozerbury High. He hit a home run off you."

We all shook hands and I begun asking Ed about his baseball career because people appreciate you asking, but he interrupted me first, saying "Do you have a fence around your house because you certainly should?"

"Wait in till you hear the cost of fences before answering," said Jack. "I thought a fence was where you hired Ed and he bought some boards and stuck them in the ground, but now he tells me that my fence will cost $600."

"Fences do not cost a god dam thing," said Ed, "when compared to the cost of not having a fence and the blowing and the damage of the wind as a result." He asked me several questions concerning my property. Was I protected by trees? How close was I to the road? Did children walk across my property on their way to school? Was I in the path of the winds? He drew a sketch of my property and I said, "You never seen my property, Ed, how can you draw a sketch of it?"

"From memory," he said. "I estimate I will build you a fence for $1,200."

"You are building a fence for Jack for $600," I said.

"You got a much bigger property," he said.

"Jack got more wind," I said.

"I will build you a fence for $1,100," said Ed, "and keep the bastards out."

"I just remembered," I said, "we all ready got a fence."

"Oh," said he, "that is different," and tore up the sketch he drew.

"Ed," said Jack, "how come you are not more impressed that I got Henry Wiggen right here in my own house?"

"If you had a fence you could kept him out," Ed replied.

"I would not wish to kept him out," said Jack, "because he is going to be my left hand late relief, he is going to save 25 or 30 games during the season ahead and we are going to win it all. I will bet you are starving for dinner," said Jack.

"Like I said, Jack," I replied, "I ate dinner all ready."

"Marva darling," said Jack, "Author ate but if you will throw an extra steak on the fire for me I will appreciate it. It been a long day and my tongue is falling out. I been 10 hours on the telephone with Mr. Alexander if you can believe it, mostly regarding you. Maybe 9 hours regarding you and 1 hour regarding the rest. The telephone company served me lunch and 2 pitchers of water while I talked." He made many notes of his conversation and begun fishing them out of his pockets.

Hilary went off to bed, stopping first to say "Good night." "I am pleased to meet my father's new manager," said she to Jack.

"My daughter is anxious to see me play ball," I said.

"Hilary darling," said Jack to her, "if it was up to me you would see your father play plenty. However, 1 of the things worrying Mr. Alexander is just that." He now turned to me. "You went and said to him exactly that. You wished to play ball for your daughter's sake. Mr. Alexander does not under stand that kind of *motivation*. He wishes you to be *motivated* by money only." He now turned back to Hilary. "Hilary darling," he said, "you under stand that you and me and your father under stand wishing to play for your sake. But Mr. Alexander is another problem."

"I am always agreeable to what ever adults decide," said Hilary.

"I can see that by looking at you," Jack said.

"I actually do not recall speaking to Mr. Alexander regarding my daughter," I said.

"Well, he got it on the tape," said Jack. "He played it to me. That is what took up a good deal of our talking time, them bushwack tapes he can prove every thing with. Here it was, you said to him some thing like this. 'I am not too interested in the money, Mr. Alexander. It is a family matter with me. I wish to have my darling daughter see me play.'"

"That sounds like my father," said Hilary.

"I am sure it was," I said. "He called me some time ago following Dutch's funeral. We had a mix up over golf clubs. He did not mention he was *taping* the conversation."

"He is not libel to mention it to any body," said Jack, "but now that you know you will speak accordingly if you get him on the phone. Do not let him know you know, for this can work to our advantage as well. If you wish him to think you believe the moon is cheese you say to him over and over, 'the moon is cheese,' and he plays it over and over to him self in till he believes you believe it, for he has heard you say it not once but 100 times. I tell you he is a genius on the tapes. Well, we will talk about these things and many more when the dinner gets going."

"You were there when I talked to him," I said.

"You got a memory as good as a tape," said Jack. "There is no explaining his reasons for any thing he does. He only replies, 'I won a World Series, did I not?' and whips out his bank book and shows it to you."

"He showed it to me at Dutch's funeral," I said.

"It is a wonder he did not show it to Dutch him self laying all prepared," said Jack. "Speaking no ill of the dead, I wish Dutch died about 24 hours earlier and never ended up playing golf with Mr. Alexander. The last person they talked about while golfing was you. Dutch said, 'You would not want him for any thing, he saved every penny since the day he was born, he got nothing to win having all ready won it all, his wife teaches school and flowers her garden, he would as soon walk away as fight you for it.' But the thing that is *saving* you and giving you a fighting chance in the mind of Mr. Alexander was Dutch saying *you saved every penny since the day you were born.* There is *motivation.* There you got a grand moment of sharing with Mr. Alexander. We will build it up over the weeks ahead, developing the idea what a *tight wad* you are with the dollar and eager for more in till you can corner all the dollars in the world and bury them in your back yard pretending all the while that what you are doing out there is helping your wife in her garden."

"Then if I under stand correctly," I said, "we are not about to sign a contract right away."

Him and Ed Lewis were measuring the wall. Jack had a hard time looking at me. "Not right away," said Jack.

"Well, it is late," I said, "and I have got a bit of a drive home through scenic Minnow, so leave me gather up my daughter and leave."

"Please, Author," said Jack. "Relax. We had a trying moment today, but every thing is going to be up hill and down hill from this minute forward. Stretch out on that sofa by the fire place. I got my way on several points with him all winter and we will win this 1 yet. We will find a way of dealing with the key word."

"*Motivation,*" I said.

"Yes," said Jack. "You see how close together you and me are. Mr. Alexander believes you got no *motivation,* you are too rich, and we have got to give him some answers to his questions. Why would you wish to play ball for us? How could he pay such a rich man as you?"

"By check," I said.

"That is the kind of an answer that will not get us any place. It is not that he him self is a tight wad. He wishes to pay people a lot of money, but they have got to need it very badly. He is convinced that no body is going to want it unless they need it and never had it. Simply wanting to do it for the thrill of it is nothing he can under stand. He never played ball, so he does not know what it feels like. If he hears of any body doing any thing free he laughs up his sleeve. If I had my choice I would never play ball for a man that never played ball. But what can we do? He is changing our life. After all our life in Tozerbury we are moving to California."

"I would not move too quick," I said. "Once you unpack your bags they got you at their mercy."

This went in and out his head with out stopping.

"In till this year we never had a penny in the bank," said Jack. "I show him how delirious I am with the money he pays me. I got stock in the club. I got travel money and pocket expenses and all these things make me appreciate him. Some body like *me* he can under stand. You got no idea what a big salary I am making and how it compares with my finances in the past. As soon as Ed leaves I will tell you how much I make."

"You owe me for 2 hours use of my telephone," said Ed.

"I went to Ed's house after the telephone company closed," Jack said. "Mr. Alexander *likes* to pay people. It is not true that he is a tight wad and cheap skate which so many people say. He is the world's most *generous* tight wad and cheap skate."

"I heard he runs and turns out the lights in the ball park the minute the game is over," I said.

"You heard right," said Jack, "and many other similar things that we all laugh over. He does not mind looking like a fool. He says, 'They will not think I am such a fool when they read my bank book,' and he will shove it in your hand at the drop of a hat and sit there while you read it and give you more or less of a little question and answer test on it afterwards."

"He showed it to me at Dutch's funeral," I said. "As I recall it showed a certain sum of money out at interest and never touched."

"A ½ a $1,000,000 is correct," said Jack, "never been touched, simply drawed interest year after year."

"As I recall," I said, "it was not a very good use of his money."

"He does not need to make any use of it at all," said Jack. "He proves it to you by showing you he does not even need to touch them gosh dingly dollars. I am drooling looking at ½ a $1,000,000 he does not even need to touch. In that situation you know who is the king and who is the simple working stiff. No body can speak for him or against him as far as it matters to him. His mind takes a long time to arrive at a decision but once it is there it is the Rocks of Gibraltar."

"Believe me, Jack," said I, "I am grateful for the way you have give me a line on dealing with him. I will explain to him how badly I need the money. I got no money now. I formerly had it."

"You got no money now?" Jack asked. I would say "his chin fell open" but he got no chin.

"Oh no," I replied. "I am talking for the benefit of Suicide Alexander. Formerly I had it. I lost it or some thing like that."

"You need it *now*. You *must* have it. That is your *motivation*."

"My lawyer will plead with him."

"Yes," said Jack, "he respects lawyers."

"My funds are at the bottom of the barrel."

"You could give up the telephone in your car," said Ed Lewis. "You could sell back your horse."

"The trouble with my lawyer," I said, "is she will ask for deferred payment."

"Oh no, for God sake no," said Jack. "You do not wish to have money deferred. You must have it right in your hand right this minute. A single word about deferred payment will set every thing back to where his mind was yesterday. Leave us hold the line. Approach him with suspicion. Look around you like the collectors are following. Ask him for certain quantities of cash under the table free of taxes. Show him that you want more now and less later, you got a hot deal on the fire now, you need money to put it in and you and I will have some happy years together on the California ball club. I see it. You are going to be a wonderful and stable influence on my young players and you are going to save me game after game with short relief."

I relaxed on the sofa by the fire place. The house become chilly. All the houses of ball players in modest circumstances are always chilly, the rooms are small, the floors are bare, the roast beef is cut very thin, the stairs creak to the second floor, and the banisters are libel to come off in your hand. Marva come down the stairs from seeing the children in bed. She changed in to another house coat and her face looked much healthier from breathing out the window. The dogs quieted down some where and I said to Jack, "How would you feel about a tremendous request?"

"Request away," said he.

"I would love to turn off the TV," I said.

"There is only 1 of them on," he said, laughing and jumping up and turning it off. "Marva loves the morning stories."

"It is not morning any more," said I. "I have got a slight head ache."

"I will get you an aspirin," he said. "Maybe you are hungry. Marva will throw an extra steak on the fire."

"I been thinking about telling you a little story about throwing an extra steak on the fire," I said. "You got a boy on your ball club name of Tom Roguski. I and his father come up through Queen City together. We were very close buddies in the early 50's, you could not of separated us with a crow bar."

"He was a shortstop," said Jack, "1 of the best people I ever saw charging the hop."

"You got it," I said.

"His son is a catcher," Jack said, "and he can really hit the ball. But people like you and me have got to teach him control of his temper."

"His father had a bit of an odd streak in him," said I. I told Jack and Marva the following incident. Coker Roguski left baseball in the late 1950's, returning home to West Virginia. Then 1 cold winter night 6 or 8 years later we received a telephone call, hello, hello, it is Coker Roguski, he is a traveling man now, driving down through Perkinsville from Albany. "Holy God," I cried out, "we will throw another steak on the fire," and I give him all these particular directions on reaching our house, and we go down in the fire proof trophy room and find certain old films showing him making some fantastic plays as well as a base hit up the middle winning the third game of the 1957 World Series and so forth, bearing in mind that some people do not care for pictures of them self. We never force film on people like some people do. Well, we wait and we wait all evening. He never arrives, never telephones, never drops a line afterwards. I telephoned him several times, but I never reached him, and he never returned my messages.

"It is 1 of them mysteries of life," said Marva, "which life is full of."

"I hate them," said I.

Up jumped Jack with a hot idea. "An idea crossed my mind," he said. "It would be wonderful if you really *stole* Mr. Alexander's golf clubs. He would respect you for that."

"Do you know what I am thinking about," I asked, "now that the children are safe in their bed? It been a long day for me and I would be refreshed by a small glass of wine or a liqueur if you by chance have any close by."

"Yes," said Jack, "I am never too happy to oblige. I do not drink it my self but you will enjoy a glass by the roaring fire," and from the coat closet he brang a bottle of Vine Hill White from the Santa Cruz Mountains, California, or any how a *bottle,* for what was in the bottle was some thing else again. I do not know what. It had that Kool Aid taste. I made it last all night. "I realize white wine should be kept in the ice box," said Jack, "but the boys are always going there whereas they never go in the coat closet."

"They throw every thing on the floor," said Marva.

"I under stand," I said.

"I am sure that girls never throw their coats on the floor," said Marva.

"Girls throw coats on the floor," said I. "I learned 1 lesson in life that been very help full, which is this. Every thing boys got going in their minds and bodies girls got the same."

"You are a rare man," said Marva.

"I do not even think it is true," said Jack. "Never mind that mental material." He brung his steak to the fire place and pulled up a chair and ate off his knees and we talked a long time. "This whole day is coming back to me," he said. "Mr. Alexander argued you pitched only against the weaker clubs last year."

"I pitched better and worse both," I said.

"I proved it to him," Jack said. "We went over you last year game by game. About 10 times you pitched with out ever giving up a run the first 2 innings. You are a sure thing for 2 innings. What else have we got that is a sure thing? I said to Mr. Alexander, 'We should not make him fight for this job, we should be running after him on bended knee,' for if we need 1 thing in the world it is dependable short relief. 'Any body can pitch 2 innings of relief,' said Mr. Alexander, so the next thing I am doing is I am going over the records of how many people come out for an inning or 2 short relief and got bombed to hail St. Mary and beyond. Oh, Author, when you rung that phone I knew my future was made. Then he starts in giving me this argument concerning *motivation*. I tell him, 'Look, up in Perkinsville Henry is fighting to keep hold of a little park, he is engaged in a terrible quarrel with the city. Concerning what? Concerning money. Just dollars, that is all.' I made many arguments I did not believe in. I said, 'Mr. Alexander, some time we can even announce him as a starting pitcher and that will draw many 1,000's of people to the ball parks, specially in cities that have not saw too much of him such as expansion cities. He is big and popular in New York and California both, which is where all the people are to begin with.' I think he went for arguments along those lines although I my self was ashamed of them. 'Mr. Alexander,' said I, 'was there ever a breath of scandal regarding Henry Wiggen? Never. He is the cleanest liver known. So we do not worry that we are getting a fellow in bad health. He is a responsible family man with 6 daughters.'"

"4," I said, correcting him.

"Well, boost it to 6," Jack said. "Do not make a liar out of me."

"What is 2 female girls more or less?" Marva inquired.

"I hit him time and time again with the statement Dutch Schnell made to him with his dying breath. You saved every penny you ever owned. You will be good public relations. You have give 1,000's and 1,000's of talks in the schools against drugs, liquor, and other bad vices. You are the author of printed books. Your wife runs a school bringing in a few extra family bucks. You never run with any woman but her. You were never arrested in a fight in a saloon or any thing close to it. 'Mr. Alexander,' said I, 'this is the missing connection we been looking for all winter. You did not win a pennant in 20 years, but I am telling you on my honor with every bit of knowledge I possess that if you hire Henry Wiggen for me you will be at the start of a new bank book.'"

After a while the chill went out of the room, and I was warm, like the fire been real. Maybe it was the wine. No, more likely it was the heat of Jack's enthusiasm. It was all real to him, his ball club, his future, my future, his family life in California. "Marva will take to the streets again in California," he said. He named the players on his club, going up and down the list and telling me their good points and their bad, naming off their names like they were kings. All this time his plate was on his knees. By 1 o'clock in the morning he had not yet ate his steak. His face was red and shining and sweating. It was the first time I seen any body sweat since the Japanese hot springs. "Every thing is ready to go," he said. "I am prepared for the big opportunity."

Maybe once or twice I rose and went to the bath room up stairs. In the bed rooms where the children were the dogs growled when I walked past. I went to the bath room very casually, concealing the fact that the pressure on my bladder troubled me. I did not wish Jack to have any questions in his mind about my health. "A few hours ago," I said, "I was feeling down on you, thinking you owed me 10,000 apologies."

"More than that," said Jack.

"No, if any body in the world owes me nothing at all it is you."

"We would be talking yet," said Jack, "for he loves to talk on the telephone."

"But you become too exhausted," I said.

"No, he never exhausts," said Jack, "he run out of tape."

"Where did you put my daughter?" I inquired.

"Come on up stairs and we will find her together," said Jack.

"Finish your dinner," said Marva, and she went up stairs with me instead while Jack finished his dinner at 2 o'clock in the morning. In front of the room where Hilary was Marva placed her hand on my back. "Come again," she said. When we opened the door 1 of the dogs was guarding Hilary's bed, growling at me and flashing his teeth in the dark. He was up on the bed standing over Hilary. Marva talked to him nicely for a while and he followed her away and I picked Hilary up and carried her down, and at 2 o'clock in the morning we were driving home. "The ball is in Mr. Alexander's court now," said Jack. "He will reach you. Wait for his little old ring a ling." I felt like I was back in baseball again. I felt like the word "California" was wrote across my shirt.

7

Where was this "little old ring a ling" I was suppose to hear any minute? There was no hot line from Suicide Alexander to Perkinsville. Or if there was it was as hot as the fire in the fire place that did not yet exist but was soon to be built by Ed Lewis in case the time and money could be arranged.

Some things were true, how ever. I seen by an old scrap book in my cellar that Ed Lewis did hit a home run off me in the last high school game I ever played, and "Vernon Sprat" hit a single by which I assumed they meant "Jack." In that game Perkinsville High beat Tozerbury High by a score of 5-1. At Jack's house that night they could not remember how the game come out, although they could remember their own hits. Ball players can not separate them self from the situation. I seen that happen all the time. I remember every boy in the Perkinsville line up very clearly. Where have they all went I do not know. Arthur La Frenais and Mort Finnegan were killed in the war against Korea. Dennis Folb become rather rich as a stock broker in New York, give several nice gifts to Mrs. Wiggen's School for Privileged Children, stopped giving gifts when the children marched against Vietnam and now begun giving gifts again, but smaller.

"Ring a ling, where are you?" I inquired for many days while walking around the house. "What a totally chinless bastard he is," said I to Holly. "Never trust a man that hides wine in the closet."

"Storming around and abusing Jack Sprat's face is not a productive activity," my wife replied. "His face is not his fault. A week ago you thought he was 1 of the finest men living."

"What am I going to do with the rest of my life?" I inquired.

"Now is our chance to do a 1,000,000 things," she replied. "We will flower my garden, which will soon be peeking out from under all the snow, or we can visit vineyards in Spain or California as discussed with the thought of living there and watching the trees grow, or we can move to some other climate which is better for the growing aches and pains of younger older men like your self, or we can taste a sample of Paris and Europe as discussed."

"Hilary would love to go and live in horse country," I said.

"Hilary will go where we drag her," said Holly.

"I might buy a horse my self and take up riding," I said.

"Because you are charmed with Miss Horse Shit Ankles of 1971," said my wife.

"I suppose it might be taking Jack Sprat time to clear his roster," I suggested.

"No," she replied, "my guess is that what is taking his time is discovering he can not accomplish what he told you he could accomplish while the 3 of you were sitting by the fire place drinking bad wine and growing red in the face and sweating streams down the side of his head in the middle of the winter."

"He did not drink any wine," I said.

"All the more proof," Holly said. "A man that does not even need to drink to be drunk is carried away by the flow of his own dreams. In the light of day he does not have the power he told you he had in the middle of the night. Poor Jack, his pride is broke. Soon he will be as smart and mean as Ben Crowder."

"It is that fucking money mad Suicide Alexander," said I, "who does not believe I have the *motivation* to play ball because I socked a few dollars away."

We invited Barbara up and she spent several whole days off and on trying to reach Jack Sprat or Alexander in California, but she could not get them on the line. "I begin to get the feeling they are avoiding me," she said. "They will not return my call. I reached as far as the club house in California. I could hear the lockers slamming in the back ground. I could hear the steam in the showers and the young men running around all naked. I could hear the trainer massaging the stiffness of winter out of their dear young bones, but I could not get Jack Sprat or Mr. Alexander on the line."

"I will bet Marva can get Jack on the phone," I said. This was the only good idea I had all month. Barbara telephoned Marva, but that was not as good as an idea as the first 1. They did not seem to get along too well, becoming jealous and suspicious from the start. I could under stand it. They were both very anxious to help me and wished to be first in the field, which I deeply appreciated. "I do not think we will depend entirely on her," said Barbara. "Leave us use her as we see fit. Be patient, sit tight, and behave your self and you will play ball yet and show them all."

"I do not wish to show them all," I said. "I only wish to show Hilary."

While in Perkinsville Barbara done 1 specially profitable thing, diving in my fire proof room in the cellar and coming up with various materials I long since forgot concerning Henry W. Wiggen Mini Park. She found newspaper clippings and a rolled up scroll and odds and ends of things that might save me from the City Attorney, who claimed that the park was not mine and never been. Well, he had a surprise coming.

Another thing Barbara done was make a thorough study of the word "improve." This may not sound like much to you, and it certainly sounded like 0 to me, but she discovered that the Town and City would have a harder time taking the park if I "improved" it. I certainly *had* improved it with lawn mowing and seats and benches from ball parks all over the country. "Another fine way of improving it," I said, "is by building a fence around it."

"Oh with out doubt," said Barbara, "a fence is a definite improvement. You could build a fence and hire some children or other artists to paint it. That certainly *improves* things over what they were."

"How ever," said I, "I do not like a fence that keeps people out."

"The law does not say how high the fence must be," Barbara explained.

"It happens," said I, "that I know 1 of the world's best fence builders living near by in Tozerbury. I will spin up there and negotiate with him."

"You go get the fence builder," Barbara said, "and I will dig further in your fire proof room and keep ringing Mr. Alexander and Jack Sprat in California besides."

I and Hilary went up again to Tozerbury. We visited her horse name of Dutch and I attended to other business there. I never went near Tozerbury in the 22 years since high school, and now I was going there fairly regular. Driving along, Hilary told me every thing there was to know about horses, and I kept shaking my head and nodding and showing her I was listening very deeply. Some times my mind wandered from horses to matters more personal to me. I was running up and down all the clubs in baseball wondering who might truly need a late relief and sign me with out so much hesitation. I had fantasies pitching against California and knocking them out of the running, costing them 1,000,000's and 1,000,000's. Suicide Alexander fired Jack Sprat. Jack Sprat shot Suicide in revenge and went to jail for life. I always opposed capital punishment. I was really quite angry about this run around I felt that I was getting. Now and again I asked a little question to show Hilary I was listening, such as, "You mean to say *all* horses do?" or "Would this apply to other beasts or only horses?"

When we arrived at the horse lady's stable I honestly could not of told 1 horse from another. Yet Hilary described them by color and size and habits all the way. They were all brown or mostly so. Some were browner than others, but they all looked the same to me except 1 which was black. If only we bought the black 1 I would of knew it right off.

"Dutch missed you while you were gone," said the horse lady.

"I missed him, too," said Hilary, kissing him warmly on the mouth.

I dropped over and seen Ed Lewis. He was in a state of irritation concerning some thing or other. As time went by I realized he was always in a state of irritation over some thing or other. "I hope you come by to talk fence," he said.

"Yes I did," I said, "but not house fence."

"Then what?" he inquired.

"Park fence," I said. "I also thought I would mention some thing else."

"Mention it," he said. He was drawing long lines on boards. He could draw them very straight with out any sort of ruler or yard stick.

"I went down in my scrap books and read over the games of Perkinsville High vs. Tozerbury."

"I hit a home run off you," he said.

"Yes, you hit a home run off me and Jack hit a single off me."

"And we beat you," he said.

"No," said I, "we beat you."

"That is possible," he said. "I do not care too much about that but do not deny the home run, for I remember it like yesterday. It was a smash. It went over the canoe shop and in the lake. How ever, leave me add on some thing to all this. I been thinking for a long time about Jack's hit. You say it was a single. Are you sure it was not a base on an error because if it was a single it was a very *scratchy* single as I recall. Jack was never beyond the truth, you know."

"That is what I come to ask you about," I said.

"About Jack's hit?" he inquired. He put his pencil down and

paid a lot of attention to me, and his eyes were excited. I think he thought there was some way now after 22 years of taking away Jack's single from him and calling it a base on an error.

"No, not about Jack's hit exactly," said I, "but about Jack him self and whether he was ever beyond the truth."

"Beyond the truth," said Ed.

"Using your expression," I said.

"This is serious," he said. "Jack is beyond the truth remembering where he hit the ball. He might raise numbers a little bit and make it a better story. But Jack is never beyond the truth as a man. He is the most honest man that ever lived. You walk up and down the streets of this town and see if you can find some body that will tell you the opposite about him and you will not."

"That was what I was asking," I said.

Having time to spend while Hilary was cleaning out the stables after 8 horses I dropped over and seen Marva Sprat. "You said 'Come again' so I thought I would come again," I said.

"I thought you might," she said. She was watching the morning stories on TV. After she answered the door she went back and sat in front of them again, filling me in on this 1 and that 1, who was who and what they were up to. "And what they are up to is no god dam good," she said, "for they are not in love with each other and yet they are telling each other how god dam deeply in love they are. It is often horse shit."

"You have not got Jack's objections against swearing," I said.

"We are different," she said. "In many cases being different works best. These opposites attract." She flipped the TV to another channel showing a clear case of opposites.

"My main business in coming," I said, "apart from monkey business, is to inquire why we can not reach Jack on the telephone in California. Where is that little ring a ling that was suppose to occur?"

"I guess he does not wish to speak to you for the moment," Marva said. "About ½ the time I can not get a hold of him my self. Now on to the monkey business."

"Suppose there was an emergency," I said.

"I could get him in an emergency," Marva said. "But there is no emergency. Give him time to work it out with Mr. Alexander."

"I have gave him quite a bit of time all ready," I said.

"Give him more," she said.

"You have got more color in your face today than you had," I said. "You were looking very pale."

"I drink a little more wine when Jack is gone," she said. "It keeps my color up."

"Do all wives live different when their husband is gone?" I inquired.

"They could put on a story about ball players' wives," she said, "but they never will. It would be too unbelievable."

"Holly should of put you in her book," I said.

"I am ready to be wrote up," she said.

"Speaking of wine," I said, "I hope you will not mind me mentioning it, but the wine you poured out of the bottle of Vine Hill White the other night was simply not Vine Hill White. There fore I will send you several bottles of very good wine from California the next time I am there."

"I hope it will be soon," she said. I was not sure what she meant by that exactly. I am sure she meant she hoped I would be there and playing ball. The wine was a bonus. "Would you care for wine at the moment?" she inquired.

"Is it the same bottle from the other night?" I inquired.

"It is the same bottle but not the same wine," she replied. "I been refilling it over the years. Jack thinks it is the same wine."

"Do you think Jack might be avoiding me?" I inquired. "I had several experiences all ready this year of being avoided and double crossed and I am a little bit scorched."

"Who scorched you?" she inquired, rising from her chair during a commercial and taking the bottle of wine from the hall closet.

"Patricia Moors to begin with," I said. "Japan. Ben Crowder."

"Jack is not Patricia Moors or Japan or Ben Crowder," said Marva. "He never told a lie in his life or dealed a double deal. Jack is what he looks like, with the purest heart ever. He supports his wife and his children and so many sick relatives gone bonkers I lost count of them. He will be a great manager because every body will soon see his good character."

"Then he was telling me the truth as far as he knew it," I said.

"On every subject," she said.

"But of course he might be over ruled by Suicide Alexander," I said.

"Mr. Alexander writes the checks," she said. She did not open the wine bottle. She done 1 thing every commercial, rising from the chair 1 time and getting the wine from the hall closet, uncorking it the next commercial, going for a glass the third commercial, simply taking her sweet time, making a glass of wine last 2 hours or more. "Keeping down the costs," she said, "although Jack is making so much money now we are swimming in it. It will take a while to get use to."

"When you get use to it you will drink faster," I suggested.

"Are you sleeping with your lawyer?" she inquired.

"Certainly not," I said.

"Yes or no," she said.

"No," said I.

"I never heard such a city voice," she said.

"She been my attorney for many years," I said, "and is a grand mother and a widow." I give Marva the impression Barbara was a small lady with a cane leaning back on her heels in the bank cashing coupons clipped from her tax free municipal bonds. The joke of it is I use to *laugh* at municipal bonds. Then I begun buying them. The older I grew the better I knew what things lasted and what things didn't. I lost faith in over night sensations, ignoring all spectacular developments. People are always saying to me, "Ain't that So And So a fantastic ball player?" and I reply, "Well, we do not know yet, he has not been around long enough yet."

"She sounded to me like she was trying to figure out who I was," said Marva.

"You are Jack's wife," I said.

"We all know that much," she said. "Tell me how old she is as well as a widow and a grand mother. I could be a widow and a grand mother any minute. There is no telling what children are up to these days. Would you say I am an older or a younger woman?"

"I think of you as a younger older woman," I said. "That is what the doctor told me I was. It puts us the same age."

"I am older than you," she said, "for your age is in the record books whereas mine is not."

"I am stunned," I said.

"All right," said Marva, "if she is your attorney I will help her all I can in making the connection to California through Mr. Alexander through Jack. You can count on me for any thing. Mean while look on the brighter side of things. During the period Jack is putting the influence on Mr. Alexander you can come down now and again during school hours and feed your horse and see Ed about the fence and drop by for a glass of wine. There is usually no body here just you and me and the dogs."

"I am just wondering if I come all the way up from Perkinsville now and again if you will ever take your eye off the TV?" I inquired.

"That is easy enough," she said, looking at me.

"You might even turn it off all together," I suggested.

"I do not know you that well," she said.

"Even if you only turned down the sound," I said, "so that you could pay your full attention to some body that come all the way up from Perkinsville to see you."

She turned the machine off all together, but it was hard for her to keep from looking at it. She expected it to come back on by it self. The dogs picked up their ears and looked very suspiciously at us. "Now that you got all this quiet," she said, "say some thing sensational."

"I will win the pennant for Jack," I said.

She become very enthusiastic about that. "Jack thinks so, too," she said. "He believes you will save 25 or 30 games in short relief. He also got great faith in that new hitter, Alan Tibbles, which he thinks will hit 40 home runs for him."

"He is just a boy," I said, "so we will see about that, whereas I am a known product. I wish he would sign me soon. I am losing time. I wish I was out there getting in shape this very minute."

"Then you would not be here," she said.

"I will be here another time," I said. "First things first. The most wonderful thing of all about younger older women like your self is the way they know how to put first things first. They can take things or leave them if necessary. They know that if some thing does not happen Tuesday night it will happen as good or better on Thursday afternoon."

"During school hours," said Marva.

"Lately I find my self becoming more and more interested in younger older women. They got more sense of the importance of business. Older women strike me as less trouble than they are worth whereas younger women are more trouble than they are worth unless you are as young as they are and do not know any more than them."

"Why are you in such a hurry to go get in shape?" she inquired. "You admire younger older women for having the patience of a saint but you do not have it your self. May be Thursday is as good as Tuesday which you said your self. How

long will it take you to be in shape? You look in shape right
now. I do not even believe ball players go in training $\frac{1}{2}$ so much
to get in shape as to get away from their wife." She seemed to be
getting angry. "Tell me just exactly what you think we do to
keep our self alive and amused from February in till October.
Years ago Jack took me to the South with him. Those were
grand years and the babies were small and you could throw
them on the beach all day. Now they are in school for an education. I suppose it is necessary, but I am stuck in these 4 walls.
Maybe we will go to California, although I hate to give up the
weather here."

"The weather *here?*" I inquired politely. "It is *cold* here."

"Not in the house," she said.

"Jack says you will take to the streets again in California."

"Jack is the fountain of hope," she said. "I go out now and
then. I am not some sort of odd ball freak or queer. I was out
only 1 month ago to the market and liked it very well. Jack is the
shopper. I suppose Holly goes out more than once a month if
that."

"She is always on the go," I said.

"Going where?" Marva inquired.

"To the schools and shops and such," I replied.

"Can you reach her if you want her?" Marva asked.

"I can always leave a message at her office."

"Can she always reach you? *That* is the question."

"I did not know it was the question," I said. "My telephone is
always on Call Forwarding."

"Including in your car?" she inquired. "I got to see that
phone in side your car 1 of these days when the weather is
warmer. We got Call Forwarding but I can never make it work."

"I showed her how Call Forwarding worked on her telephone. "It is as easy as swallowing ice cream," I explained, but
she was not too mechanical. "All right," I said, "leave us punch
out Jack's number in the club house in California," which we
done. "Now when it rings here they will answer it there."

"How amazing," she said, although I do not think she was actually too amazed. I got the feeling nothing much amazed her. She knew every thing there was to know with out ever leaving the house. "They all come to me," she said. I thought she meant through the TV. "No," she said, "in person in the flesh."

"Who all come to you?"

"Ball players," she said, "from up in New York and as far away as Buffalo."

"I would say *down* in New York," I said. "Is it any body I know?"

"You would know their name," she said, "or may be met them here and there. They are retired. How ever, they are not too retired. 1 of them is all ready in the Hall of Fame and another will be coming up for election next year."

"You should be in the Hall of Fame your self," said I, "in case they had a category."

"The woman most ball players made love to," said Marva, "could be the category."

"The woman most ball players made love to in 1 season," said I, "could be another category."

"The woman most left hand ball players made love to in 1 season," said she, "could be yet another category, and so forth. I played around with those thoughts and wrote them down some where."

"Well," said I, "I must be getting back over to the stables."

"You think I am lying," she said.

"I am thinking no such a thing," I said.

"You think old ball players do not come to see me from as far away as Buffalo."

"I believe you," I said, "for you are a most attractive woman."

"You come," she said, "and you are the 27th winning pitcher of all time."

"I come to see Jack," I said.

"Jack is not here today," she said.

"I come today because you put your hand on my back and said 'Come again,' standing up stairs out side the bed rooms, but I do not wish to get the business and the pleasure mixed in. Leave us do the business first and enjoy the pleasure after."

"Your face has grew all red and flustered," she said. "Your pulse rate is exceeding all speed limits." She held her hand on my beating heart. "Your heart is moving along with out delay."

"Tell Jack what a healthy young man I am," I said.

"Except for your prostrate," she said.

"Do not mention my prostrate," I said. How did she know about my prostrate? Hilary mentioned it to Stuffy Sprat.

"I will not mention it," said Marva.

"We will keep our various secrets from the wrong people," I said.

"Whereas you are hoping to play ball for my husband, so we must work together and not complicate things while the negotiations are in progress," she said, "and be the kind of people that can put off in till Thursday what is best for them, and not run around sleeping with lawyers."

"A manager does not wish to have a relief pitcher on his ball club that is sleeping with his wife behind his back," I said.

"Although it been known to happen, I am sure," said she. "What else is baseball for?"

"Baseball also requires control," I said, "and I am known as a master of control."

"Now that your fast ball is gone you better concentrate on the control," she said.

"When I was very young," I said, "it was all or nothing. Every woman I seen I said to my self, 'What would it be like to marry her?' But I never really cared to marry her, and so I asked my self, 'What would it be like 1 quick fuck with her and split for ever?'"

"But you never married any body new," said Marva. "You stood with the 1 right wife for you."

"And am no longer interested in the 1 quick fuck," said I.

"Who is?" she inquired. "Then what you are looking for is the love affair, where you and I become acquainted over a long period of time, where we begin by first sitting on the sofa 2 cushions apart, drinking a little wine and watching a little TV, and on the next occasion we move in to the point where we are only 1 cushion apart, and you are coming and going between Perkinsville and Hilary's horses and Ed Lewis's fences and dropping around during school hours between February in till October while Jack is away, or on a different schedule in case you end up playing ball again. You use to be the wild young man. But now you are suggesting a very old fashion way of doing things. All right, Author, be my guest. I will try any thing once."

How do I know if some body is sincere or not? Should I call them or will they call me? It was impossible for me to believe that Jack Sprat would tell me a lie, and Marva said the same. But of course Marva was full of surprises her self.

Hilary felt confident she would see me playing yet for California. She soon read 144 books on California, including 1 about a naked Indian that stood in the woods for many years rather than come in and meet the white men. Who could blame him? The white men murdered every body in his tribe for the gold there abouts. No body was left but him, but he would not give in, he would not surrender, the whole world might consider that his days of being an Indian was over, that *he had no fast ball and was therefore through,* but not Ishi. He could still shoot his bow and arrow and he knew it. (I hope you are getting the point here.)

"Did he have a telephone in his car?" asked Holly. "Did he buy a new horse from the horse lady every time he went to Tozerbury?" We bought a second horse name of Dr. Schiff.

I mapped out a little telephone schedule. Every day I would press some body for an answer, and if they had no answer I would press them to press some body else. How ever, I never kept to my schedule. I tried out guessing what people would say

ahead of time, carrying on such long conversations with them in
my mind that I forgot I didn't call them. Then when I telephoned
them I hoped they wouldn't answer. I telephoned Barbara. She
had spoke to Suicide Alexander, discussing my *motivation*. "He
will be dammed if he can see why any body of your situation
would wish to pitch in the heat and the grime and the swearing
and the stinking and the traveling around in dirty air planes
where the lavatories do not work," she said. "I told him in reply
that he did not under stand your situation, that you were more
or less flat broke due to bad investments."

"What did he reply to that?" I inquired.

"He replied that rich men's lawyers always lie," she replied.

"And you said what?"

"Nothing. He hung up."

I was furious beyond words. I telephoned Marva. A young
man with an educated voice answered the telephone, and I
thought to my self, "She is certainly serious, gentle men certainly come from far and near for a sip of wine and the morning
stories in Tozerbury," but it was not Tozerbury, for we had
forgot to take the telephone off Call Forwarding. It was the club
house in California and the speaker was Tom Roguski, son of my
old friend Coker Roguski that I played with in Queen City and
in the early years with the Mammoths. Coker was a shortstop.
Tom was a catcher.

"How are you, Tom?" I inquired. "This is Henry Wiggen."

"I can not believe it," he said. "No body will believe it when
I tell them. My father will drop dead and my mother as well.
Every body here is a gog to think you might be joining us."

We chatted back and forth to some extent, and finally I
inquired, "What are the chances of me getting a hold of Jack?"

"You are making me feel important," he said. "Jack is not
around but I will be pleased to write down your message."

"Ask him to call me," I said. I give him my number. "How
did I get California when I telephoned Tozerbury?"

"It been happening," he said. "I got a couple calls before you. A little kid calls and says tell Robert we are going ice skating this afternoon. Another kid left his lunch in Stuffy's sheep skin coat."

I telephoned Ed Lewis in Tozerbury. "I wish to get a message to Marva Sprat," I said.

"Telephone her, same as me," said Ed.

"If I telephone her I get California," I said.

"I rather get California any way," said Ed. "I never speak to Marva."

"You spoke to her the night I was there," I said.

"Because Jack was there," said Ed.

"Can you not simply carry a message to her for me," I asked, "simply telling her take her telephone off Call Forwarding? If she does not under stand how to do it she can have Stuffy read the instructions and *he* will do it."

"I will not carry any message to her," said Ed. "It is policy."

"This is 1 hell of a note. I am not asking you to do some big favor. I am only asking you to carry a message 1 mile or less. I am not asking you for a free fence or some thing like that."

"It is nothing personal," said Ed. "Do not mix it up with the fence business. I will carry a message 10 miles for you or 50 miles for you or 100 miles or twice around the world expenses paid, but I will not carry a message or any thing else to Marva Sprat's house with her in it."

"I see," said I quite stumped.

"But what I can do," he said, "is I can collar 1 of the kids to and from on the way to school or the ice rink or what have you and give them the message. Which was what?"

"Take her phone off the Call Forwarding," I said, "and give me a little ring a ling down here in Perkinsville."

"Got it," he said. "Glad to do it."

Within 1 hour Marva telephoned me, speaking in her family voice. "Victory," said she, "I have spoke to Jack, he spoke to

Mr. Alexander, with in a matter of hours you will be flying through the air to California."

"You are wonderful," I said.

"You do not know that yet," she said. "By the by, I mentioned to Jack that you paid a courtesy call to this house."

"I am sure that you know how to handle such things best," I said.

"Perhaps you would like to know the particulars of what I said," she said, "so that all 3 interested persons will know the exact truth of the situation from the same point of view."

"If it is difficult for you to speak now," said I, "I can call you back at a more convenient time."

"It is always difficult to speak," she said, "since you have always got a certain number of children at the age of intelligence. They are very cute before their brains grow in. Some times I wonder why I even bother to keep my voice down."

"All right, the particulars were what?" I inquired.

"I told Jack you come down to Tozerbury to buy a second horse to go with the first, you seen Ed about some fence, and you dropped by the house to tell me you were hanging in suspense, never knowing what was happening to cause all this delay. You said to me, 'I will win the pennant for Jack,' which Jack also believed. So why not get started? Why not get in shape in California? Where was the contract? You were in agony. Never the less, you did not even take your coat off, Hilary was sitting in the car out side, you stood in the door way."

"All that was very kind of you," I said. "I want to mention 1 other little matter. I hope you will not be offended."

"Oh my God," she said, "what have I did?"

"You speak of *down* to Tozerbury," I said, "whereas I think of it as *up*. You are north, and north is *up*. We are south of you and south is *down*. New York is farther south yet. You should say *down* to Perkinsville and *down* to New York and so forth."

"When you go from Tozerbury to New York you are going *up* in the world," Marva said. "It is not a question of north and south but where you are. Tozerbury is low *down*. Every place in the world is *up* from Tozerbury. I would think this is some thing we could talk about more in the winter time. Right now you are expecting calls from California."

"I got Call Waiting," I said.

"What is that?" she inquired.

"If a call is coming in you get a signal," I said. "It comes in the package with Call Forwarding."

"Good by and good luck," she said. "Keep me informed. Come down soon and visit your horses. And why not leave Hilary home, leave it be just you and me and the dogs?"

The day before we left for California we met in Judge Kendall Phillips's office, which he referred to as "chambers," regarding Henry W. Wiggen Mini Park, also known as Depot Park. I took the Judge the photo of our high school class showing him in the very front row petting our school mascot, a dog name of Bozo. He appreciated the photo and stood it on his desk and from time to time looked at it and switched the lamp on to see it better. He had bad eyes. "If it was not for my eyes," he said, "I would of been some what of a ball player myself."

There were 5 of us, 1 of them and 3 of us and the Judge. I did not under stand why we sat in his crowded office when we could of moved to the court room which had long tables and better ventilation, but the Judge said we were not a trial and could not sit in court. O. K.

What was the question? The question was, "Was I or was I not a baseball player?" Point 2, "If I was not a baseball player did Henry W. Wiggen Mini Park, also known as Depot Park, return to the Town and City of Perkinsville?"

"If he is not a baseball player," Barbara inquired, "what else could he possibly be, for he played baseball last year and will play again this. During the present winter he traveled to various parts of the country as well as over seas discussing arrangements for the forth coming season. At this moment we are on the eve of a trip to California for the same purpose. You will hear the

announcement of him playing any hour. We are even surprised
that the announcement has not all ready been made."

"Nothing come in on the radio yet," said Judge Phillips, "or
I would of heard it, for I keep my ear tuned to all the latest
sports developments."

"How do we know the announcement will be forth coming?" the City Attorney, Myron Smallman, inquired. Mr.
Smallman and the Judge come to the house not long before,
asking me to run for Commissioner of Real Estate, and I believe
they were angry that I did not. They were in cahoots together.
Yet on every point they argued. "Oh yes," said Barbara, "they
will disagree on every thing except the bottom line."

"We know that the announcement will be forth coming,"
said the Judge, "because Mr. Wiggen told us so through his
attorney and he is a person of honor. He is not some bum in the
park."

"His playing days will end soon 1 way or the other," said Mr.
Smallman. "We might as well settle it this year as next."

"In baseball," said Holly, "the people say they are playing
ball long after they are finished playing. A manager is 'playing
ball' even when he is only managing."

"Even if he was totally unemployed," said Barbara, "you got
no right to take back what you give him once up on a time."

"You can not deprive an unemployed man of his property,"
said the Judge.

"When we give the park to him," said the City Attorney,
"we give it to 'Henry Wiggen the baseball player,' according to
the language of the agreement. We did not give it to 'Henry
Wiggen the unemployed man' or 'Henry Wiggen the self employed speculator and financier.' "

"Leave me see those papers you hold in your hand," said the
Judge. "These are not official papers. These are your own papers
to your self." He took the papers from the City Attorney,
Myron Smallman, and flicked on this little lamp on his desk and
begun reading them over. From the Judge's window I could see

the very park we were litigating over. Right at the moment it was empty of all life and the ground was hard and the trees were bare and there was 1 little winter bird hopping along on 1 foot it looked like to me. Maybe not, though. Would you rather have 1 foot froze or 2 feet ½ froze? Then the bird flew up on a bench that was once in the grand stand at Seals Stadium in San Francisco, 3 seats, what they call a "section of 3." "This paper only describes him as a baseball player," said the Judge at last. "It does not say he loses the park when he changes in to some thing else."

"Your Honor," said the City Attorney, "I did not say other wise."

"Then I have misinterpreted some thing in your opinion," said the Judge sarcastically.

"No, your Honor, nothing at all."

"I should hope not."

"Therefore," said Barbara, "the City should not refer to the park as 'temporarily known as Henry W. Wiggen Mini Park' but *permanently* known."

"So ordered," said the Judge. Never the less, about 5 minutes later the City Attorney again referred to the park as "temporarily known," but the Judge did not seem to hear him say it. The Judge made a ruling and forgot it 5 minutes later. It was a trick. He give Barbara every point she made, but it was all in the air, none of it on paper. Suppose an umpire called a man out but the man remained on the base any how and the umpire did not object? Would you come to the opinion the umpire was definitely favoring 1 team over the other? Are you surprised that we were 6 years in the courts to prove the park was mine?

"The park pays no taxes to the city and produces no revenue," said the City Attorney. "Old men are sitting on the benches all the time and some old women now a days as well. The park been a gathering place for people smoking drugs and other bad and illegal things and during the various recent parades been a place where many people planned riots and swore through microphones."

"To some people," Barbara said, "old men and women sitting on benches may be an eye saw and to other people persons gathering protesting 1 thing and another such as the war may be an eye saw. Yet to certain other people such activities may be very productive."

"Your Honor," said the City Attorney, "I did not finish my remarks and was once again interrupted by the defendant's mother."

"He is not a defendant," said the Judge. "He is a baseball player."

"Wonderful," said Barbara, "I appreciate Your Honor referring to my client as a baseball player, which we argued from the beginning was the case."

"If he was a baseball player," said the City Attorney, "he would now be on the way to Florida, for that is where all the players go at this time of the year."

"And a mighty baseball player he was," said the Judge. "This town sat up many a night these years watching a New York Mammoths game to the end, the more so when their pitcher was Henry. We said to our self, 'There is some body who is 1 of us, who knows our streets and houses and schools and stores, who was a child of this town and his family before him, and yet there he is down in New York or else where on the TV pitching with all his might. You can see his face close up. You can see him saunter off once he done his inning, putting them down 1, 2, 3.' We treasured hearing the name of Perkinsville mentioned time and time again over the years on the national broad cast, for example, 'Henry Wiggen, the wiley left hander from Perkinsville, New York,' or 'the slender southpaw from Perkinsville.'"

"I might interrupt to say that I been told by the electric company how consumption increased 30 per cent on nights that Henry Wiggen pitched," said Myron Smallman.

"I am sorry if I was carried away by the sound of my words," said the Judge.

"Your Honor," said Barbara, "if I may interrupt to raise a point of courtesy."

"Please do so," said the Judge.

"I will appreciate you asking the City Attorney to refer to me as my client's lawyer and not as my client's mother."

Holly smiled.

"It was a slip of the tongue," said Mr. Smallman, "only because it was obvious to me that the defendant's lawyer is a person of so much maturity."

"Your Honor," said Barbara, "you have instructed the City Attorney that my client is not a defendant."

"I am sorry if I referred to him as a defendant," said the City Attorney, "but he will be so soon so we might as well start now."

"What is he guilty of?" Barbara asked. "The park was gave to my client on a certain day 12 years ago or so along with a wrist watch, a traveling bag, a suit of expensive clothes, government bonds worth $300 which was more money then than it is now, plus $500 in credit on enthusiastic merchants and 4 new tires for the car he had all ready been gave as a gift by some body else, not to mention this scroll," she said.

Holly been sitting there with the scroll and other papers and now passed them to Barbara. She unrolled the scroll, reading out loud, "'Presented to Henry W. Wiggen, athlete, author, proprietor and owner for ever of Henry W. Wiggen Mini Park, in till yesterday known as Depot Park, in gratitude for his having contributed more than any one else to the eternal fame and celebrity of Perkinsville, New York,' and signed by every store keeper and politician that could possibly get his hands on the scroll to sign it. At the height of your enthusiasm you give him the only thing you knew how to give, which was goods and money and finally a piece of land you had no more use for any how, and as time passed you decided you wished you had it back. That is called Indian giving. I do not know why. Probably it is unfair to Indians. You were very enthusiastic about my client making his way to the big leagues, but you become so accustom to his name in the papers and his face on the TV screen that you begun to think him over, saying to your self, 'He is only some body that we see around all the time any how.' Besides, some of the things he said you did not like concerning the war and 1 thing and another, but above all you seen that *you made a property mistake,* that the 3,150 square feet of dirt and earth you give him free were now worth some thing after all, and so you are trying to take it back. Besides, he is not such a big winner any more. It is some time since he won 20 games all in 1 year. You had your use of him. You could make money off him. You heard the name of Perkinsville on the TV broad cast and your electric use increased by 30 per cent. In my opinion, what Henry learned in the world was this. That you loved him only as long as you thought he done you some good. That you thought he brought you power by being famous. That you thought you loved him but all you loved was something in your self.

"Well, Your Honor, we are all some times sorry afterwards for some thing we done before, but the way to deal with this is to go on and do better and never make the same mistake twice. Instead, what you are trying to do is take back from him the only thing you can, which is this little piece of land 75 by 42. At least you are not as illegal as the girl with the weapon system."

"This scroll is not a legal document," said the City Attorney, who been studying it all along. "The men that signed it did not own the land and you can not give away what you do not own. It is amazing how many of these persons now are dead."

"I am dying to know what team you will be signing with," said Judge Phillips. "In the mean while I am ordering that Henry W. Wiggen Mini Park go back to the Town and City of Perkinsville. So ordered."

"No, sir," said Barbara, "it can not be so ordered as I have an injunction preventing you from doing so."

"I *thought* you would remember that," said the Judge.

Hilary flew first class with plenty of room for spreading her books around. Her favorite topics at that period were California, horses, and California horses. "She is the most spoiled child I ever saw or heard of," Barbara said.

"All the world is agreed on that," said I, "except Hilary and I and Dr. Schiff. We are doing what the doctor ordered."

"You are wasting your money on that so called doctor," Barbara said. She did not approve of Dr. Schiff although she never met her. Dr. Schiff did not approve of Barbara. Holly *hated* Dr. Schiff but approved of Barbara, having the right idea but the wrong woman. Holly also disliked the horse woman of Tozerbury but approved of Marva Sprat. She still seen me as pursuing younger women when I had all ready moved on to older, which probably ought to been a warning to me regarding baseball as well. "Hilary could of stood home for all of me," said Barbara. Hilary and her did not get along too well.

"Hilary is improving," I argued. "She has not screamed once since some days ago on the road to Tozerbury when I sat up ½ the night with Jack Sprat by the fire place."

Barbara and I flew coach. You will ask why. We were flying coach because Suicide Alexander agreed to pay 2 coach and nothing more to bring our "negotiating team" to California, remembering to remind Barbara in the same breath to remind me to bring his golf clubs which I by mistake took home with me from Dutch's funeral. "Tell him you stole them," Barbara said. Jack Sprat advised the same thing. "He is a worried man," she said. "If you do not cheat him he does not under stand you. If you play fair and square with him he can not under stand your *motivation.* We must keep a track of every penny of expense and charge him for it but pad the items slightly so that he under stands we are dependable." We charged him $4 for 2 glasses of wine apiece on the air plane but he would not pay for the second glass. He had his rules. He was suspicious of employees that missed the opportunity of cheating him, but if he caught them he fired them. He was not easy to work with.

Jack Sprat emphasized to Suicide how cheap and narrow and economical I was. I kept my daughter out of school because of the expense. I was so cheap I kept the telephone in the car for fear that my family would call long distance while I was away from home. He was fascinated by the phone in the car. "Speaking of fascinated," I said to Barbara, "if Suicide shows you his bank book study it with great fascination. He was unhappy I give it only a glance at Dutch's funeral."

"He will show it to us," said Barbara, "from all reports."

"It was the cleanest book I ever seen," I said, "1 deposit, no with draws."

"He hung up on me," she said, "and I can not forgive him for that no matter how much money he got."

"Rich as that," I said, "I suppose he can hang up on a number of girls." She liked it when I called her "girls."

Hilary never really been to San Francisco before, and we walked across the Golden Gate Bridge in the fog and the wind and back again, too, and I felt very good for the walk though my feet were tired and my bladder was full. Barbara did not prefer to walk with us, for she was being drove out of her mind by such questions as "Would you rather be a tug boat or a ferry boat?" A ferry boat, because I rather carry people than pull ships. I could answer these questions with no strain on my mind any more, but Barbara lost her patience, saying, "Henry, I raised all my children all ready doing my share for the world, and I do not under stand why I am now once again marching up and down the Coast with a little girl."

"Because she is mine," I replied.

"People are looking at us all over this town," she said, "from your face to mine and from my face to Hilary's and they can not figure it out. Who am I? Possibly I am her grand mother. This makes me your mother in their mind. They are saying 'She must work night and day keeping her self looking so younger for an older woman, poor thing.' I can see it in their eye."

"No," said I, "what I see in their eye is they are thinking you are the extremely young mother of his extremely young wife, for he must of married practically a *child,* which is the way men do these days when they do not know any better."

"That is a very sweet thing for you to say," she said, "and I hope that I can live up to it."

Returning from the Golden Gate Bridge we drove up Twin Peaks in a taxi cab and looked down on every thing, the first high place we been since the Washington Monument, continuing by cab and viewing Candlestick Park and over the *Bay* Bridge and seen the Oakland park. Later in the week we seen Los Angeles, Anaheim, and San Diego. Hilary had now saw every major league baseball park in the United States of America. She believed she was the only girl could make such a claim. "Or if some other girl can make such a claim," she said, "I do not think they can also claim that their father played ball in every single 1 of them." In several parks I played only 1 game, or part of 1 game, such as an All Star Game. "A game is a game," said Hilary, "and part of a game goes in the record like a game it self," which was true. No, racking my brain I could not think of any girl who could make the claim she now seen every park in America or her father played in every 1. I knew several men that probably played 1 game or more in every park, but either they had no children or they never took their children any where.

At a good shop down town I purchased a very fine quantity of wine from Domaine Chandon north of the city, sending several bottles to Marva Sprat as promised with a note enclosed reading, "For you and me and the dogs," and out to Golden Gate Park right afterwards with Hilary and Barbara. "It is certainly some what bigger than Henry W. Wiggen Mini Park in Perkinsville," I said.

Hilary did not appreciate this statement. Some thing was

eating on her. "I am only thinking," she said, "that I am the only daughter that has saw almost every ball park in America, but I am also the only daughter that has never saw you play ball in any single 1 of them." I was afraid she planned on screaming and I did not know what I could do about it. "You could of bought her Golden Gate Park," said Barbara afterwards.

"Your record is a record in it self," said I to Hilary.

"But it is not a record to be proud of," said Hilary. "It is a negative record."

"Hold off screaming," said I, "for that is why we come, to agree on terms with Suicide Alexander."

"I am trying," she said. She was some what angry having been *forced* to sit in the first class seat in the air plane where she was *lonesome* and *deserted*. "We should of brung Dr. Schiff with us," she said.

"Why not?" inquired Barbara in a sarcastic voice.

In the aquarium in Golden Gate Park we seen 1,000's of fish of every variety, color, size, shape, and strength, from little fish no bigger than your finger to sharks I personally rather stay out of the Japanese hot springs with. "Would you rather be a salt water fish or a fresh water fish?" Hilary inquired. A fresh water fish. Why? Because I find I am healthier going light on salt. Very good. Would you rather be a Sword Tail or a Giant Fresh Water Prawn? A prawn. Would you rather be a Tiger Barb or a Harlequin Fish? Would you rather be a Scissors Tail Fish or a Speckled Mouthbrooder?

After many years we passed from the aquarium in to the museum. My feet were about to fall off. I was thirsty but did not wish to drink for fear of filling up my bladder too soon again. Soon we come to some thing I had saw in the past with 1 daughter or another. I am still not sure I under stand it. It is called a Foucalt Pendulum swinging from the ceiling back and force across a pit in the floor. Around the pit are many little wooden pegs, and 1 by 1 the pendulum will knock down the pegs in till in 24 hours it has knocked down them all. You see, what happens is this. Every time the pendulum swings it changes its direction by 5/1,000 of an inch per swing. *Or so it seems.* But the pendulum is not changing its direction at all. It is the world that is changing its direction, for the pendulum is hung in such a way that it does not move with the world. The public is kept out of the pit by silver railings, but people crowd around the rail and children crouch down and watch the swinging of the pendulum, and every 22 minutes, according to the sign, the pendulum knocks down another 1 of the little pegs.

When the peg goes down the crowd breaks up. Every body is relieved. The suspense is over and the people go away and a new crowd begin to arrive. I use to stand behind the crowd and watch while my daughters crouched beside the rail, and Hilary no different than the others.

Closer and closer the pendulum comes to the next peg in the line. My feet were killing me. I leaned against the wall. "Are we going to wait for 22 minutes in till the peg is knocked down?" Barbara asked. The world only turned around so fast. There was no hurrying it. Soon you say to your self, "It is so close now it will knock it down the next swing," but it does not, and you say to your self, "Well, surely it will knock it down the *next* swing," but again it fails to do so. And once more it fails to do so. And once more. And once again, for you have got to remember that 5/1,000 of an inch is not very thick and you do not know what you are looking at 5/1,000 of an inch 1 way or another when suddenly Hilary jumped up from where she was crouching among the children and whirled her self around searching for me with her eyes on fire, and she screamed out at me, *"You might be dead before you ever play baseball again,"* screaming the bloodiest blue murder you ever heard or any body else, and all the children jumped up and went running every which way crying and screaming through the museum, and the guards come running in their uniforms from various directions, calling out, "What is this terrible disturbance here beneath the Foucalt Pendulum?" Hilary her self now turned around in a very lady like way and was watching the pendulum swinging back and forth in till at last it knocked down the peg, and she breathed out a sigh, saying, "At last."

We drove down by Hertz car from San Francisco to Los Angeles. I hope no body will correct me Los Angeles is *up* from San Francisco. The weather all the way was warm and clear. The sky was never bluer. It is an extra long distance in the winter from Perkinsville to the coast of California. We attended the Los Angeles Zoo, and we seen the Watts Towers, 100 feet high made out of old broken glass and tiles, sticks and stones and what not else by a single man name of Simon Rodia. He done it all alone. It is 1 of the best things I ever seen, and Hilary said the same. She was feeling very good.

In Los Angeles Hilary stood with the Petrotones. Len Petrotone played for us awhile, infield and outfield. He once threw a man out at first base from right field, but he was rather rich and never needed to play ball. We like each other. I like his wife and he likes mine and our children get along good and when they come east they look us up and visa versa. They go sight seeing all over the world. I dropped Hilary at their door, saying, "I got a crowded schedule to meet, I am here on a negotiation," and they under stood, and Hilary walked in the front door between them with her books in her arm.

Barbara and I doubled back north about 25 miles to a "Spanish town" name of Newhall. Suicide Alexander called it that. He liked to think he lived in "a little Spanish town." It was not much more Spanish than Perkinsville. It had several tacos shops on the main street. Barbara and I bought some carry out Spanish type foods over the counter from a blonde American girl that took our money with out ever looking at us, and we raced off looking for Suicide Alexander eating while we drove.

He lived in the La Casa de los Conquistadores, which in Spanish refers to the house of the conquerors, which in Newhall was a small apartment house with a knight in steel armor standing in the vestibule, his sword aimed up in the air. People stabbed messages through the sword. Upstairs Suicide lived by him self in a 2 room apartment looking out on a golf course. May be this was not his real home. May be he lived some place else. He had 4 telephones on his bed all rigged up to a tape recorder. He had a type writer on a rolling table in the bath room. He wore the same pea green polyester wash pants that he had wore to the funeral in December. "At last you brung me my golf clubs," he said.

"I brung ½ of them," I said. "I give ½ of them away to a bell boy in the hotel before I even knew they were yours."

"In what hotel?" he inquired. "What was the name of the bell boy?"

I thought he was joking. "Have bell boys got names?" I inquired.

"You and the bell boy together," he said.

"Together what?" I inquired.

"We are not getting off to a good beginning," Barbara said.

"Stole them," he said.

"Yes," said I, "but my conscience got me and I am returning ½ to you. I always meant to return them."

"I will *bet* you always meant to return them," he said, but he respected me for taking a run at stealing any how and brung out a cold bottle of "French supply" wine. Living in the middle of Spain he drunk "French" wine. He scraped the label off. It was not bad, how ever, and it made difficult minutes some what easier. He showed us his telephone set up and how he filed away his tapes in boxes on shelves with every thing numbered and color coated.

"Are you not afraid of being sued?" Barbara inquired. "I believe it is illegal to tape people unless asked."

"I got so many people suing me 1 more can never hurt," he said. He swung around on me very suddenly. "How is the wine?" he inquired. "Who ever heard of a ball player that was an authority on wine? Where is such a ball player's motivation for

Christ sake? Ball players with opinions on wine are ready for managing. Jack is afraid you wish to take away his job managing. I suppose you think you will make it in California now that you got dumped in New York."

"Sir," said I, "it never for 1 minute occurred to me. I wish to play for Jack and not manage and help you win your first pennant in 20 years and intend to do so."

"You thought you would manage New York. He advised her against hiring you as manager. The last thing I talked about with Dutch prior to the moment he dropped dead on the golf course was you, my dear friend. What do you think of that? How does it feel to be a man that your name was on a man's lips in the moment of his death?"

"Mr. Alexander," said Barbara, "it is my experience as an experienced negotiator, which I know that you are, too, that we will do best by taking up matters 1 by 1 in an orderly procedure."

"I apologize for every thing," he said. "I always begin negotiating by hitting the ceiling in till I come down again."

"When negotiating you should remain seated with your seat belt fastened in till the air plane has come to a complete stand still at the terminal and the captain has turned off the motor," she said.

Well, this broke the ice. Suicide Alexander laughed in a snappy way. "If we had more negotiators like you, Barbara," said he, "the world would be a pleasanter place. What this world needs is a sense of humor."

"I am interested what Dutch might of said about me prior to his tragic death," I said.

"I imagine you would be," said Suicide. "Who would not? We were simply running several names. I was looking for people to help out Jack Sprat and your name rose along with others. 'No,' said Dutch, 'you got 2 nice men there back to back. They have not got the heart to give a boy a ticket to back home, saying good by, kid, you were big in Central High.' I think he was out of his mind, for Jack Sprat is very tough running around chewing that big black tobacco all the time, and it was just about then when it happened. He sat down on the ground, feeling around in his breast pocket. I thought he was feeling for a pencil. He was choking."

"You know what he died?" I thought to my self. "He died laughing."

"If I do not play the World Series in the next year or 2 I am going to jump off the tallest convenient location with the usual results," said Suicide. "This is why I live in a Spanish town. There are no high buildings. Some place I heard not only that you are not too much interested in managing but you are only looking to play to please your daughter."

"Ridiculous beyond words," I said.

"Well then," said he, leaping up from his chair, "leave us listen to the words them self," switching on a tape recorder and playing the following conversation between I and him several days following the funeral.

> I understand you took a bag of golf clubs home from St. Louis. They were mine.
> I took home ½ a bag. I give ½ the bag away. I thought they were Dutch's.
> Give them to me when you see me.
> I would love to see you and talk about playing ball for you.
> I am open to that idea but I suppose you would wish a lot of money.
> I am not interested in the money. It is a family matter. I wish to have my little girl see me play.
> Talk to Jack. He lives near you, does he not?
> A wonderful idea for Jack and I are friends from way back.

"Of course," said Barbara, "that is a little replay of Henry speaking in a highly emotional state following Dutch Schnell's death. We are here all the way from New York and ready to sign."

"I am not ready to sign, how ever," said Suicide. "Those remarks bother me concerning his *motivation*. I am worried about a pitcher too deep in the study of wine."

"He has passed the age of beer," said Barbara.

"That might be the problem," said Suicide.

"If we leave here," said Barbara, "and go exploring other offers which have come our way you will lose Henry and Henry will lose the opportunity of winning a pennant for his old friend Jack Sprat."

"You got no where to go," he said. "No body wants him but possibly me."

"Our time is valuable," Barbara said.

"Then spend it exploring all those other offers coming your way. Mean while I will wait and see what the trading dead lines bring."

"You will lose Henry and people will say what a fool you are," said Barbara, "for he will pitch against you in the stretch and knock you out completely."

"If I hear of people saying what a fool I am," said Suicide Alexander, "I whip out this World Series bank book which I am eager to show you." He handed me his bank book and I took it.

"You showed it to me at the funeral," I said, "but I am always eager for another look at exciting reading."

"Look extra special," Suicide said, "because you will see that since the funeral a new line of interest been added," and I done so and there it was.

01 04 1971 $42,136.99

The balance was well above $1,000,000, beginning with $500,000 he deposited 20 years before when he won the World Series. "Author," he continued, "write another book and put a picture of this in. This is *my* book when people say I am a fool. Take it with you and take a picture of it and send it back." He addressed an envelope to him self and stamped it.

"I will value it," I said, "and return it to you safe."

"I know that you will," he said.

"The main thing that you 2 gentle men got in common," said Barbara, "is your love of *motivation*."

"I do not care for the money," said Suicide, "only for the numbers. What do I need money for? I got no family any more. I booted them out. *He* is the 1 that needs the money with 6 daughters specially eating all the money with never a look back. It is too bad you never had sons. I would buy you off your self if it was legal and put you out to breeding sons by women with strong arms them self. How many of those bank books would I own then? You knocked us out time and again, you and Dutch and your god dam Italian brothers and your god dam Jewish first baseman and your god dam colored second baseman and your god dam Spaniard at third. In a whole life in baseball should I not be in title to more than 1 World Series?"

"Some people never play any," I said.

"I am not talking about them," said Suicide.

"We come all the way to California to sign," said Barbara.

"Your way was paid," he said. "I inquired around plenty. The only person in the world that is absolutely sold on you is Jack Sprat and he can not move with out me, and the only other person sold on you is Jack Sprat's wife and she is a woman."

"When will we know your decision?" Barbara inquired.

"I will wait and see what the trading dead lines bring," said Suicide Alexander, "and after that I will give you a little ring a ling."

8

Nobody screamed. I telephoned Hilary from a telephone on the street in Newhall. The sun was very hot, 80 degrees warmer than Perkinsville that day. Suicide Alexander had 4 telephones on his bed but I would not use a 1 of them. I wanted to be out of there as fast as I could. I never felt so double crossed in my life, my stomach weighed me down like I swallowed a rock, I was gasping for air and hoping it would not be Len Petrotone answering the phone because I did not think I could of carried on a polite conversation at that moment with any body.

I wished to go home and stay there. I thought I would go in my house and pull it down on top of me. I seen my self playing ball in the evenings in the Perkinsville No Pitch League. I seen my self Commissioner of Parks and Recreation answering the telephone saying, "No, thank you, I simply never leave Perkinsville." Luckily it was a child answered the phone at the Petrotones, I asked for Hilary, and the child called out to her, saying, "Hilary Margaret Wiggen, it is some man for you."

"Did you sign up?" Hilary inquired.

"Hilary," said I.

"You sound awful," she said.

"Hilary," said I, "you will be a tremendous help to your father if you will be out in front of the house with all your gear because I do not feel like talking to any body in about 45 minutes, and I do not wish to make any big explanations to any body why we are leaving 1 day ahead of schedule and so forth."

"Then you did not sign up," she said.

"You hit the button on the head," I said, "but you are in the quiet and peaceful house of dear and devoted friends."

"I will not scream," she said.

With the same dime I telephoned Holly saying I now intended returning home and planned on never leaving Perkinsville again on baseball business. So she said. I honestly do not remember speaking in those terms. I remember sweating on the telephone and feeling like I had a high fever. My arms and 1 side of my face become sun burned and the Spanish tacos and the "French supply" wine were sticking in my throat.

"So it did not go good," said Holly.

"It went bad," I said.

"Bad for you is good for me," said Holly. "Ain't that awful? How is Barbara taking it?"

Barbara took it very bad along lines I could not explain to Holly. "If you were double crossed," said Barbara, "I was double crossed twice, which you can add up on your little electric pocket calculator. I am informed by Suicide Alexander that negotiations are all called off for the present and I am informed by you that we are now joining up again with Hilary instead of spending the night in Los Angeles. I been looking forward to it. I been prepared. No woman was ever more prepared. I am more prepared for a night in Los Angeles than you are prepared to play baseball if you care to know the bitter truth. You deserve to be beat with in 1" of your life," and she smashed me on my arm with her fist. It was the first hard words we ever had.

"When you are in trouble," I said, "you report in to your family. Hilary is my nearest family."

"You all ready reported in to her," said she. "You and *Hilary* spent a wonderful night in Los Angeles last night. Oh, you and *Hilary* seen the bright lights of Hollywood and the in sides of McDonald's and I will never forget them 2 hours of the wildest joy at the Wax Museum."

"Hamburger Hamlet," I said, "not McDonald's. Hilary's taste is moving forward. I promise you that you and I will spend a happy night some other night in Los Angeles."

"We will never be back," she said.

"I will be back before the summer is out with 1 ball club or another," I said.

"No body wants you," she said.

"So he said," I said, "but I got ideas of my own."

"You just told your wife you were coming home for ever."

"If you are interested in a legal case I wish to bring a case against Suicide Alexander for $10,000,000 for taping my telephone calls," I said.

"I am returning to New York by my self," she said. "Drop me at the air port."

"Hilary is waiting in the hot sun in front of the Petrotones," I said.

"Telephone her go back in," said Barbara.

"No," said I, "she needs me like I need her."

"Then you do not need me. Leave me out."

"We are in the middle of the free way," I replied.

"Drive *off* the free way," she said.

"There is no where," I said. "We are in the middle of the wilderness. It is Van Nuys."

"*Drive the fuck off*," she said, beating on my arm, but I declined to do so.

"You are right," I said. "No body wants me, including you."

"There is a song," she said, "Da da da dum dum, no body loves you when you are old and gray."

"Will you play it for me on your $15,000 piano?" I inquired.

"If I ever again invite you to my house," she said.

We drove very quietly down from Los Angeles to San Diego. Every body was thinking their own thoughts. The 1 thing we all agreed on no body said, which was this. I was through playing ball, and that was a fact. I was very mad. We seen Sea World. We seen the ball park. Hilary now seen every major league baseball park then existing. We seen Shamu, the whale, open up his mouth while his trainer stuck his head in. Many many jobs I would not care to have. After all, how lucky could a person be? I played ball 21 years counting the 2 in Queen City, I was never hurt, I was mainly a winner and seldom a loser, I could retire rich under 40 if I cared to, but never the less sitting in Sea World watching some poor chap stick his head in a whale's mouth I was feeling deeply sorry for my self. I had fans around the world. Walking near the lagoons with dolphins some body cried out, "Hello, Henry Wiggen," and I stood there giving out autographs for 20 minutes. The dolphins were mad I took away their crowd.

We seen these very young fellows diving off very high platforms in to very small pools of water. "I will certainly not scream for fear of making them nervous," said Hilary, "all though I certainly feel like it." It was 1 of the most terrible ways of earning a living I ever heard of, and I felt like screaming my self and calling out a message to those poor young fellows, saying, "Hey, listen, do not do that for *my* sake. Do not dive. Climb down. I will not even ask for my money back." In that kind of a game 1 error and you are dead. I prefer baseball. In the whole history of baseball only 1 man ever died of it, a chap name of Chapman in 1920. Hilary did not scream and neither did I. But flying to New York she was so very quiet she worried me, and we checked in to Dr. Schiff for repairs.

"It is about time you and your wonderful daughter showed up again," said Dr. Schiff, but looking at Hilary, not at me. She was really a very good doctor, just right for Hilary. "How many horses did you make him buy you? How was your trip to Tozerbury?"

"We been several places since Tozerbury," said Hilary, "including San Francisco, Los Angeles, and San Diego."

"If I know my California facts," said Dr. Schiff, "all 3 of them places are there and I am dying for you to come in and tell me about what you seen and what you hit up the old man for. As for you," said Dr. Schiff to me, "you may sit here a while and think about your sins in my waiting room."

Instead I went down in the lobby of her building and Zeroxed Suicide Alexander's World Series bank book and dropped it back in the mail for him in the self addressed stamped envelope he give me back there in the La Casa de los Conquistadores in Newhall, thinking, "You bastard, just where do you come off living in the house of the conquerors, just what in the fuck did you exactly ever conquer?" He played 1 World Series. That was 20 years ago in a franchise he soon run out of business due to bad management. In 7 years in California he never finished higher than third place. In another 7 years he would never play another World Series because he would never win another pennant. He would be 27 years in baseball playing only 1 World Series before he would finally hang up his telephones. He never committed suicide, either. When he retired from baseball recently he said, "I decided instead of jumping off the highest convenient locations I would buy them for some body else to jump off," which he done, owning a great deal of real estate north of the San Fernando Valley whereas he him self continued to live in a 2 room walk up apartment in the La Casa de los Conquistadores.

So what insanity was I up to? Here was a man that never threw a baseball 2 feet in his life telling me what my future was. He surveyed the field and he seen that I was not needed. Why was I allowing him to make a survey I should of made my self? Poor Hilary, she had give up on me, taking other people's word for every thing. "Your father is through playing ball." How could she of knew any better, and so it was up to me to know better and survey the field my self.

How Do You Do? Come On in and Meet Your Self

Never Break a Promise to a Child

Who knew me better than I knew my self? I agreed with the posters on Dr. Schiff's wall. No body surveys your own condition like you survey it your self. I knew that some ball club needed me some where. I knew that I could save some body many ball games with 2 innings at a time and even step in and pitch longer with plenty of rest against weak clubs and offer a lot of instruction to younger players. I was experienced and balanced and healthy and I would make people sorry they double crossed me, such as Patricia and Ben Crowder and Suicide Alexander. Look at those magazines on the rack in the lobby near the Zerox. I bought 1 containing a survey of the ball clubs in training in Florida, Arizona, and California. What did the magazine know? It was old stuff. I seen it every year. Why don't they read in September what they wrote in March?

No body could make a survey for me like I could make it for my self. If I got on my horse and kept close to every thing day by day I would soon see where I was needed most and sell my self, and the best way of doing that was by announcing. I was dialing the telephone when the mail man come across the lobby and opened up the box and carried away Suicide Alexander's World Series bank book with him.

"Friday Night Baseball," said a young man on the phone. He was their secretary.

"Henry Wiggen here," I said.

"How are you, Henry?" the man inquired.

It irritated me. I don't know why. People will call you by your first name 1 minute and double cross you the next. "Are we acquainted?" I inquired.

"I wish we were," he said.

"Because you are designating me by my first name I thought we already been," I said.

"Leave us take it from the top," he said. "You are dialing the telephone. It is ringing, b-d-r-r-r-r-p. Pause. Suddenly some body answers. He says, 'Friday Night Baseball.'"

"Henry Wiggen here," I said.

"How are you, Mr. Wiggen?"

"I am fine. I wish to speak to Jerry or Suzanne."

"They are in the South," the young man said. "I can hook

Suicide Alexander's World Series bank book

DATE	WITHDRAWALS	DEPOSITS	INTEREST	BALANCE	TI
Dec. 29, 1950		$500,000		$500,000	M
1-2-52			20,000 00	520,000 00	ah
Jan. 2, 1953			$20,800	$540,800	M
Jan. 4, 1954			$21,632	$562,432	M
1-4-55			22,497 28	584,929 28	ah
1/3/56			23,397 17	608,326 45	J
1/2/57			24,333 06	632,659 51	J
1-2-58			25,306 38	657,965 89	ah
1/5/59			26,318 63	684,284 53	J
1/4/60			27,371 38	711,655 91	MD

1-3-61			28,466.24	740,122.15	DF
1-2-62			29,604.89	769,727.04	DF
1-2-63			30,789.08	800,516.12	MD
1-2-64			32,020.65	832,536.76	NL
1-4-65			33,301.49	868,838.23	NL
JAN 8 - 66			34,638.55	900,471.76	HH
1-3-67			36,018.87	936,490 63	NL
JAN 8 68			37,459.63	973,950.26	HH
JAN 8 69			38,958.01	1,012,908.30	HH
5 70			40,516.33	1,053,424.60	HH

DATE	WITHDRAWALS	DEPOSITS	INTEREST	BALANCE	TI
01 04 1971			42,136.99	$1,095,561.59	M

you up with them if you wish in a flash. Hang on the line, *sir,* and I will get them on their beeper. Do you know that if you join us you will get a beeper, too?"

"Very nice," I said, "but there is no need me speaking to them live and direct or beepers. Will you take a message?"

"I will take a message for Miz Winograd and Mr. Divine," he said.

"Tell them 5 little words."

"Which are?"

"Tell them *Jerry, just count me in*," I said.

"Eureka," the young man shouted in my ear, "the Lord is on the job today."

I went back up again. Hilary and Dr. Schiff were waiting for me in the waiting room. "We were beginning to wonder," said Dr. Schiff, "if this was 1 more promise broke. Where were you?"

"I was not beginning to wonder," said Hilary. "*You* were."

"Putting money in blue chip slots," I replied, "first in the Zerox and next in the telephone."

"While we been waiting here patiently on pins and needles," said Dr. Schiff, "I and Hilary been having a long and confidential talk just between the 2 of us. Lock the door." The nurse locked the door. "No," said Dr. Schiff, "lock your self on the out side of it."

"Patients are coming," said the nurse.

"Leave them heal them self," said Dr. Schiff. "Tell them take 2 tranquilizers and read a copy of *Psychology Today,* for here we have a really and truly sick man been leading his poor little daughter all over the country by the nose in till she screams her head off every place they go."

"I screamed only twice since we were here," said Hilary. "Once on the road to Tozerbury."

"Where you got 2 horses for your pain," said Dr. Schiff, "1 named for your father's dead manager and 1 for me. How do you think I enjoy being named for a dead horse?"

"The other time in San Francisco," said Hilary.

"Beneath the Foucalt Pendulum," said Dr. Schiff.

"He is not leading me around by the nose," said Hilary very calmly. "He is trying to fill his promise to me."

"We are waiting to see you play ball," said Dr. Schiff, beginning to sound like screaming her self. "The men are all ready down South practicing in the Grape Fruit League and else where and where are you? Why are you not practicing with the rest of them? You were in California. Why did you not just don your togs and start playing with the rest of them?"

"Because I have not signed," I said.

"You can not play in till you sign," said Hilary.

"Then *sign*," said the doctor.

"No body thinks I am good enough any more," I said.

"I think you are good enough," said Dr. Schiff, "for I seen you pitch 2 innings last September and you certainly pitched perfect. When the manager took you out of the game I booed with all the rest. A manager like that deserved to die."

"This is encouraging," I said. "I wish you owned a club."

"If I owned a club I would beat you over the head with it," said Dr. Schiff.

"He means a baseball club," said Hilary.

"Is that what he means? Why does he not say what he means so I can under stand him?"

"Any body under stands him that under stands any thing about baseball," said Hilary. "You know nothing about baseball. You think that Tozerbury is in the big leagues." Hilary was laughing at the ignorance of Dr. Schiff and losing patience as well. Her eyes were wet.

"Jack Sprat is the manager and you seen him in Tozerbury. Therefore Tozerbury is in the big leagues," said Dr. Schiff, folding her arms and curling up her lip. "Unless your father is once again lying to us as usual."

"He does not tell lies," said Hilary.

"He told you he would play ball again."

"It is not that easy."

"It is extremely easy," said Dr. Schiff.

"You are making a scream come on," said Hilary.

But this did not stop Dr. Schiff, who continued. "Any body can play ball that puts their mind to it."

"No," said Hilary, "that is not true." She was holding back her screaming, fighting and struggling, and I had a mind to rush over and pick her up and kiss her 100 times in both eyes.

"Father, stay where you are," said Dr. Schiff.

"I can give you an example," said Hilary, "showing that you can not play ball simply by putting your mind to it. In Los Angeles I was visiting with my good friend Cynthia Petrotone. Her father played ball for 5 years. He would go on playing ball if he could, but he is all slowed down now from head to toe."

"You are also a friend of Stuffy Sprat," said Dr. Schiff, "and his father is the manager. Make him make his father give your father a job. My father owned a shop and give neighbor kids a job sweeping up."

"It is not that easy," Hilary cried out. "There are 1,000,000's of people can sweep up but only a very few can play in the big leagues."

"If you really wished to have your father play ball," said the doctor, "you could make it happen by using your influence on Stuffy Sprat, and if your father really wished to play ball he could make it happen by using his influence on Mr. Alexander. Your father is rich and famous. He can make any thing happen. I seen him pitch. He is so strong he can make the world slow down the Foucalt Pendulum."

Hilary glanced at me. "Does she believe what she is saying?" she inquired. She then screamed at Dr. Schiff, who put her hands over her ears and leaned back in her chair with her feet off the ground and begun kicking her feet in the air like she was riding a bicycle in till Hilary stopped screaming. The nurse unlocked the door from the out side.

"You are an extremely intelligent young lady," said Dr. Schiff.

Hilary thought this over. She enjoyed being considered intelligent because she considered her sisters intelligent. On the other hand, look who was saying so. "In my opinion," said Hilary to Dr. Schiff, "1 of the most disgusting things the human eye can see is some body putting out cigarettes in Coca Cola cans."

"There is hardly any left," said Dr. Schiff. "Leave us all go to McDonald's."

In McDonald's Hilary and Dr. Schiff heard my name on a radio some body was carrying. "Ask the person what it said," I said, and Hilary asked but the person replied, "We do not listen to the talking."

"Maybe some club signed you up," said Dr. Schiff.

"I thought we have gave up hope of that happening any more," said Hilary, but even so she was excited and got up from the table and begun walking all over McDonald's looking for people with radios.

"*She* may have gave up hope," said Dr. Schiff to me, "but I could sit by the hour and watch you pitch the baseball, throwing your leg up in the air like that and the poor batter trying to hit the ball, which you will not leave him do. When you are back in action I will go to every game you play where ever you play it."

"How do you find Hilary?" I inquired.

"She is much recovered," said Dr. Schiff.

"She just screamed again," I said.

"At me," the doctor said, "because I behaved as stupid as she formerly behaved. She has saw her self in me. You, on the other hand, are totally cracked and we must talk *incessantly*."

"I will call and make an appointment," I said.

"Tonight," she said.

"All right, I will call tonight."

"No, start talking tonight," she said.

"Every body says they heard your name," said Hilary, returning from touring all over McDonald's, "but no body knows what it said."

"It undoubtably has some thing to do with baseball," said Dr. Schiff.

"Very logical," said Hilary.

"I will visit you at your apartment tonight," said Dr. Schiff, "once you have give your wonderful daughter time to drifted off to the land of nod."

"Only if you promise you will not bust up the apartment like the last time," I agreed.

Therefore, instead of returning to Perkinsville that night I and Hilary stood in the apartment. She carried up a Big Mac and a Hot Caramel Sunday and many trimmings and Coca Cola, showering in our marble shower once showered in by some of the best ball players playing ball between 1955 and 1965 and friends and starting in reading about vineyards, wine, and wineries in the Encyclopedia Britannica. She was looking for the best place to begin a winery and she was also selling stock in same.

Holly telephoned, saying she heard my name on the radio, it was not too clear but clear enough. "You are announced as definite for Friday Night Baseball," she said, "which disappoints me."

"I am only surveying the field," I said, "seeing where I might fit in on some body's ball club."

"Why is your wife the last to know?" she inquired. "You will remember how angry you were when the ball club give your release to the news before giving it to you."

"I made 1 telephone call," I said. "I did not know it would be announced so soon."

"They announced it quick to keep you from backing out, I suppose. You will be gone again from February in till September. I hoped that was over with. I thought you would remain in Perkinsville as promised and watch your daughters grow that in the past grew up hardly seeing you. Also, staying home will help you cure other bad habits you developed in a life spent on the road."

"It will be a lot of money," I said.

"The 1 dam thing no body argues with," said Holly. "How did Hilary make out at the doctor?"

"Wonderful," said I. "I truly believe we will hear less screaming in the future."

"Is she asleep?" my wife inquired.

"Long since," I said, "for we are exhausted from running all over the country looking for honest work."

"Even if you get work," she said, "I am sorry to say I see you shelled out of there in quick time. Henry, I have got to tell you this. I watched an exhibition on the tube today out of Florida and I can not believe you care to work that hard any more. It looks to me like pitchers throw faster than ever."

"The older you get the faster it seems," I said. "You must be getting old."

"Who will be keeping you company this grand evening while Hilary is sleeping?" she inquired.

"I am alone," I said.

"Doing what?"

"I am sitting by the window in the dark with my feet on the ledge drinking a glass of wine from Domaine Chandon I bought in San Francisco and watching the snow melt off the Waldorf-Astoria."

"Spell it," she said, for she thought my French was poor.

Dr. Schiff thought I was *impotent.* "Impotent, impotent," I said, "I believe it means I can not have any children."

"You are thinking of *barren*," she said, speaking in a loud whisper so as not to wake Hilary. "Impotent is worse. It means you can not even *think* about having any children," jumping up and running in and looking at Hilary sleeping, and I thought to my self, "Ain't that the sweetest thing the way the doctor runs and looks at her patient," and she come out of Hilary's room with Hilary's left over Coca Cola and poured it in her own. "It is no wonder your wife walked out on you."

"I was not aware my wife walked out on me," I said.

"When Hilary screamed in the Washington air port your wife walked out on you," said Dr. Schiff.

"Walked *off*," I said. "Not out. I do not blame her. She had enough of Hilary right about then."

"I may be off on the wrong track here," she said. "It was my impression you were having an affair with Suzanne in the hotel in Washington."

"I can not imagine Suzanne telling you such a thing," I said.

"She did not. Hilary told me."

"Hilary told you I was having an affair with Suzanne?"

"Hilary told me you were in the hotel with Suzanne."

"I and Suzanne and my wife and 2 girls and 2 government people," I said.

"I may be off on the wrong track there as well," she said.

"Go on," said I, "I love talking about my love life."

"Then why do you do it with your child in the next room?" Dr. Schiff inquired. "The place to talk about your love life is some place where no body is present but you and your conversationalist."

"I prefer to not leave her alone at the moment," I said.

"Same as before," she said, "because you are afraid some body else will find out how impotent you are. You are avoiding the test. Your confidence is shot to shit because you are no longer a manly baseball player. You got prostrate problems and gray hair curling down your neck and contact lenses and you have not got a single love affair going. This is what I call sick, sick, sick. You feel that you failed as a manly father because you got no sons to go on playing baseball. So you must go on your self. You wish to believe it is your wife's fault you could not conceive of sons and so you returned to the hot springs of Japan but could not repeat the act."

"Repeat what act," said I, "if I may inquire?"

"Fucking your wife in the hot springs," she said, "as you done in the earlier days."

"We were not unable," I said. "It was only our prejudice against fucking on busted glass which people threw in the hot springs of Oyasumi. In earlier days we went to better places than Oyasumi where people did not throw bottles in the springs."

"You are dodging the truth," said the doctor. "You did not lay a single hand on the beautiful Italian voiced horse lady of Tozerbury. You run in the stable, leaving Hilary there, and run over and visited your baseball friends, the Sprats. When you finally busted down and took a woman with you some where you took an old lady lawyer 75 years old. You just made an important life decision. It is coming as a shock to your system and making you impotent. You must prove to people that you can make love and I will present you with a clean bill of health."

"What makes you think my lawyer is 75?" I inquired.

"Hilary's estimate," said Dr. Schiff.

"She is much younger than 75," I said.

"And you run off with this young lawyer on a joy ride to California while exiling your very own daughter in the front of the air plane. It is a wonder this child has any marbles left at all. About how old was this young lawyer?"

"In my opinion," I said, "you been a very good doctor for Hilary, but I am wondering if you got exactly the straight line on me."

"I been a little girl in my time," said Dr. Schiff, "but never a man of 40. It is possible that I am on the wrong track."

"I am not yet 40," I said.

"What is your sign?" she inquired.

"You know," said I, "I lived through all the Vietnam days and always refused to answer that 1 question. I never believed in it. I will be 40 years old July 4 and hope to be playing baseball some where on that day. I can not remember the July 4 I was not playing baseball."

"You are my perfect sign," she said.

"But not the perfect age," I said, and we sat for a long time with our feet on the ledge watching the lights go out in the hotel. She done a fine job with Hilary and I told her so.

"Recommend me to others," she said.

"I certainly will," I said.

"Unless you think I am on the wrong track too much," she said.

"You are on the right track," I said, "but you are not yet at the station."

"I will report back to you when I am older," she said.

"I see us a hot item when you are 50 and I am 60," I said.

"I will be counting the days," she said with a some what sarcastic sound in her voice, but she soon forgive me and kissed me good by beside the elevator as before. It was not such a small kiss this time, and my whole body enjoyed holding her there a moment or 2, gray hair, contact lenses, prostrate and all.

In the morning, when the garage man brung the car to the apartment, the phone was off the hook. "It kept ringing," he said, "it was driving me out of my head."

It was Marva Sprat. "You forgot to put it on Call Forwarding," she said. "I am sure your spirits are high this morning. You got nothing ahead but top options. We hurdled the biggest hurdle of all. The inter league trading dead lines flew past like a witch on her broom at midnight. Sit tight for the league dead line. No body helped Mr. Alexander out, no body got a short relief to trade him. Jack says they are going to get no help from any body, they are too strong. You sound like you are in the middle of a city street."

"I am," I said.

"You are in the driver seat," she said. "I will be listening to your wonderful voice every Friday night hence forth in till the league dead line has come and went. On the following day you will be pitching for my own Jack."

"Last evening," I said, "I just about counted my self out. Hilary counted me out, too. Hilary is right here in the car with me, hanging on our every word."

"I under stand," said Marva. "That is why school was invented to clear the house during school hours."

"I thought our meeting with Suicide Alexander was a disaster," I said.

"*Disaster?*" she replied. "The man was *charmed* with you. Your lawyer's sense of humor knocked him off his feet, he dreams about marrying her. It is only in fairness to the stock holders he is waiting for the second dead line. He wants you. He was delighted how you grabbed a hold of his bank book and become so excited reading it you plan to put it in a book. Send him an autograph copy."

"Having friends like you, Marva, is the only thing keeping me afloat these days."

"Where are you now?" she inquired.

"Driving across 57th," I said.

"I hear them fucking buses hissing like 10,000 snakes," she said. "Is it any wonder I never leave the house? Remember this and say it over and over to your self. 'It will never be Jack who double crosses me. If any body double crosses me it will be Mr. Alexander.' But he will not double cross you, either, my darling boy, for he sees how things are hanging and he will *need* you. Should I tell you what I see ahead of us?"

"Keeping it clean," I said.

"I see ahead of us a historic first. You will be the first man that ever come down out of the broad cast booth and went back in the game it self. You will save game after game after game for Jack. I see ahead of us the sweetest pennant ever won followed by the grandest World Series party that was ever threw, a celebration floating back and forth all winter between Tozerbury and Perkinsville."

"Should I tell you what I see ahead of us?" I inquired.

"Clean or dirty I do not care," she said.

"The East River Drive," I said.

"The best of luck," she said. "If any body ever deserved it it was you. When are you coming down and feed your horses?"

"Up," I said.

"Your way is my way," she said.

When I and Hilary arrived home young ladies were hanging from every corner of the house. These were friends of my daughters of all ages come for a glimpse of Suzanne Winograd. They brung autograph books to sign except 1 girl name of Gwendolyn Biheller with a leg in her cast from skiing. Every body signed her cast. At 1 time there must of been as many as 20 girls in the house, and when Suzanne arrived she signed them all and talked in a very patient way with them, giving them very good advice on running their lives. She was less insane than she been during the winter. In some body's house she was usually very sensible. When she got in public she shrieked and insulted every body, making a show of her self like she done when she was a child and went over big with the adults. Working with Dr. Schiff she had now grew up 20 years in 18 months, her game was better than ever, and she was beginning to rise out of debt.

As the weeks went by I become very good friends with her daughter Bertilia. Suzanne often become so carried away hearing her self being interviewed or listening to the sound of cameras clicking off photos of her self that she forgot Bertilia. I and Bertilia drifted off to the back of things, wandering around among wires and cables and technical workers and crew, or out in the street all together. Some times we wandered through ball parks together. She wore her beautiful white sweater reading *Friday Night Baseball* across her little breast. We were both rather bored with baseball games. Now and then I took an inning off, leaving the job to Jerry and Suzanne, strolling with Bertilia up and down the ball park ramps, or we walked along to some far corner of the park where no body was sitting and we sat there. If any body missed my voice no body said. I received $10,333.33 for every Friday night I announced less military taxes and this and that and the other in till you were dizzy.

Arriving at the house Suzanne was brown and sun burned from visiting the baseball camps in the South and I was sun burned from the telephone call in Newhall, California. Jerry Divine arrived on the following day bringing 2 network negotiators with him, and Barbara come up on the same train carrying the wine glass she kept her memorandums in.

While the negotiators were negotiating I and Holly and Suzanne hit golf balls on the range and passed the time in other ways. On the golf range Suzanne become very war like, hitting the balls very far and sneering at Holly, saying, "You are certainly no athlete, my dear. Now watch *this* son of a bitch," rotating her shoulders and moving in on the ball in the most casual way and blasting it out of sight. Holly hits a ball rather well, but not consistent. She does not care enough. She does not concentrate, or any how she concentrates on some thing else, such as Mrs. Wiggen's School for Privileged Children. My self I like to fantasize I am a baseball player hitting home runs, driving the balls nothing less than 750 or a 1,000 feet. No ball park can hold me. I give pitchers night mares. "I am no lady playing sports," said Suzanne.

"I was never a big competitor," said Holly.

"You must of knew what you were doing," said Suzanne, "for look at the husband you bagged. When you got him you got every thing but Christmas bells. I would give every cup and medal I ever owned for a man who was at least ½ a man instead of all pig. Figure every 1 of these balls is the head of a former husband," she said, lining up balls on a row of tees. She danced down the line, driving them out of sight 1 after the other, *whoop, whack, whup,* no sweat, never aiming, hardly looking, hitting every ball absolutely clean, every ball far. "God give me the fucking gift of co ordination," she said, "I wish He had gave me a tea spoon full of mental balance. I can play tennis, golf, row boats, skate on ice, skate on wood, shoot rifles and pistols, dive and swim and jump double summer salts on the trampoleum by sticking with my diet. When I was 10 years old I dressed up like a boy 15 and won the marbles champion ship of Michigan and all surrounding states. But the minute I go off my diet I can not do 1 thing good any more, my whole system whacks out of balance and I am ready to go under taking 3 or 4 people with me. Certain people deserve the worst." Bertilia often said to her, "You know that you must set a good example for me." "I try," said Suzanne to me 1 day, "but it is fucking hard. I am a chemical mess. As you get to know me in the broad cast booth you will begin to say, 'Now I see why her husbands fled the coop.'"

The negotiators met for 3 days in my fire proof room in the cellar. The 2 net work men burned holes in the arms of my chairs. Every afternoon about 5 they staggered up stairs choking with smoke and drunk a drink and commuted back in the city. Barbara come away from every session with questions for me wrote out on slips of paper fished out of her wine glass. Did I agree to this or that? Did I not agree? The negotiators made every thing more complicated than it amounted to in the long run. Suppose it rained. When was a game not a game? What was meant by "travel," all though I thought I always knew. Suppose you slandered some body on the air. Who was libel? Who owned the tapes? Suppose while sitting announcing the game you invented some thing which could be marketed for money. Who owned it? Did you invent it on Friday Night Baseball time or your own? What was the difference between Friday Night Baseball time and your own? Where did 1 stop and the other begin? Suppose you left the booth and visited the press box men's room for the purpose of draining away your Precious Golden Cleansing Fluid were you on Friday Night Baseball time or your own? Suppose you went to the *public* men's room instead of the press box? During those danger filled journeys were you covered by their insurance or yours? May be 1 insurance covered 1 and the other covered the other. Suppose on some body's time or the other you were struck in the booth by a flying baseball. Suppose the booth tore loose from the structure and fell down on the field. Suppose the stadium it self tore loose from it self and fell in to a hole in the ground and ended in Hell. Was that "travel"? I am looking at it now. I am prohibited from "printing, publishing, or selling else where in the known world and on the Earth's moon" any secrets of how we broad cast Friday Night Baseball.

This was in the middle of March. In *September* Barbara received my copy of the contract with a note from Friday Night Baseball saying "Enclosed please find and so on and so on and we hope you will find working together with us a pleasant and rewarding relationship which will be fruit full now and in the future," signed by the President of the Sporting Broad Cast Division in his absence.

I laid in bed 1 night while the negotiation was going on thinking how full the house was. It was all women. There was Holly and the girls and 2 friends of the girls plus Barbara, Suzanne, and Bertilia. That was 10. Counting servants 13. Why didn't any body ask Jerry Divine to stay? "No body asked me to ask him," Holly said. It slipped my mind. How do you like that? A person slips your mind. Since he was not a negotiator he shouldn't of been commuting with the negotiators. He was on *our* side for God sake. His limping grew worse. By the end of a few Friday nights in Friday Night Baseball he could walk only with a good deal of difficulty. Once upon a time he could run the bases in 13 seconds, but now he could hardly walk them. He stood on whiskey and pills to keep down the pain, although some body since told me he been on whiskey and pills to begin with or he wouldn't of been clipped by the car on the street in Cleveland. Who knows? All these things are buried in mysteries.

"There are 13 women in this house," I said to Holly.

"Why are you counting women?" she inquired.

"To get asleep," I said.

"Why not count sheep?" she inquired.

"I do not fuck sheep," I replied.

"Playing baseball again is a bad idea enough," she said. "Announcing is worse. With all the things in the world to look at I am wondering why you would wish to look at more baseball games."

"I am helping out Suzanne and Jerry," I said, "and surveying the field for my self. I only intend being away 2 nights a week at the most."

"I am guessing 3 or 4," she said, "by the time you finish various conversations along the way. I was hoping you would help me flower the garden now that spring is here."

"Some ball club needs me," I said, "and I am going to advertise my self. Year after year the garden will be here needing work, and all the warm climates will be out there waiting. But I have got some pitching left in me and I am going to pitch it. The only thing that can not be put off is playing ball."

"I hear that you and Hilary been talking winery," she said.

"We are reading up on them," I said.

"I rather be addicted to wine than baseball," Holly said.

"I can come back to wineries," I said, "but if I do not try this baseball now I will always say, 'You should of tried it before the time was past.' I am helping out Jack Sprat and Marva. It will be a good deed winning for Jack. I am going to save him 30 games in 2 inning jobs at a time."

"Speaking of your acquaintances in the ladies' department," said my wife, "leave me ask you a question."

"Ask."

"Was Dr. Schiff in the apartment with you the other night?"

"Never," said I.

"Hilary smelled her in the morning," Holly said.

"Now that Hilary is recovering her mind," said I, "she probably needs a nose doctor."

Getting in shape for Friday Night Baseball I trained my self for sitting 3 hours in the broad cast booth with out requiring the men's room. For men over 40 I will tell you how I handled it successfully.

I bore in mind my number 1 rule, which was this. When game time comes be empty but not thirsty. It is a simple rule like "Keep the tie run from coming to the bat." I begun working on it when rising from bed. The pressure on my bladder was great, some times unbearable, or so I thought, and if I been shorter on control than I now learned to be I would of run to the bath room immediately. How ever, I knew that the pressure was not on my bladder but in the canal blocked by the prostrate, and if I run straight from the bed to the bath room I would of stood like a fool dribbling and spraying and giving my self a delightful warm foot bath.

Instead I took my time. I was cool. I went about my business, leaving my self drain down. I telephoned people, remaining on my feet while doing so. I worked a little in the garden. I drove children to their various schools, although sitting set me back a little.

I remembered what I learned passing through Minnow that day on the road to Tozerbury. I said to my self, "Remember the difference between *a full bladder* and a *temporary traffic jam*. Think Minnow. The pain will pass." I wrote down the time on a scrap of note book paper, and when I knew my bladder was empty I give it 4 or 5 hours to fill again. I did not pamper it.

I drunk as much liquids as I cared to in till 3 or 4 hours before game time, whether broad casting or playing. When game time arrived I emptied my self. I would now last with out pain or difficulty in till after the ball game, when I could begin again drinking all the liquids I cared to and visiting the bath room as often as I cared to in till bed time, knowing that on the following morning I could easily get my self back on the schedule again.

Most of my getting in shape I done right around Perkinsville. I run the roads, I swum at the "Y," I played tennis if I could find any body, and I threw hitting practice at Perkinsville High. When we begun broad casting I worked out on Thursdays and Fridays where ever we went. Back in Perkinsville over the week end I employed 2 catchers from the high school team to catch me. They objected to taking money but I made them do it. They begun thinking it was a joke, but after they caught the first few pitches some thing in the palm of their hand told them that this old man could throw a baseball rather hard. I threw to them on the Perkinsville High diamond where I pitched more than 20 years before, and many thoughts come back to me. I noticed what quick reflexes these boys had, they learned very quick to put 2 plus 2 together, how my fast ball hopped and how my curve broke. They scooped balls out of the dirt as good as they ever would, for in some ways they were as good ball players in high school as they would ever be, and I realized now how terribly fast and hard I must of threw the ball when I was 17. I polished up my screw ball. They had never saw a screw ball before and were amazed. I also worked some what on throwing the knuckle ball, which I never threw before and ended up abanding, but I thought at the time I needed as many varieties of pitches as I could manage. The more pitches I had, *or the more pitches other people thought I had,* the better off I was. I begun to remember in my mind many pitchers I heard of that learned to go for variety when their fast ball give out, extending their career by several years in some cases. I begun to realize why old pitchers I had saw looked so very easy to hit and yet were so difficult. They had many varieties of pitches, but no fast ball. They also had wide experience.

A lot of other things come back to me as well. Stepping on the scale in the high school locker room I noticed 1 day I jiggled the weights before the next person could see what I weighed. I remembered in the old days I use to see old ball players do the same, jiggling the weights and shaking their head and stepping off. I give each of these high school catchers $200 a piece for several weeks work, both were name William, 1 was white and 1 was black, and I realized when I done my income tax I did not know their last name. We wrote in "William Williams, $400," and left it go at that.

On top of every thing my *concentration* was better than it ever been before in my life. Every thing else was shut out of my mind. I knew there was no problem in the world that could not wait in till after the ball game. It was not necessary for me to think about what my hair looked like on my head or my pants on my hips. No matter what I looked like the people that loved me would love me. I did not worry about getting through the month financially. There was no telephone call coming in or going out that could not wait. There fore my mind was ready for any thing my body might wish to do with the baseball, and as far as I could tell both my mind and my body were doing their thing as good as ever.

Working out with various ball clubs prior to Friday Night Baseball many fellows said to me, "It is easy to see that you have got games in you left, it is a wonder no body asks you." *Tell your manager,* I thought to my self. Now and then 1 fellow or another said to me, "You got plenty left, it is true, but a lot been took off your fast ball, Author."

After working out I dressed and went up in the booth and announced with Suzanne and Jerry. If Bertilia and I took a stroll through the park I carried a small 1 pint canteen of water formerly belonging to 1 of my daughters at summer camp. I kept it slung over my shoulder. Some people thought it was some kind of special TV equipment. Leave them think what they wished. Bertilia soon owned a canteen of her own and carried it with her. We had the same canteen and the same sweater and I realize she told people I was her father. I said nothing. Once in a while I called her "Hilary" by mistake. The minute the ball game was over I drained the canteen if any was left in it, and on the way out the park I drunk from every water fountain I passed. From the park we often went some place for beer or wine or other beverages, or if we flew directly home we drunk liquids through out the air plane ride.

The day before Opening Day Ed Lewis come down in his pick up from Tozerbury and took a look at Henry W. Wiggen Mini Park. It was a cold, raw, nasty, windy day. I wore an over coat. He walked around admiring the seats and benches I had brang over the years from various ball parks. He noticed how they were made, these boards or that, these bolts or the other. "You said a 1 foot fence," he said.

"Yes," I said. I told him we wished a 1 foot fence.

"You said 1 foot high and all around," he said.

"Correct," I said.

"You know," he said, "that 1 foot high is not going to keep any body or any thing out, not a small kitten or a 3 legged dog."

"We are improving the property," I said. "A fence improves it."

"I know that a fence improves it," he said. "I am sold on fences, but it has got to be high enough to matter."

"No," I said, "for my part it has only got to be high enough to matter legally. I am legally improving the park."

"You are living up to the letter of the law," said Ed, "but not the spirit. I will build any thing you wish and if they drag you in court call your lawyer, not me." He measured my park by walking it off, now and then saying, "A 1 foot fence," writing down figures, and when he was done he said, "There is 1 great advantage in building a 1 foot fence because you can multiply almost any thing by 1 with out a pencil."

"I should get a discount," I said.

"I will build you a 1 foot fence around this park for $350 less discount," Ed Lewis said.

"How much discount?" I inquired.

"For a man of your means," he said, "nothing."

*   *   *

"On the road to New York the same day I received a call from Marva Sprat. She received the Domaine Chandon I sent from San Francisco. "You are a darling boy," she said, "to thought of me out there. Where are you now?"

"Around about Mount Vernon," I replied.

"Take care in the rain," she said, "with a pennant riding along on the out come."

"In the mean while," said I, "I am feeling rather out of things. Tomorrow I will miss Opening Day after 21 years in organized baseball."

"It is a crime," she said, "but soon will be revenged by the forces of good. Should I tell you what I see ahead of us?"

"Tell me what you done with the wine," I said.

"Safe as can be," she said.

"A little bird is telling me you poured it out of the Domaine Chandon in to the Vine Hill White bottle which did not even have Vine Hill White any more in it."

"I see ahead of us another historic first," she said. "You will be the first man in the history of baseball that ever threw out the ball on Opening Day and was back in uniform playing that very same season."

"I am devoutly praying you will be right," I said.

The reason I drove down a day early was for a meeting in Patricia Moors's office with her and Barbara and the 2 net work negotiators and various TV people from other net works regarding throwing out the ball Opening Day. Various baseball broad casts such as Monday Night Baseball and Week End Baseball and Game of the Week protested the ceremony, saying it was 1 big advertisement for Friday Night Baseball. "Here is Wiggen," said 1 of the other net work men, "standing up there as big as life with *Friday Night Baseball* wrote across his sweater. Where will it end? The world will think Friday Night Baseball is the *official* baseball announcer for New York."

"The thing that pains me the most," said his friend, "is realizing that after he throws out the first ball he will be cheered by the crowd, for that is what they do. The world will think the crowd is *cheering* Friday Night Baseball. Is that justice or fairness? It does not sound like that to me."

Patricia's office was very cold. They always turned the heat off in the ball park by Opening Day, talking them self in to the idea the weather was perfect for baseball. The 2 negotiators from Friday Night Baseball that burned holes in my arm chairs back home were now burning holes in the chairs in Patricia's office. I had not saw Patricia since her and Ben Crowder pulled a fast 1 behind my back and I did not care who burned down her chairs and the whole place with it. We all crowded around a little electric heater. "I am amused," said Patricia, "hearing you say 'the world will think this and the world will think that' when the world will not be at tomorrow's ball game. We will be lucky if we sell 40,000 tickets."

"In fairness," said another net work man, "you should call off the game rather than permit the first ball to be threw out by Friday Night Baseball."

"Call off Opening Day?" Patricia inquired. "Opening Day is 1 century old in our family. You are a man of ambition."

Barbara spoke, saying, "The ball will not be threw out by Friday Night Baseball but by Henry Wiggen. It is an occasion showing respect for 1 man dead and another just now retiring."

"Possibly retiring," I said.

"If Friday Night Baseball throws out the first ball tomorrow why not Week End Baseball the next time?" inquired the man from Week End Baseball.

"Because," said Patricia, "you are making a mole hill out of a mountain. If you can tell me some body in your organization that pitched for me for 19 years I will gladly ask him to throw out the first ball on the next occasion."

Barbara spoke again, saying, "I am amusing my self thinking if every TV net work gets an opportunity of throwing out the first ball every radio station will have the right to throw out the first ball and every news paper and magazine that sits in the press box will have equal rights to throw out the first ball."

"I am only talking about net works," said 1 of the net work men. "No body is thinking about these god dam fly by night independents that are not even off the ground."

"Well now," said Patricia, "I must take a firm hand and tell you that Mr. Wiggen will throw out the first ball. Many of the tickets sold were sold to people expecting 1 last glimpse of him tomorrow, so there we are."

"May be not 1 last glimpse," I said. "Coming down in the car I heard a prediction where some body said I will throw out the first ball tomorrow and be back playing again soon after."

"I am groaning with in," said the first net work man, "to think about him standing up in front of all those people plus TV news with *Friday Night Baseball* wrote across his sweater."

"This is where we were," said Barbara. "He might take off his sweater."

That was a good idea. Barbara never suggests any thing I would not agree with. I did not plan to wear the sweater in the first place. I planned a dark blue blazer with gray light wool pants. I was thinking about a really flaming shirt, but in honor of the 1 minute silence for Dutch I planned a certain pearl gray and blue pin stripe instead. Neutral socks and a pair of tassel mocs. "Yes," I said, "I will be taking off my sweater all right. I did not plan on wearing it in the first place."

"Never the less," said 1 of the net work men, "you are associated with Friday Night Baseball now with all the advertising they have gave you sweater or no sweater."

"I was picturing my self slipping out of my jacket and leaving it in the box," I said.

"Well all right now," said the first net work man, "I am seeing a little justice through the clearing. He will not wear any sweater or other identifying marks."

"May be you would like him to change his name," said Barbara.

"Not necessary," the man replied, "but what is now beginning to disturb my conscience is the words I just heard. You are 'leaving it in the box.' What is the meaning of that?"

"I am leaving my jacket in the box," I replied, "while strolling out on the field to the box."

"What box?"

"The pitcher's box."

"This is gone from too much to much too much," said the net work man, shaking his head from side to side and giving out a little smile showing he would be brave no matter what. "He should throw the ball out from the owner's box. There he is concealed and can not be seen. A lot of people will hardly know who is doing it much less give Friday Night Baseball the credit for it. He should not be strolling slowly out in front of all those people, visible to many, walking ever so slowly at leisure across all the distance from the Owner's Box to the pitcher's box while 1,000's of people turn to 1 another and say, 'Oh, yes, he is now with Friday Night Baseball.' It is enough to make you cry what happened to justice."

"It is advertising pure and simple," said his friend. "Why does he not squirt his mouth and under his arm while walking to the box and collect a fee from the mouth wash and the under arm?"

"Any how," said the first man, "he will not wear the sweater."

"I am sure we are all parting good friends," said 1 of the net work men and we all stood up and shook hands all around. The joke of it was that every body was winners on the following day but me, if you recall the occasion, which I just as soon forget.

Opening Day was fair and clear and dry with some what of a nip in the air. It was Spring and Dutch Schnell was dead. New York in the Spring meant clear days after rain and a nip in the air, and Dutch above every body else. I kept thinking I heard him shouting in the park. Where was the center of the park now that Dutch was dead, for in the past you listened for him and you looked for him, and where ever he was the center was.

I and Barbara sat in the Owners Box. Often in the past Dutch walked down from the dugout to the box and shook hands and talked a little with some body there. Some times he kissed a lady for the camera, or a cripple child. When I was a young ball player I wondered why you done such things. When I was a more experienced ball player I thought you done it because the owner told you to. But when I was an older ball player I knew you done it not because any body told you to but only because that was where you were. Older people were not people you bowed and scraped to. They were your friends. You knew them. You partied with them. Your children were as old as their children. When my daughter Michele was 15 she went on a world tour with Stanton Moors La Vigne, son of Patricia, although we would not of knew they went together if the plane was not high jack. You under stood the same problems. You were all in it together.

Time and again as I grew older it was I they cared to meet, so it was I that strolled down from the dugout and shook their hand. I shook hands with many rich and famous people over the rail of the Owners Box, cripple children and ailing persons and foreign dignitaries, causing a commotion once when General Weiskopf was there 1 day during Vietnam. I said in an angry voice, "General, if you are having a war these days why are you not out dying with the young men instead of sitting in the sun at a baseball game?" His face become white and he looked at me like he was disappointed in me. Then he smiled and replied, "We are each of us caught up in our life, are we not?"

But on this particular Opening Day it was not Dutch Schnell but Ev McTaggart at the center of things. He was up against the dugout wall watching the drill, his hands jammed down in his ass pockets, focusing his eye on things when some body mentioned some thing to him and he begun walking down toward the Owners Box with out taking his eye off the ball field. When he arrived he greeted Patricia and Barbara by the hand, he give a warm kiss to Millie Schnell, and he shook my hand, giving me a wink like him and I knew some thing no body else knew and said, "How is it, Author?" and I replied, "Good luck, Ev," although it killed me.

I pitched my first complete big league baseball game Opening Day in 1952. I was not yet 21, the youngest pitcher in the league. I signed to play ball for $4,000 bonus and an automobile when numbers had a different sound from now and an automobile was a bigger thing. Now a days you can hardly get a ball player to spit on an automobile unless you throw in a small sum of cash, such as $400,000 for Beansy Binz. On Opening Day, 1952, Mayor Vincent R. Impellitteri of the City of New York threw out the first ball from the Owners Box, and Sid Goldman caught it, according to my book in title *The Southpaw,* and run over and got the Mayor's autograph. Later Sid him self run for Mayor and lost.

I remember Opening Day, 1952, clearer than any Opening Day since. I remember the players of that year clearer than the players of any year since, first names and bad habits. Nothing ever stuck so hard in my mind as the first year, and no day of that year so clear to my mind as the first day. I knew every body, or any how I thought I did. I can not now give you the names of 2 dozen present day ball players, and those I can give you are all past 30. I don't know any body low down any more, and I notice where fewer and fewer people call me "Author." People that knew me good enough to call me "Author" drift off in to the distance. When the telephone rings people ask for "Mr. Wiggen" and are flattened out with surprise when they hear that I answered my own phone.

Here was the Mammoths starting line up on Opening Day in 1952.

3b Gonzalez
cf Judkins
lf V. Carucci
1b Goldman

rf P. Carucci
ss Jones
2b Park
c Traphagen
p Wiggen

Where have they all went I do not know. George Gonzalez, third base and leading off, left American baseball in 1956 and returned to Cuba. Some time afterwards I heard him on the radio 1 night driving between New York and Perkinsville. Some body asked him what position he played. He said, "In U. S. A. baseball I was a third baseman but in Cuba as a patriotic player I play every thing but pitch." Lucky Judkins, center field, was soon traded away, played awhile else where, left baseball in 1957 and to the best of my knowledge lives in Oklahoma to the present day.

Vincent Carucci, left field, owns a mortuary house in San Francisco. You see his advertisement on all the bill boards there. At baseball dinners he gives out little cards that look like the bill boards. When the freezer girl was all over the news he give me a phone call warning me she was a fraud, which I already knew but thanked him all the same. "Author," he said, "have your self buried in the earth, not in no fucking refridge."

Sid Goldman, first base, quit baseball in 1960, went to work for President Kennedy, run for City Council of New York and lost, run for Borough President of Manhattan and lost, run for Congress from Manhattan and lost, run for Mayor of New York and lost, and at the present writing is the director of athletics at a small college up state.

Pasquale Carucci, right field, brother of Vincent, sat on the bench at the end of his career. It was a sad sight to see. He was very unhappy and sat with his head in his hands. He felt that he should of been used. He felt that Dutch was *prejudice* against him, that it was an *injustice*. The first time Dutch asked my opinion on any subject what so ever he asked me, "What do you think of Pasquale these days?" Maybe this was 1958, 1959. Well, I was always deeply grateful to Pasquale the way he went back for fly balls. No body caught fly balls better going away on the run or got the ball back in faster or was less afraid of the fences. He stared them down and I do not think he ever really run in to 1. But as time went by he could not turn and run back any more as good as he formerly could, and so he no longer played so shallow, and line drives he formerly caught while shallow fell in for base hits. "There been no injustice," I told Pasquale 1 time. "Dutch is prejudice against *every* body. If you are human he hates you," and Pasquale laughed a little at that, but not much. Soon he quit or was released and I and him and several other persons ate dinner together 1 night before his air plane to the Coast. I shook hands with him in front of the hotel, saying we would meet again, etc., and he replied, "If life lasts." I heard on good authority that he and Vincent fell out very badly over a business matter and stopped talking for ever. They were totally different. But when I meet Vincent 1 place or another and ask him, "How is Pasquale and why does he always stay home?" he smashes me on the back replying, "Pasquale was never greater, we are the happiest living family," but I know that is not true. Next time I will ask him for the truth if I have the courage.

Ugly Jones, shortstop, dropped from sight.

Gene Park, second base, also dropped from sight. He retired from baseball about 1960 and went home to California. A year or 2 later I met him at some sort of a get together where a fellow sold me a share in a children's game played with dice and cards and a spinning arrow called "Heads Up Baseball." The fellow said if we would put some cash in it and put our name on it we would make a lot of money. Maybe it never made a *lot* of money, but it made *some,* and I receive checks very regularly for my self and another check for Gene Park since the fellow has no address for Gene and neither do I. I put it in the bank and leave it draw interest like Suicide Alexander's account, only smaller.

This been many years now. My daughter Rosemary said she believed Jones and Park were swallowed up in the Bermuda Triangle. This was at the time the Bermuda Triangle was big in the news.

Red Traphagen, catcher, taught me a great deal about baseball. In 1953 he retired, returning to San Francisco and teaching in the university there, where he been ever since. We write back and forth every year or 2 and we visit. I consider us close. Holly has wrote about Rosemary Traphagen in her book in title *Baseball Wives.* Red him self wrote several books I am sorry to say I never read except 1 in title *Backing Up First,* his own auto biography, mentioning me as follows. Notice the terrific writing. I never realized in till this minute what a clever title it was.

I have expressed my aversion to superlatives. Nevertheless, the "best" pitcher I ever caught was Henry Wiggen.

We played together during the last year of my career, at the blossoming of his. We were twelve years apart in age—one baseball generation. I think I first knew how very good he was going to be following a small incident during our year together. He pitched a pitch. The umpire called it a ball. It was a day that had not been going well for me, and I leaped upon the umpire, as one leaps upon someone—anyone—on days not going well. To my surprise, Henry came impatiently down the line, anxious to return to work, bawling at me, "Aw, fuck it, Red, it missed." It was not that he did not wish the pitch to have been a strike. It was not even that he would have morally objected to its being called wrong in his favor—wrong calls even up. It was only that he had so keen an eye for every action of his own that he hated its distortion, whether for better or for worse.

He had the instincts of a crayfish. He came with talent and desire and health. But to deliver work so good over so long a period of time requires also an independence of character sufficient to resist the mockery of people who, never having dared an art, remain ignorant of its demands. In this independence he was

encouraged by his wife, Holly, a woman of wisdom and tolera-
tion and a genius in endurance; to each other they have been
equally loyal and faithful; and by their four daughters Henry as
father has been viewed with mingled respect and amusement.

As pitcher, he saw the game whole, the point and purpose of it.
The idea of every game was not personal distinction but winning.
Knowing this, he achieved both victory and distinction. Perfor-
mance absorbed him. He *enjoyed* playing baseball, savoring the
phenomenon of his own accruing skill. That he pitched for a full
five years after his fast ball was gone testifies to his wit, wisdom,
humor, enthusiasm, and to the keenness of his analysis of the
tricks and realities of the art of pitching against savage hitters.

The game was a game, but life was not. He was oppressed by
inequality and injustice, awed by the idea that while he was
playing baseball other young men were dying in Vietnam. Many
people told him it was "bad for baseball" to speak out. "Don't
rock the boat," they said. But he could not resist speaking when
occasions presented themselves.

"Ladies and Gentle Men. Your Attention Please. Our National Anthem." We all stood. Ev McTaggart was still walking
back to the dugout with his hands in his pockets. He did not
know whether he should stop or continue. There fore he
stopped and removed his hat and kept walking a few steps but
changed his mind and finally stopped all together, and ½ way
through the song he remembered to take his other hand out of
his pocket. The song ended and the cheering rose. Usually the
voice of the umpire follows, calling "Play ball," but on this day
the loud speaker spoke again, saying, "Ladies and Gentle Men.
Your Attention Please. In honor of the late Dutch Schnell,
whose name for 45 years was associated with the New York
Mammoths Baseball Club, Inc., may we remain standing for 1
minute of respect full silence." We all stood standing.

I felt many eyes on our box. Only Millie Schnell stood
sitting, looking down on her hands folded in her lap. I was glad I
had wore the blue pin stripe instead of the flaming shirt. I

remember smelling Barbara's perfume. Millie did not cry. Patricia cried like she cried at the funeral, but I was not angry at her now as I been before, nor angry at Ev McTaggart standing there with his hat still off and his 1 hand back in his pocket.

Soon the loud speaker spoke once more, saying, "Ladies and Gentle Men. Your Attention Please. May we ask Mr. Henry Wiggen to throw the baseball in to play," where before the sentence was out of the loud speaker's mouth the cheering of the crowd rose again. Dutch was forgot. I could feel it. In $\frac{1}{2}$ a second all the people present turned their thought from Dutch to the next item on the program, like Hilary at the funeral thinking of nothing but the Gate Way Arch. I hated the fans. I would of loved their cheering better if I didn't know it might change to hatred and booing in another $\frac{1}{2}$ a second. I sat down beside Millie, kissing her hard and sincerely and holding her close and the crowd begun to stir, becoming restless and wondering, "Well, where is he?" and I stood up and slipped off my blazer and laid it across Barbara's lap. I left my self out of the Owners Box and begun walking to the pitcher's box. I rolled up my sleeve while I walked. The cheering was very loud. If I had wore a hat I would of touched it, but wearing no hat I waved my hand instead. This felt extremely peculiar. I never before *waved* to people in a ball park. I felt insincere. Who was I waving at? I took the ball and rubbed it up and the cheering rose higher and higher. I stepped on the mound, looking in to my catcher for my sign, like this was the real thing. In my book in title *The Southpaw* I tell where Red Traphagen said to me, Opening Day, 1952, standing listening to the anthem, "Good luck, Henry, this is for the money," but today was not for the money. It was only an older ball player now retired looking in for his sign from a catcher whose name he could not even remember from September. He was the boy I pitched 2 innings to the night Dr. Schiff come to the ball game. I wound up and pitched to him and fell down.

I fell to 1 knee only, really. It must of looked worse from the seats. I popped right up again. But it could not of looked worse than it felt, falling down in the wrong clothes, all alone in front of a large crowd. The crowd first gasped. Then it laughed. Then it suddenly stopped laughing and begun cheering and applauding. Where the ball went I never knew. Every thing was standing still. No body was in motion. Suddenly from the first base side this boy Beansy Binz called out to me, "Throw it again, Author, go ahead, do it, do it," holding up a ball he was waiting to come on and pitch with, and he threw it to me and I stepped on the mound again. He was a quick thinker and I appreciated it. It was Beansy Binz actually first made me think about becoming a short relief. I should of thanked him for mentioning the idea to me, but I never did.

The reason I fell down was this. I was wearing a pair of tassel mocs by Bally. They were never meant for baseball. Maybe I should of threw from the Owners Box. But I didn't, and it never for a 1/1,000,000 of a second entered my mind to think about shoes. Who ever thought about shoes? Shoes were *on*. I pitched 4,815 innings of big league baseball and never walked out in the wrong shoes. I am not knocking Bally shoes. They are $80 shoes good for many things. I stepped off the mound where I had fell down and dug a quick hole with my toe in the grass and pitched from the hole, whipping the ball in with good speed to the catcher whose name I still can not remember. Maybe it will come to me. The crowd cheered and the umpire called out, "Play ball," and then it was for the money again, but not mine.

10

On the following night we done our first Friday Night Baseball, Cleveland vs. Atlanta. "Take in your mind," said Jerry Divine, "that we are nothing but 3 blokes at home and talk accordingly." It begun in a very enjoyable way. I talked softly in the microphone, thinking of my voice going out to all the states in the United States and over seas and around the world by satellite and what not. "Take a certain person in your mind," said Jerry, "and talk to that person and it will keep you natural." I took Holly and my daughters in my mind, I took Barbara and Marva Sprat and Dr. Schiff in my mind. Talking to them kept my voice soft.

Suzanne also enjoyed her self at the start. "The most wonderful thing about it," she said, "is that no body can see me." She had went off her diet and was eating every thing in sight. The TV booth smelled like mustard, she gained 20 pounds, and she threw her tennis rackets down the insinerator in her apartment house, or any how she said she did. Bertilia said she did not. Many things Suzanne threw down the insinerator over time poor little Bertilia went down in the cellar of the house and saved and brang back up again. "She will need to go back and play tennis 1 of these days," Bertilia said. In the mean time, how ever, Suzanne grew fatter and fatter week by week and 1,000 times easier to get along with. She followed Jerry's instructions to the tee and we were all feeling totally optimistic about Friday Night Baseball at the start. The very first night after 3 or 4 innings Jerry received a report from some body at head quarters some place saying polls showed that many people were tuning in and chuckling and telling their neighbors the same. At 1 point in time we gained 1,000,000 viewers in 14 seconds. That was the report. How they know such things I do not know. Some times I think they make it up and tell it to them self and bring smiles to their own face.

When Jerry heard the news we gained 1,000,000 viewers in 14 seconds his whole face lit up and he clapped his hands in the air and done victory signs over his head, but as soon as he done those things he looked down cast again and said, "It can not keep up, I am not a winner but a loser."

"I wish you told us you were a loser before hand," said Suzanne.

"Keep gaining 1,000,000 viewers every 14 seconds and you will be a winner," I said. Here is a little tape of a few minutes of our first broad cast playing the part of 3 blokes at home, Cleveland at Atlanta. At this point we were trying to speak only 1 sentence at a time.

"Friday Night Baseball knew what it was doing when it chose to start off with Cleveland at Atlanta," said Jerry, "for this is an exciting ball game."

"What is the name of the present batter?" Suzanne asked.

"That is a boy name of Dennis Gedgaudis," I said, "of parents from Lithuania."

"I did not know they played baseball in Lithuania." said Jerry Divine, smiling and holding up his hands in a victory sign, and saying to us off the microphone, "We are going real good now, gang. Stay positive."

"He excites me," said Suzanne.

"If you notice how far he chokes up on his bat you will see that he does not expect to hit a long ball," I said.

"You mean that he is an exciting player," said Jerry.

"I mean that he is an exciting player," Suzanne replied, "and got an exciting face in an exciting body."

"He is trying to punch the ball in to right field behind the runner," I said.

"Friday Night Baseball knew what it was doing calling in the expert authority of Henry Wiggen," said Jerry Divine.

"While you are self advertising," said Suzanne, "the runner is stealing second base."

"It is a pitch out," I said.

"The pitcher fooled them by throwing it where the batter could not reach it," said Jerry.

"The runner is out," said Suzanne.

"The pitcher was smart to got ahead of the hitter in the first place," said I.

"That way he could afford the pitch out," said Jerry.

"I give the runner credit for getting down there as fast as he could never the less," said Suzanne, "and sliding so gracefully."

"Now the batter is no longer choking up on his bat," said I, "because the strategy is changed from hit and run to hit away."

"He has also widened his stance some what," said Jerry.

"Were you ever hit by a baseball?" Suzanne asked.

"No," said I, "for I was not a hard enough hitter for any body to throw at."

"You some times been hit by enemy batters," said Jerry.

"There goes a ground ball to shortstop," said Suzanne, "for a sure out unless some body flubs it."

"On several occasions enemy batters hit the ball at me too fast for me to field and it bounced off 1 or another of my personal parts," said I.

"Now we must stop for just a few moments for advertisements," said Jerry.

Before the first night was over Jerry changed his mind about talking only 1 sentence at a time per person. "Start talking 2 sentences at a time," he said, "it is more natural than 1." I don't know what made him change his mind. May be he took too much advice. Every time he spoke on the phone he took in a new idea or 2, hanging up and saying to us, "Listen, I got a bran new thought."

"Back in Atlanta," said Suzanne when the advertisement ended, "waiting to greet the lead off man in the top of the fifth inning."

Was that 1 sentence or 2? It depended on where you put the period. Holly says it isn't even 1. By the following week we were talking 2 sentences each in turn, April 16, Washington at Chicago. Here are some snippings that catch my ear.

"What is the name of the pitcher?" Suzanne asked. "He has got a form divine."

"It is funny you put it that way," said I. "His name is Jesus Columbiana."

"I am sure he pronounces it another way," said Jerry. "Here he comes with the pitch."

"It is a very nice pitch, too," said Suzanne. "The umpire calls it a strike.

"No," said I, "he pronounces it *Jesus* like the original. I talked to him before the game and asked him."

"I suppose we will just call him *Columbiana* here after," said Jerry. "He is going in to a big wind up."

"Poor fellow," said Suzanne, "he missed the plate. Does his manager become angry at him when he misses the plate?"

"He was probably not trying for the plate," I said, "since he all ready got 2 strikes on the batter." I stopped speaking, thinking I had spoke 2 sentences. Jerry give me the sign, go on, go on. "He said he prefers being called *Jesus* rather than *Columbiana*," I said.

"May be he will be knocked out of the box and we will not need to face the problem," Jerry said. "Friday Night Baseball chose the best man in the world to tell us what goes on in side the head of a pitcher."

"He might even waste another pitch," I said. "We will see."

"You spoke out of turn," said Jerry off the microphone, or so he thought. It was on the microphone and went out over the air. All right then, if I spoke out of turn what now? Who would pick it up? How would we get back in turn? Suzanne and Jerry both begun speaking at once.

"You do the same in tennis," said Suzanne once Jerry give her the go ahead. "When you are ahead of the other person you make her go for the risk if you can."

"Pitching is the old psychology," I said. "How ever, you have also got to have a fast ball or you are in trouble."

"This fellow *Columbiana* takes his time," said Jerry. "Here comes the pitch at last."

"Struck him out," said Suzanne. "He would pitch faster if he did not spend so much time scratching him self all over."

"He fooled him," I said, "by coming in with the good pitch when he could of wasted yet another. Notice on the instant replay how late the batter swang."

"I suppose the batter is feeling down cast in his mind," said Suzanne. Then she stopped, realizing she had spoke out of turn. How ever, Jerry did not realize she had spoke out of turn and waited for her to complete the second sentence. As a result, no body spoke for awhile.

"After every pitch," I said, "1 person or the other is going to be down cast in their mind."

"You are talking out of turn," said Jerry off the mike, or so he thought. "It is too bad we can not have games where no body is ever down cast in their mind."

"Now here comes Dee Carabatso," said Suzanne. "Listen to the fans cheer for Dee."

"He is a hitter worth watching," I said. "He can hit fast balls or curves no matter where you throw them."

"Then what is the best thing to do with Carabatso?" asked Suzanne. "Is Jesus worrying about him?"

"You can not face him with out worrying," I said. "The best thing to do is stay in bed."

"What would you throw him if you were pitching against

him in this situation?" Jerry inquired, looking at me. But it was not my turn to speak.

"I would pitch around him," said Suzanne, "if no body else is going to speak. That is 1 sentence and this is the second."

"I would rather walk him than leave him hit it out of the park," I said. "The problem is bringing the tie run to the plate."

"That is very clear," said Jerry. "You would make a good school teacher."

"Here comes the pitch," said Suzanne, "and there it goes." Columbiana tried to jam Carabatso with an in side pitch and Carabatso hit it out of there. "The pitcher failed to do what Henry Wiggen advised."

"If people would follow my advice they would win the pennant," I said. "What both these ball clubs need is a left hand relief pitcher my age and experience."

"Now we will stop for just a few moments of advertisements," said Jerry, "of the kind that are *actually paid for*." He did not like me advertising my self on the air. He smiled when I done so, but as the weeks wore on he become peeved and annoyed.

I was on the road over night only 1 night for the first Friday Night Baseball and 2 nights for the second Friday Night Baseball and 3 nights for the third. It was libel to be more before it got less. The easy style went out of it, Jerry Divine become tense, and Suzanne become extremely irritable due to returning to a reducing diet due to the extremely popular reaction to the film we done for the President's Committee Focusing on Aging.

I was sitting home 1 night between Friday Night Baseballs when some body called out from another room, "Hey daddy, here is the film with you and Suzanne Winograd," and up I jumped and run in and looked at it. I had ½ forgot all about it and ½ wondered if I could stand hearing my self say "I have hung up my glove" and ½ decided I would not even look at it in case it come on the air. But when I was called I went. "Hi, there, my name is Henry Wiggen and I was a baseball pitcher for 19 years for the New York Mammoths."

"It is not your voice," said 1 of my daughters.

"I was hoarse from shouting over Ben Crowder's furnace all day," I said. When I see that film I taste that gargle I gargled while Suzanne sat on the edge of the bath tub planning a revolution against the President. Now that I heard the film the thing that bothered me more than hanging up my glove was the sentence, "You will never see me play baseball again."

"That is not true," said I, arguing back at my self on the TV.

"You are competing against your self," said Holly, "and I can not figure out who I am rooting for."

Oh well, it would mount to nothing, it would run a few times and drop from sight like every thing else. Holly said on the following morning she knew it was going to be a great long running success because she met a neighbor name of Gil Gadt that said he went nuts and out of his mind besides watching that girl in the sweater rotating her shoulders and serving the tennis ball. " This does not seem to me," said I, "like the kind of thing people are going to sit up late at night dialing around on the TV for."

"You had more opportunities in life than Gil Gadt," said Holly to me.

The only really wonderful memory of the film I have is my various daughters being so proud of me for going down to Washington and making a film focusing on helping old age people. They never give a thought to Suzanne's sweater. They said there was more sex appeal in my hoarse throat. May be that was what done it. Mainly they said how fine I was for what I done, and I soon begun receiving 100's of letters asking me for further information on aging. Many letters said they tried writing directly to Washington and got no reply. People had the idea there was some great big friendly help full government agency out there standing ready day and night to help people out with their old age problems, but there was *nothing*, there was only me throwing my glove away and Suzanne serving the tennis ball, and after the President him self left Washington, or got booted out you might as well say, they cut him out of the film all together leaving me ending up saying "Good morning, Mr. President" to no body in particular.

"Never the less," said my daughters, "if you did not do a good thing you did not *mean* to do a bad 1."

"I earned $50,000 for 2 minutes of film," said I. "I suppose you could look at it that way." (I was including there the second film also.)

"Then what will all the aging people do?" Hilary asked.

"Why," said I, "they can stay home and watch Suzanne and I jump around like that."

Due to the extremely popular reaction to the film Deck Roberts wished to make a second film with out delay. "Same cast," he said, "same story line, same every thing."

"But not the same money," Suzanne said, which he seemed to be expecting. Barbara negotiated the sum for her, and we were paid a lump together to split as we seen fit. As the star of the show Suzanne believed she should of received a great deal more than 50%, but we settled for 50% and as soon as she was thin enough we flew down to Washington with Barbara and Bertilia between 1 Friday Night Baseball and the next, and once more Deck Roberts come to the hotel with the script, and once more we fussed and argued about it, and once more he begun mentioning his baseball experiences, saying he was called "Deck" because he decked people with his fast ball. I smile even yet to think of it. He was too thin. I can see the batter sticking up their hand and catching Deck Roberts's fast ball and throwing it back to him saying, "Throw it so it does not loop."

By diet and exercise Suzanne thinned her self down, becoming at the same time more and more crankier and irritable in till at the very worst of it Jerry Divine told her take the night off with pay, May 14, Cleveland at Washington. She was a jolly fat lady and a mean thin woman in till the day come when Dr. Schiff helped her be jolly though thin. "I wish I was the fat lady in the side show," Suzanne said, "sitting there all day and never moving." Then she remembered Bertilia, adding, "Just me and my little chipmunk," hugging her and kissing her.

"I can see that you got no faith in my baseball career," said Deck Roberts to me, adding sarcastically, "I never claimed my name was *Henry Wiggen* if that is what you are driving at."

"I wish we would not have any arguments in till the fees are paid," said Suzanne.

The President him self did not actually appear on the scene when we shot the second film, and if he been there you might not of noticed him, for whereas we had possibly 6 or 8 people made the first film we now had 20 or 30, and whereas we spent about 3 hours at the most making the first film we now worked from morning to night of a very long day, and whereas the budget for the first film was in the neighborhood of $50,000 according to what I heard the budget for the second film was in the neighborhood of $250,000 *plus* distribution costs. Where did it all go? I never seen the second film on the air and I never heard of any body that did.

Friday Night Baseball was in San Francisco, Chicago vs. San Francisco, when the freezer girl announced in West Des Moines, Iowa, that I chose the middle of June to enter her freezer and lay down on her ice and not wake up for 125 years. I no sooner heard the news when Hilary was on the phone to San Francisco saying, "If you are doing any such thing do you not think you should inform your family first."

"If I *was* doing it I *would*," I said, "but you know that I am not doing it."

"How do I know?" she inquired.

"Because you know me," I said, "and I keep my promises."

"She said you promised her," said Hilary.

"Who said?"

"The lady in Iowa."

"Yes," said I, "she *said* I promised her, but you *know* I promised you."

"I am glad to hear it," said Hilary, "because I sold more than $50 stock all ready in our winery."

Even so, she was greatly up set and worried to the end and now and then cried to think about it. After it was over she said she never been upset about it, never worried, and was laughing all the time.

The freezer girl was wrote up as follows according to the paper I seen that evening in San Francisco.

The spokesman for the Iceoleum said that Wiggen chose mid-June because of the normally hot weather at that time of year. He has been disappointed with his career, she said, citing as an additional reason his frustration with his inability to find a cure for prostate trouble. "He knows," said she, "that in 125 years they will have found cures for that disease and many others."

She named other people who have already entered the Iceoleum of Life After in West Des Moines or who have signified their intention to do so. Among these are Walt Disney, former Republican President Eisenhower, Jane Fonda, Muhammed Ali, Howard Cosell, House Majority Leader Hale Boggs (D. La.), Kate Millett, Ralph Nader, Democratic National Chairman Lawrence F. O'Brien, Bobby G. Seale, Abby Hoffman, Paul Newman, Senator Edward Kennedy (D. Mass.), Elvis Presley, and famed TV dog star Lassie.

Besides Hilary the only person taking it seriously was Suzanne. She immediately got her self the assignment from the net work to be present in West Des Moines, Iowa, when I walked in the Iceoleum. "I am going to be there," she said, "and I am going to see for my self. And further more—" she said.

"Further more what?" I inquired. We were flying on the air plane back from San Francisco following the ball game.

"I will tell you further more what," she said, waking up

Bertilia on the seat and changing positions with her so I and her could sit close together and whisper. "This," she said. "If you are going in the ice I am going in with you."

"I am taking my family and pets with me," I said.

"I am simply going as company," she said. "No romance intended. You are aware that I have destroyed my life up to a point or else give it away to various husbands of mine in conspiracy with crooks and promoters and lawyers and government men such as Deck Roberts, but you are also aware that I am not a wild woman. I *marry* the son of a bitches. There fore I am entering the ice with you as a friend only, which we been in the past only, and I will be laying there with you and your family and my own little chipmunk Bertilia in till all the men of my past are dead and gone. After 125 years there will be no body left from my crowd except me and Bertilia and we can start life all a new." She woke up Bertilia and kissed her all over the head, calling her "my little chipmunk."

"My dear Suzanne," I said, "I am not going out in that ice."

"She sounded pretty confident," said Suzanne, "like she knew what she was doing."

"Never the less," I said.

"She set the *date*," said Suzanne, "and the net work OK'd it and Barbara accepted the fee for me. In the middle of June you are going away for 125 years and some of us are going with you, by gum."

"It is easy to see why you been conned out of your fortune," I said.

"There is nothing wrong or wild about laying together in our clothes fully dressed unconscious on the fucking *ice* is there, specially with your whole family present?"

"Plus Bertilia," I said.

"Plus Bertilia, too," she said. "I slept in your house before."

"With the heat up," I said.

"She gives you a scientific injection and wakes you up in 125 years," she said, "and life will be trouble free ever after."

"Are you sure that she her self will be standing by to do the job in 125 years?" I inquired.

"I am going to sleep right now," Suzanne said, sticking a pillow under the back of her head, "some where over California and I will wake up when we land on the ground in New York 3,000 miles away. I am confident that once you buy your ticket some body or other will be standing by," and off she went to sleep in 5 seconds leaving me and Bertilia conversing through the night.

We were back in California the following Friday, Washington vs. California. This was the third time we broad cast Washington. Don't ask me why. On previous occasions I worked out before hand with the other ball club, avoiding Ben Crowder. This night, how ever, I worked out with Washington, avoiding Jack Sprat, although Tom Roguski and other people of Jack's come and said "Hello" and said they heard I would be joining them after the trading dead line. Jack come out of the dugout and seen me and turned around and went back. This worried me, for I knew he knew more than his people did. He never come out for good in till I was up in the broad cast booth.

Ben Crowder was some body else again. Personal relations meant nothing to him. We stood in the dugout talking. Soon afterwards we went back in his office. "I wish *you* was my pitcher coach," he said to me, although Andy Whedon was standing beside him. Andy and I were acquainted from Mammoths days and we liked each other and talked a little, how was your wife, etc. But it never mattered to Ben who he was standing next to. May be that is the best way. May be I should be that way.

"You got a mighty fine pitcher coach in Andy," said I, "so your problem is solved."

"Leaves me only 10,000 more problems," he said.

"You will lick them all," I said.

"Yes I will," said Ben, "but not this year." His ball club was sunk low in the standings but I thought they would rise higher soon. "That is true," said Ben, "I did not know you observed things so good." He looked at me for several seconds, sizing me up, like may be he mixed me up with some body else.

"May be I got dimensions you did not know about," I said.

"Yes," he said, "may be you got a motivation that slipped my mind when we spoke in February."

"Probably January," I said.

"You are arguing," he said, "and that is what stopped me in my thinking. Are you standing there and telling me that there is 1 fucking bit of difference between February and January? I am assuming you are free and I am god dam tempted. This god dam Andy Whedon that I bought off your ex boss turns out to be a No Name pitcher coach matching my No Name pitcher staff. Tell me, Andy," he said, not looking at Andy, "how in the world you are doing any good for your country standing here at my elbow all after noon."

"It is evening," I said. We walked back in his clubhouse and I showered and sat in a towel wrapped around me in his office. A number of young ball players were running around the clubhouse naked, and I remember doing the same in the past, but now I kept a towel around me.

"Then it is evening," said Ben, "and I am thinking over our conversation from January and February and remembering nothing about baseball and every thing about Japanese cherry trees blossoming in the spring and this fucking little dish with a flame under it we keep on the dining room table. Ever since that time when ever I sat down at the table and begun thinking about you as a possibility I seen that fucking flame and I remembered you asking me where it was bought and how interesting it was in till I realized your mind is not on baseball but on Japanese cherry trees and flames. Why did you not take the job in Japan? The streets are not safe around here any more. I would of went to Japan my self if there were not so many fucking Japanese there. I would of come out here and managed for Suicide Alexander if there were not so many drug attics. Then he settled for Jack Sprat instead."

"He is doing very good," I said.

"And the month is barely June," said Ben. "Suicide got too many permission men in 1 place. Would you care to make a small bet they do not win?"

"I will bet you $10,000," I said, knowing he never bet.

"Whereas what they need is an electric chair man balancing it out. Jack Sprat is a permission man.He is too open minded. He is ready for a discussion at the drop of a bat. They are so soft hearted they will keep dead wood. If a young player is having a hard time Jack sits down with him and cries along together instead of throwing the switch and scorching his ass with electric power lines. It is too much money. I will bet you only $3. I meant it only as a gentle man's bet. I hear he addresses his players as 'gentle men.' Look at them wild savages running around with their cock flying in the breeze and tell me if they are gentle men." I turned around and looked down the row between the lockers. It looked like it always looked, coming and going, shouting and bragging, pushing and shoving.

"Ben," said I, "were you a gentle man to invite me in your house when you all ready made a deal with Patricia on the telephone? Why did you do that to me behind my back?"

"That is the best way," said Ben. "If you do things in front of people's eyes they can see what you are doing. Speaking of eyes, tell me if it is true your eyes went bad. You do not wish to pitch with bad eyes or these naked savages will hit it back at you with a stick. Pitching is not a safe game any more. Your head, your skull, your between your legs, down you go, you are a vegetable ever after. Why are you arguing with life? When you are dead lay down."

"Still and all," said I, "think it over. Clear your roster. You need a short relief." I seen it was time to get dressed.

"Broad cast good," he said, "and do not run off with that girl on the ice skates."

I was back in Moors Stadium, home of the New York Mammoths, 2 weeks later. Announcing. Patricia had tore out a

section of grand stand and put in new chairs and saved 1 old
chair for me for Henry W. Wiggen Mini Park in Perkinsville,
New York, which I carried up to the broad cast booth with me.
To my surprise this made Jerry Divine extremely angry. Something was wrong. His leg was hurting him those days worse than
before and he leaned heavier than ever on his cane, but that was
not what the problem was.

"The problem is," he said, "it is not done."

"What is not done, Jerry?" I inquired, although I knew what
he meant by the way he looked at the chair.

"It is not professional," he said, "lugging lumber and timber
around like a furniture mover from the Mayflower when you are
suppose to be a classy baseball and sports announcer wearing the
sweater of Friday Night Baseball."

"Jerry," said I, "I apologize." It stuns people. They never
know what to say next when you apologize.

He softened his voice a few notches, saying sadly, "You been
making us look awful stupid all along."

"In what way, Jerry," I inquired, "have I been making you
look stupid all along?"

"He has not been making me look stupid," said Suzanne.
She was dieting, eating nothing but her finger nails, which Bertilia was manicuring with some very strong smelling liquid out of
a bottle. The week before, in Montreal, I said I preferred the
smell of the manicure liquid to the smell of mustard, but now
we had both, for Jerry was eating sandwiches, saying, "I have not
gave up eating simply because Suzanne is dieting again." He had
not gave up drinking, either. In Montreal he drunk more than
he should of for good broad casting. Drink is the ruin of many
people, players and broad casters alike.

"You certainly made us look awful stupid right here in this
park on Opening Day," said Jerry, "falling down flat while trying
to throw a baseball."

"*While trying to throw a baseball,*" I exclaimed.

"Thank God you were not wearing your Friday Night

Baseball sweater," he said, "while laying out there while 1,000's of people gazed down on you."

"How about the following?" I inquired. "How about if you and I have a duel with baseballs? You take 10 or a dozen balls and I will take 10 or a dozen and we will stand 60 feet 6 inches apart and throw baseballs at each other in till 1 of us is dead or surrenders or what you may. Then we will see who is who *while trying to throw a baseball.*"

"You stung Henry in the wrong place," said Suzanne, "but I think such a thing would make a terrific TV special or pre game."

"You know," said Jerry, "it *would.*" His face lit up and he forgot that he was irritated with me over some thing or other. "A duel of baseballs, 1 on 1," he said. "It is too bad they do not have between the ½s in baseball. I can see the baseballs hitting in the air. I can see 1 contestant crowned and down. Then what? You need some rules. No throwing at a man when he is down. The contestant on his feet must go to his own corner while the contestant that is down has got to get up on his feet by a certain count. I can see it."

"Not long ago," said I, "the thing you could see was me and you and Suzanne sweeping the country on Friday Night Baseball. Judging by your irritable mood you have lost some of your enthusiasm for the subject."

"It is not going as good as we expected," said Jerry.

"We did not empty out the temples and the synagogues," said Suzanne.

"The Catholics wound up with all their energy in spite of eating fish," I said.

"The down town crowd stood down town," said Jerry, "instead of rushing home and diving for their TV switch and listening to our magic voice. Telling you the truth, the survey shows that only a small percentage of the people could name all 3 of us, most people could name only 1 of us or *less,* and some women that viewed a whole ball game where we called Suzanne by name 75 or 100 times still believed she was dozens of other women including Eleanor Roosevelt, Lady Bird Johnson, Helen Keller, or Mary Tyler Moore. As for you, Author, many people did not know who you were even when the poll *told* them who you were. No body under age 15 thought you were still living and this freezer girl in Iowa is not helping your image as an actual person. Last week only 18,000,000 people tuned us in, or 28,000,000, it ended in 8 but not enough to pay the freight."

"If it cancels," said Suzanne, "I get paid off in full so I do not care. I can get rich making films for the President's Program Focusing on Aging and when that dries up I am sure that crook Deck Roberts will have another program focusing on some shit or another."

"Ladies and gentle men," said I, "start your ear phones, for it is pre game warm up time."

"By the way," said Jerry, "these ear phones are not 2 way systems any more but 1 way systems. I can speak to you but you can not speak to me."

"I can spit at you," said Suzanne. She rotated her shoulders and give a good imitation of spitting at him, all though I do not think she did. Her back was towards me.

"This is not my fault," Jerry said. "These are instructions and suggestions from the net work. I apologize deeply but I am going to have to be tough from now on. If you do not like any thing tell me and we will talk about."

"How can I talk to you," I inquired, "if you cut me off from the 2 way system?"

"Sorry I can not hear you," said Jerry off air. "Pass me a note."

"I do not think you are getting at your problem," said I to Jerry off air.

"You can not speak off air," he said, "or it will go out live, so watch what you are doing every minute."

"We can speak by beeper," said Suzanne, but the comical thing was that we never used the beepers for any thing at all except playing. Bertilia and I took long walks up and down the ramps in 10 ball parks talking to each other by beeper.

"Friday Night Baseball," said Jerry on the air, coming across with a lot of excitement. "And here we *are* in old New *York*, Jerry Divine speaking *for* him self *and* his partners Suzanne Winograd *and* Henry Wiggen, athletes all, just us 3 blokes sitting by the screen like you folks at home are doing. And what a night this is *for* baseball, believe me." I know he did not like the sound of doing it that way, and it tore him up to do it. It was really *not* a good night for baseball or for any thing. It was a good night for showering in your marble shower in your apartment with a friend. It was hot, damp, humid, and sticky.

"This is Henry Wiggen's old ball club," said Suzanne. "I guess he knows a thing or 2 about it."

"Friday Night Baseball is lucky to have a person of such wide baseball experience as Henry Wiggen," said Jerry. "Tell us a bit about the Mammoths." Off air he said we should not do the 2 sentences by turn any more. "Just speak," he said. "No body appreciated our efforts." It was 1 of your easier habits to break.

"I played for them 19 years," I said, "and then they cruelly cut me loose. Lucky for me I hope to go with another club very soon."

"This is another thing we have got to cut out," said Jerry off air. "This personal advertising. If you want a job go out and get it personally, not announce it every few minutes on this show." On the air he said, "This Mammoths ball club has been somewhat of a surprise to us, has it not?"

"It was certainly a surprise to me," said Suzanne. "I thought tonight was suppose to be Pittsburgh."

"Leave us get a hold of our selves, gang," said Jerry off air. I thought the same, writing him a little note which I have in front of me this very minute saying, "Do not panic. Get through tonight. Talk over the week end," passing it to Suzanne. She passed it back to me. She refused to pass it or she did not under stand what it was, plus she was angry our 2 way system was cut off. I could not get a word to Jerry unless he asked me some thing and switched me on his ear phone long enough to answer. It was possible for me to talk in a soft voice around the world and in to space by satellite but it was extremely difficult getting a message through Suzanne to Jerry 5 feet away. "Henry Wiggen," said Jerry, "tell us some thing about this Mammoths ball club that been some what of a surprise to us."

I told what I knew. The Mammoths of that year were far better than any body expected them to be. Ev McTaggart was doing a good job on the field for her, the No Name players she got from Ben Crowder were doing superb, and several young players were proving out that had rose through the Mammoths organization. Beansy Binz won 9 games by June 10 and another young fellow won 8 but has since disappeared. Thinking about Jerry I said on the air, "The secret of their success is they do not panic. When things go wrong Patricia Moors catches a hold of her self and thinks things through. She does not drink or yell at her fellow associates," for I liked Jerry and wished to help him if I could, but in reply to my talking he come at me off air soon after, saying, "Never mind using this show for selling your own friends. And further more, put a little laugh in your voice."

"Nothing is funny," I said.

"Put more excitement in your voice," Jerry said.

"I am bored," I said.

"Why do you wish to play ball any more if it bores you?" he inquired.

"I love playing," I said, "but watching other people do it is getting me down," which he never heard, having turned me off the 2 way system.

After 7 innings Jerry's face lit up, 2,000,000 people suddenly tuned in, and 2,000,000 more after 8 innings, we were talking to 20,000,000 or 30,000,000 people smelling of finger nail polish and mustard and my daughter's canteen full of water from camp, and Jerry's spirits zoomed to the sky when ever another 1,000,000 people joined us. "If only it went in to extra innings," he said, "we would of had the world," but it did not, and our system went down and our lights went off and we begun straggling out of there to the parking lot. "We have got to meet and talk things over," Jerry said.

"That is what I thought," I said. "I wrote you a note."

"I did not get it," he said. "The mail is slow these days. We are pressured by the net work to do some things a little different."

"I have not got the time to meet," said Suzanne.

Never the less we went to my apartment and drunk a bit of wine in a good mood, opening the balcony porch and leaving the breeze drift in. Bertilia took a shower in the marble shower and went to bed in Hilary's bed, saying, "This bed smells like onions." I took her a Coca Cola. She said she definitely hoped I would invite her and Suzanne along if and when I went in the ice for 125 years, and I said I would.

"When will we meet?" Jerry asked. "We have got to talk over our needs vs. the net work needs and plan our strategy."

"The easiest thing is doing it their way," said Suzanne. "I can not meet during the week. I got phsychiatrist 1 day and conditioning another day and Iowa Tuesday and Bertilia's class is performing some shit brings us to Friday all ready and another exciting night of Friday Night Baseball."

"We can drift their way some what," said I, "and do things our own way, too. May be we will catch on as time goes by. I look at 30,000,000 people as some what of a start."

"People say we are catching that natural sound of 3 blokes at home," said Jerry, "but we are not sufficiently fact filled. We have got to give them more statistics. We have got to talk averages. The net work says 'More numbers, less joking around,' because people do not yet under stand the game enough to catch the humor of it. They are too deadly serious. The poll shows the average viewer is 2 kids 15 ¾ years old sitting on a sofa holding hands. They been going steady since 15½ and they are *serious*, they want hard facts and numbers. It has got to sound *important* to them. Frankly, Author, the thing I am hearing most from the net work is this. 'Henry Wiggen is not sounding *serious* enough. It does not sound like baseball is *important* to him any more.'"

"Well that of course is a bunch of horse shit," I said.

"How do you keep your apartment so beautiful?" asked Suzanne. "I had a husband once that bought new dishes rather than wash the set we owned."

"Who was that?" Bertilia asked over the beeper.

"Just 1 of your fathers," Suzanne said.

"People are not looking at the game as close as we are," said Jerry. "We are running too much stuff on replay. Put more volume in your voice. *Care* more."

"I suppose we are too interested in the fine points," I said.

"Exactly," said Jerry. "We are too interested in the game and not enough in the score. The net work said we went 3½ innings in California on May 28 with out once telling the score. The name of the game is winning. We have got to believe that even if we do not. We can not go on being *students* of the game and *artists* of the game when that is not what is needed or we will be canceled."

"What will we do if we are canceled?" Suzanne inquired.

"Not receive money," Jerry replied.

"I might be able to meet Wednesday," said Suzanne. "Put me down. I am willing." She drunk my wine like water. The next day she told me she thought it *was* water. It was Domaine Chandon champagne and it was not water. She sat all evening on the old grand stand chair.

"Author," said Jerry, "the burden is on you."

"Thank God," said Suzanne.

"How is the burden on me if I may inquire?" I inquired.

"You have got to be our expert. You have got to talk in a voice of excitement and enthusiasm predicting the way things will go from pitch to pitch and in the long haul as well. You have got to sound positive. Never mind this modesty."

"I got no idea how the future will go," I said.

"It is our ace in the trump," said Jerry. "We are the only baseball broad cast featuring some body on their way to the Hall of Fame. Any body can be 3 blokes at home but only you got the right to predict the future and criticize the players."

"I would never criticize players," I said. "Certainly not on the air."

"Neither would I," said Jerry.

"When will we meet?" Suzanne inquired.

"Actually, I feel that we all ready met," said Jerry. "We know what the problem is. The problem is that we lack leader ship. I can not even call a meeting and Author can not take a firm stand on the subject all though he knows more about it than any body in the world."

"He takes firm stands where it counts," said Suzanne. "I wish he was my husband."

"The trouble with us," I said, "is the 3 of us are permission men. If only 1 of us was an electric chair man our fortune would be made. If only 1 of us could make the other 2 do the right thing, but you are not going to do it and I am not going to do it. That is why our children are in phsychiatrists, because we are permission men."

"My children are not in phsychiatrists," said Jerry.

"I am sorry to hear it," I said.

"They use to be," he said.

I walked with them to the elevator and they went down, and I returned to the apartment and Bertilia was sleeping in Hilary's bed. I thought Suzanne would remember and come back and get her. I waited an hour or more and when she did not come back I my self went to bed.

11

Driving home in the morning I telephoned Marva Sprat. "How I love to hear your fabulous voice," she said.

"You got a certain fabulous in yours, too," I said.

"No," said she, "I mean last night. I had the TV on all over the place, listening to you in living stereo color. You made the last the best."

"I got no indication yet it was the last," said I.

"Back you go in the old harness," she said. "Within 1 week from now you will be saving baseball games for my own Jack. Leave me tell you what I got in mind for you. I am dwelling in my mind on nothing less than a triple historic first."

"Which is exactly what?" I inquired.

"You will be the first man in the history of baseball that ever threw out the first ball on Opening Day and was back in action by season's end. All right, that much you all ready done."

"*Done!*" I exclaimed.

"Threw out the first ball," she said, "but not yet back in action. You will receive that little ring a ling when the dead line passes. Number 2. You will be the first man in baseball that ever broad cast 10 baseball games in living stereo color and was back in action by season's end. Now you accomplished that all ready, moving down the line on schedule. Number 3. You will be the first man in the history of baseball that ever played in an Old

Timers baseball game and was back in action pitching by season's
end. Is that or is that not a triple historic first? I ask you."

"Do you hear these hissing busses on 57th?" I inquired.

"They can not touch me," she said.

"Marva, my friend," I said, "I am thinking I might drive up
from Perkinsville this afternoon and bring another horse back
home."

"Make it tomorrow instead," she said, "during Sunday
School hours."

I and Hilary drove up to Tozerbury on Sunday. "It is a lot
different in the summer," I said. "For all these years I never seen
much of this country side by summer."

"Do you remember 1 day along here last winter I
screamed?" said Hilary.

"I can hear it yet," I replied.

"I think I might be over my screaming fits," she said. "I have
not screamed since I screamed in Dr. Schiff's face. Any how I
hope so."

"It will be a convenience to every body."

Hilary wore horse boots and horse pants like the horse lady
of Tozerbury and she was reading a book in title *California
Wineries.* "Of course," said she, controlling her crying, "there
will not be wineries or any other kind of happiness for any body
if you go in the ice in Iowa on Tuesday night."

"I will be in the city Tuesday night," I said, "and there fore
will not be in Iowa for ice, heat, or luke warm."

"She says she will bury you Tuesday night."

"I knew it was some time soon," I said. "I wish on Tuesday
night you would be my guest at the Old Timers Game at Moors
Stadium. Take a day off from school, books, horses, and stock
selling, come to New York, and we will hit the various
McDonald's."

"No way Old Timers Game," she said. "I wish to see you in a
championship game or nothing at all. Mother seen you in many

many *dozens* of games and Michele seen you in dozens at least, and Rosemary and Millicent seen you in many. Rosemary and Millicent seen you in the World Series as well."

"Suppose I never play again?" I inquired.

"If you go in the ice?" she inquired in reply.

"No. Simply if no body hires me. The owners of the various baseball clubs are not exactly standing in a long line with their hand folded in prayer begging me to pitch for them. I am 39 going on 40."

"How can that lady go around saying you will be buried in her ice?" Hilary inquired.

"Because I can not stop her spouting off," I said. "I am a public character and pay the price. People can say any thing about me they please. I see where people that never once seen me play offer opinions about how good I was. You can be sure the less they played the more opinions they got, 'Oh, he was not so good, he only won this, he only done that, he never done this, he had a good organization behind him.' Sweet heart, *I won 247 big league baseball games* leaving only 26 pitchers ahead of me *in the history of baseball*. It could not be all 1 total accident. Some body named Patricia Moors father and then Patricia her self must of thought I was good, for they paid me several million dollars to do this, out of which I put it all in the bank for your mother and you and your sisters except a few dimes I kept out for telephone calls in till I put the phone in the car. Over time you will hear from people or read in books and magazines where I was this or that or where I said this or that, or I done this or that, and there is not the least bit of sense in the world trying to fight it. For example, you will read where I am going on the ice in Iowa. Or you will read where a certain famous man was in love with a certain woman not in his family if you know what I mean."

"You mean a certain man took a mistress," said Hilary.

"That is what I mean," said I, "you have certainly learned a lot since you are back in school. I must send money to the various schools. There fore no matter what you ever hear about me when I am dead and gone you will know that there were only 5 ladies I ever truly loved and you know what all their names are."

"Yet others you liked and give a kiss to," said Hilary.

"Oh, well," said I.

While Hilary visited the horse lady of Tozerbury I dropped over and visited awhile with Marva Sprat. The day was so glorious I could not under stand how she could remain in doors, but there she was. "The out doors would improve your complexion," I said.

"Love improves my complexion," she said. "A woman surrounded by such a loving family as I got got no need for other air."

"Never the less come on out in the sun shine," I begged her.

"If you speak to Sun Shine Briscoe Tuesday night extend him my regards for old time sake. He is a bundle of 1,000 laughs." Sun Shine Briscoe is a 1 time ball player that says he was ruined by night ball. He is the president of an organization to out law night baseball but I see no evidence that he made any progress.

"Come out in the sun shine now."

"Never."

"Can you imagine what love plus sun shine will do for you?"

"Give me the sun burn," she replied.

"Today has such a glorious and beautiful odor in the air," I said.

"Nothing can beat the odor of wine fumes racing through the air condition system," she replied. "Also extend my regards and best wishes to Swanee Wilks," she said.

"I did not know you knew him," I said.

"I knew him very well. I knew him as well as I know you. Tell him Marva Sprat greets him and says 'Hello' for old time sake. Is 1 message all you can carry or can you carry another?"

"I got a whole horse trailer on the back of me," I said, "whereby I can carry as many messages as you care to send."

"Some day I will stroll out and see the telephone in your

car," she said. "In the mean time I will appreciate you also carrying a message to Scotty Burns, telling him Marva greets him and says 'Hello' for old time sake."

"Same message to both," I said.

"Same message to every body," she said, "but do not tell Swanee you are carrying the same message to Scotty, for he is a jealous fellow."

"Are those all?" I inquired.

"3 people out of 9 on 1 Old Timers ball club is a good average for a girl with a pale complexion," she said.

"Now leave me express a matter that worries me," I said. "I seen Jack 2 weeks ago in California and he could not of helped but seen me. Yet he never met my eye, never give me a wave, but simply stood in the clubhouse in till I went up in the broad cast booth."

"Jack is handling matters the way he must," she said, "holding the line while praying the dead line for trades will come and go in your favor. He is embarrassed to his toes. He made a promise to you he is not able to fill as quickly as he wishes, but Jack is Jack and you have got to keep saying over and over what I told you in your mind."

"Which was what?" I inquired.

"Did you forget?"

"Give me just the barest hint."

"I told you. It will never be Jack who double crosses you. If any body double crosses you it will be Mr. Alexander. But he will not double cross you, either, for Jack keeps explaining to him how things are."

"I will be waiting for the little ring a ling," I said.

"Mr. Alexander will be on the other end," she said.

"I hope this is not some sort of a pipe dream of yours," I said. "My daughter Hilary will be extremely grief stricken if she does not get to see me play again."

"We only stay alive by pipe dreams," said Marva.

"It worries me," I said, "seeing your fire place for example. There *is* no fire place."

"Of the pipe dreams I kept going," said Marva, "there was 1 where I thought to my self 1 of these days Henry Wiggen will walk in my house off the street in the middle of the winter. Or Jack and I dreamed beside this fire place that 1 day he would become manager of a club. We can make every thing happen we put our shoulder to."

"All right," said I, "I have got to load up a horse. Are you sure that those are all the messages you are asking me to carry?"

"Those are all the old Mammoths," she said. "I would not expect you to go carrying messages to the visiting team."

Old Timers Day was a bad evening and I do not care for the memory. I was not grace full. I was not a gentle man. I dropped by Patricia's office. Millie Schnell was on the way out the door. We kissed many times. "You are here again," I said.

"As many times as they send me a ticket and a hotel room is as many times as I will fly in," she said. Tonight was another 1 minute of respect full silence for Dutch.

"It went over very good Opening Day," said Patricia. "We got a lot of good mail on it." I sat with her awhile facing her over her desk. The electric heater we all crouched around in April was standing in a corner, the plug was out and dragging on the floor. While we talked she kept glancing at all the papers on her desk, picking up a paper weight and reading underneath, and putting it down and reading under another.

"That music on the loud speaker is worse than any thing I ever heard yet," I said.

"You are fighting the forces of nature down to the music on the speaker," she said. "It is waltzes pure and simple, chose with care. I rest assure you we did not do this thing with out thinking. By the time this evening's grand ceremony is over you will be bathed in tears like every body else. Do you know what we are planning?" she inquired.

"Tear gas?"

"Better than that," she said, "we are planning 55,000 hearts and voices singing together in a chorus with the organ 'When

Your Hair Has Turned to Silver I Will Love You Just the Same.'"

"55,000 people on Tuesday night?" I inquired.

"For *you*," she said, "and maybe that is an under estimate. It is fantastic considering school is still in session."

"Then I am still paying my way," I said.

"You will for awhile," she said.

"Then I will fade away," I said.

"Oh, dear," said she, "I was not made for this."

"But fading slow," I said. "I expect to be going back on the active list tomorrow."

"Are you hoping some body will pick you up after the dead line?" she inquired. "I hope you are not hoping it is me."

"Did you ever hear of any body went from an Old Timers Game back on the active list?" I inquired.

"No," said she, "I never heard of any body that done so and I never expect to."

Both teams dressed in the visiting clubhouse. I was early. All my life I been early to ball games, and the first person I seen was an old man name of Jay Pringle wearing the word "Philadelphia" across his shirt. *"Hey,"* said I, "how *are* you? Believe me you are looking *great*. When did I see you last? It seems like *ages*," slapping him on the back and grabbing him by both hands by the shoulder and looking him square in the eye and trying to think if I even seen him before and who he might be if I did.

"How are you, kid?" he inquired.

"You know," I said, "I never dressed in this clubhouse before."

"You will start doing a lot of things you never done before," he said.

He had a right hand glove, small and old fashion which ball players laugh at now a days and wonder how you could of caught any thing in them. They were on the way out when I come up. In walked Benjamin Scotland, known as "Big Ben." He threw out the first ball on Opening Day, 1955, the year

Bruce Pearson played to the end as you seen in the film in title
Bang the Drum Slowly, with Robert DeNiro, Michael Moriarty,
and Beatrice Manley. *Big* Ben. My God. *Small* Ben you might as
well say, all shrivel up and dried out like a piece of old leather,
91 years old, and he said to Jay Pringle, "How are you, kid?"

Big Ben was the oldest man in the game that night, and I was
the youngest. I was the youngest pitcher in the league in 1952
and the youngest Old Timer in 1971. Shit. He carried an old
time Mammoths suit in a paper bag and he begun dressing. I did
not care to see Big Ben Scotland naked or even in his under
wear. People kept arriving and running up to each other crying
out, *"Hey,* how *are* you, believe me you are looking *great.* When
was it we seen you last?"

I heard 1 fellow say, "This is the game that really counts.
What is that small time act known as the World Series?" Every
body laughed.

I heard 1 fellow say, "My home address is the same as the
home address of all retired ball players. It is Porch View,
U. S. A."

Jay Pringle of "Philadelphia" said to me, "Hey, kid, are you
going to pitch? I could not hit you then and I will not be able to
hit you tonight, I am sure." I still did not know who he was. "I
hit against you my last year I played," he said. "I could not see
the ball you threw. I was 42 years old. I could not even see curve
balls people threw. I was all ready a grand father." He took a
paper out of his bag and showed it to me and I sat in my locker
and read it.

Play in old-timers' games. I figured, why? I got the store and I
got to work at it, but Fern said, "Go ahead. See the guys you
played with." I went. I put on spikes. I'd been off 'em ten years. I
rocked. I thought I was gonna fall over. I couldn't walk on
spikes. I made it to the outfield. Someone hit a little fly. I ain't
caught a fly in ten years. Son of a bitch, the ball looked as though
it was six miles up. I said to myself, "See the old guys if you want

to, but for Christ's sakes, don't do this no more. Don't ever put on spikes again."

"Who said this?" I inquired. I thought it was some good writing and I wished to take it home and save it and maybe put it in a book about retiring if I wrote it. I slid the paper in my own locker.

"No body wrote it," said Jay, "it is out of a book."

"You played to 42," I said. "I might play a couple years yet."

"I saw you fell down Opening Day," said Jay.

"You saw no such a thing," I said.

"It was from being off the spikes," said Jay. "He was off them 10 years."

I become in rage. "I was never wearing spikes," I said. "I was wearing god dam street shoes. What in the hell do you know about any thing?"

He blinked his eyes like I slapped him in the face and turned around, never looking again in my direction. In the game he come to bat and looked at 3 pitches and turned away. You could see he did not like me. I had took the spirit out of every thing for him, *ruined* it for him, and I regretted it a great deal and never done any thing about it. For awhile I thought I might send him a Christmas card and never done so. I could not get out of that clubhouse quick enough. It was torture, believe me. I never seen so many naked old men in 1 place before or since. Did I look as old as that to Ben Crowder's boys in the clubhouse in California on May 28? It was not possible, I am sure.

I felt peculiar coming up on the ball field out of the visiting dugout. I felt like some sort of a trader to my country. I crossed over to our side and got a hold of Ev McTaggart there and said, "I believe you are my catcher tonight," which he was. Ev caught for us for several years before he went in to coaching and managing. He last caught me 6 or 7 years ago, and we begun warming again now, but after I threw 4 or 5 pitches he come walking down to me and said, "Author, telling you the truth, I really can not see with my eyes in the shape they are in and I am going to look bad in the eyes of my players." He winked at me like I and him knew some thing no body else knew.

"I under stand perfectly," I said.

"You still throw fast," he said.

"I am available in till midnight tonight," I said.

He called out the name of 1 of his catchers. It was the same boy that I pitched to in September and then again Opening Day and fell down and I *still* can not remember his name. I threw some. "You have lost nothing off it since last year," said the boy.

"I been staying in shape," I said. "I hope to be back yet this year."

Some how this scared him and he stood up. "With us?" he inquired. "In place of who?"

"No," said I, "probably not with you but else where in the league," and he crouched back down again.

How ever, after several more pitches he stood up once more. "Then you changed your mind about going in the ice," he said.

Soon come the ceremony. The old time Mammoths crossed the field and lined up in front of the Mammoths dugout. The old time visitors lined up in front of the visiting dugout. The anthem played. Following the anthem come another announcement, same as Opening Day. "Ladies and Gentle Men. Your attention please. In honor of the late Dutch Schnell, whose name for 45 years was associated with the New York Mammoths Baseball Club, Inc., may we remain standing for 1 minute of respect full silence." I stood between Swanee Wilks and Scotty Burns. They were both on the bench on the day I pitched Opening Day, 1952. I was coming up while they were going down and I never got to know them much. They made me feel like a kid again and behave like 1 as well. "The music is so god dam loud I am out of my mind," I said, clapping my hands over my ears like a kid will do. "Ladies and Gentle Men," the loud speaker called, "Your Attention Please. Introducing the members of the All Star Visiting Old Timers," naming each person by name and the principal club they played with, and mentioning a certain out standing event of their life, such as "Jay Pringle, Philadelphia, hit 5 singles and scored 4 runs in a single game against Boston, 1946." For each man the crowd applauded politely.

"Ladies and Gentle Men. Your Attention Please. Now introducing to our record breaking audience this night members of the New York Mammoths Old Timers so recent and so beloved to our minds and memories." Up come the music, trumpets and drums like we were heroes back from the all time final war, and my blood rushed through me in to my finger tips, for I could feel them tingling, and I was unable to breathe for a moment, and my knees shook, but why this was I do not know. I do not know if I was angry or excited or sad or filled with joy. "Ladies and Gentle Men, New York Mammoths Old Timer lead off batter Big Benjamin Scotland, elected member of the Hall of Fame, struck out 312 batters in the year 1901. By the way, ladies and gentle men, Big Ben will be 91 years young tomorrow. Happy birth day, Big Ben. Ladies and gentle men, Big Ben Scotland, to rest his pitching arm for a future game, has chose to play right field tonight." Cheers, cheers, cheers for Big Ben Scotland. Between the clubhouse and the ball field he had grew several inches smaller, or so it seemed to me, but he was all sparkle and pep, hustling right along from the dugout to the line up on the foul line, his old fashion uniform hanging off him like rags in a sack while people blew horns and clapped their hands, and I certainly clapped a good bit my self, watching him go, although I seen that Swanee and Scotty kept their arm folded, whereby I felt more like a kid than ever, the year was 1952 and I was fresh up from Queen City still looking down the line in the dugout to see how the real ball players done it, and my father was alive and well yet and I and Holly might get married in the winter.

I turned and said to Swanee, "By the way, Marva Sprat asks me to say 'Hello' to you and extend her best regards and good wishes for old time sake," feeling like a kid in 1952 *talking on equal bases with the famous Swanee Wilks, I must be a regular big league baseball player after all knowing the same people he knows.*

"Who?" he inquired.

"Marva Sprat," said I.

"How are you spelling it?" he inquired.

Like a fool I spelled it.

"Jack's wife?" he inquired.

"Right," said I.

"Do I know her?" he inquired.

There I was, the young kid, acting like a big shot, passing along a message, whereas a real ball player like Swanee Wilks did not know some little dreaming girl name of Marva Sprat no matter how you spelled it. To the present day I never knew the truth of it. I felt stupid and foolish. All right then, if I was to be in the part of a fresh kid down from the country I might as well play it, and I begun to holler and clap and whistle and cheer for each and every Mammoth Old Timer when their name was called. Off they trotted as well as they could to the foul line, possibly moving a little stiff in their legs or any how not use to running every day, and taking rather a while to get there.

I was the last man called. I sprang away. I ran. I sprinted to the foul line. The whole stadium roared like thunder, and I might of thought, "Patricia was right, they come for *me*," but good sense told me they roared with happiness because the introductions were over at last. You could see old men running short distances at any bus stop. Here was the Mammoths starting line up on Old Timers Day.

rf	Benjamin Scotland	born	1880
1b	Harry Hazelton		1916
cf	Allen Burns		1919
lf	Brendan Wilks		1917
2b	David Curran		1924

3b	Philip Galluze	1929
ss	Michael DeLowry	1909
c	Everett McTaggart	1930
p	Henry Wiggen	1931

I stood beside Ev McTaggart along the foul line. "That must feel good," he said.

"What must?" I asked like I had no idea any body cheered me.

He shook his head from side to side. He was glad he would never need to put up with me.

"Ladies and Gentle Men. Your Attention Please. Leave us sing an old song together honoring the hearty and talented men before us who give their every thing for 1 team or another among the many fine teams flying the flags of baseball. For some of our younger fans the song might be unfamiliar. Follow the words on our score board by singing along with the bouncing arrow. Or you may follow the words on your souvenir score card."

55,000 people is a mighty chorus. I never heard such tremendous booming music in my life. I wished Hilary been there. It seemed to me like the singing was holding the world up, that as long as the people kept singing every thing would stay in place, but when the music ended the world would fall apart and the second $\frac{1}{2}$ of my life would begin. So I wished it would go on for ever, for it raised me out of the ball park, lifting us all up in to the air, where the world was nothing but music and singing voices. I sung as loud as any body and Ev McTaggart looked at me like I was mad. "You are not suppose to sing in honor of your self," he said. What did I care? I sung on. Then again. Then a second time through.

> When your hair has turned to silver,
> I will love you just the same;
> I will only call you sweetheart,
> That will always be your name. . . .

Then all was silent, and I heard a sound I never heard before in a ball park full of people. I thought nothing could happen in a ball park I had not saw or heard before, but there it was. Finally I placed it. It was the sound of many people crying. It all been crying since Dutch's funeral. And who were they crying for? Was Patricia crying for Dutch? Were all these people crying for Big Ben Scotland and me? No, I was crying for my self. Every body was crying for them self.

"Play ball," the umpire shouted. He was an old time umpire name of Austin Colopy while another old time umpire umpired from behind second base like they do in school games but I never knew his name, and Big Ben Scotland went scooting along to right field on his little legs 91 years young tomorrow, and Scotty Burns jogged in to center field and Swanee Wilks in to left which I last seen either of them do 19 years before and now seen for the last time ever, and Ev McTaggart crouched down behind the plate. He was very out of shape. I threw several pitches to him and he could not move very good. "Author," he said, "you are throwing too hard."

Well, fuck *that*, I thought, I would throw them as hard as I cared to. I was a mad man. I was a maniac. I was not grace full or a gentle man. I did not behave well and I do not care for the memory. I was certainly immature. I begun the evening stealing a piece of paper off Jay Pringle, born 1910, and there he was in front of me again with his bat on his shoulder. By his own story he was unable to see a baseball coming at him 20 years before and there was no reason to believe his eye sight suddenly improved tonight. I fired at him like a rocket. "Leave him hit it," Ev McTaggart called out to me. I fired again. The third time I fired the ball Jay Pringle backed up and left before the ball was ½ way to the plate. The umpire called him out, yelling "St-eeee-rike" and making these immense motions and wavings with his arms like we were all having a giant size package of fun playing our little 2 inning game which we were not. How could any body have fun? No body could hit the ball. Therefore no

Music Sung Prior to the Old Timers Game

When your hair has turned to sil - ver, I will love you just the same; I will
on - ly call you sweet-heart, That will al-ways be your name. Through a
gar - den filled with ros - es Down the sun - set trail we'll stray: When your hair has
turned to sil - ver I will love you as to - day. - day.

fielders got the chance of fielding the ball. It was a game of catch between me and Ev. Ev come down the line to the box saying, "Author, this is just in fun here, sail them in easy, the idea is letting them hit it so every body can run around on their legs a little."

"What idea?" I inquired. "That is not *my* idea."

"This is just a *game*," he said. "This is not an actual game. Use your sense."

Up come the next hitter, name of Sun Shine Briscoe carrying a huge flash light shaped like a bat which he shone and waved about. This made the park laugh. Sun Shine shows up at many baseball functions, claiming he was ruined by night baseball. His motto was, "Sun shine and I went out of baseball together." He put down his flash light and stepped in with his bat and I poured 1 down the middle. He jumped back, throwing down his bat and picking up the flash light and stepping in the box again. This was disgusting. It really was. "Go ahead and throw," he said. I never threw at a hitter carrying a flash light and I was not about to begin now. "May be we better play ball," the umpire said, "and stop all these comical doings. May be we just better get it over with," and Sun Shine changed his flash light for a bat again and stepped in the batter's box, and I threw the ball very hard again, and Ev McTaggart said again, "Come along, Author, this is not right, serve it up where we can all see it good," but the next ball I also threw as before. Sun Shine swung his bat around on it after Ev all ready caught the pitch.

Ev come out to the box again. His gear was clanking on him. His shin guards were borrowed and did not fit him. "I am amazed at you," he said, "firing the ball in like that at these old men. You are busting my hand besides."

"There is only 1 way to pitch a baseball," I said, "and that is to pitch it the most effective way every time."

"No," said he, "the best way is to throw it like I am telling you."

"Ev," said I, "whereas I am personally fond of you and admire your soft spoken ways it would be a very cold day before I would follow your advice re pitching."

"That is why," said Ev, "I would never have you on a ball club I was managing and told her so, and this proves it." He whipped off his mask and stared me down eye to eye. "I would not have took this job if you went with it. The day she hired me she released you because you never stop arguing and complaining and refusing. Dr. Schiff tells me you are madder than a March hornet." He jammed his mask on again and run back behind the plate. The batter was Christopher Sweeney. He got a sister lives in Perkinsville.

He swung at all 3 pitches and missed. I had struck out the side on 9 pitches. This happened only once before in my life, in the sixth inning of a game against Brooklyn, July 1, 1956, and I was knocked out of the box in the following inning. I did it again in the second inning Old Timers Day, which was the end of the game for me. I run in to the clubhouse and dressed and left with out even showering. I never before left a ball park with out showering unless I was sick. Driving home I dried my self by air condition.

It is 1 whole memory I can do with out except the singing. I will remember the singing. Even while I am writing this I am singing to my self.

> When your hair has turned to silver,
> I will love you just the same;
> I will only call you sweetheart,
> That will always be your name.
>
> Through a garden filled with roses
> Down the sunset trail we'll stray:
> When your hair has turned to silver
> I will love you as today.

I wished to be home. I wished to be sitting in front of the TV with Hilary on my lap. I wished to take a shower. Driving home

I tuned in and out of the ball game. I seen 2 girls hitch hiking by the side of the road and I thought about Raney Nelson, long since dropped from sight. Him and I once picked up a beautiful hitch hiking girl driving south. May be Raney Nelson would be looking in on the Iceoleum in West Des Moines tonight. Suppose you actually did fall off to sleep for 125 years. Suppose some body forgot to set their clock. Then what? Then you over slept. When you woke up you jumped up, saying, "Oh my, I forgot to set my clock, what year is this? Oh well, I only over slept a few years, I can catch up by skipping breakfast."

The telephone rung. It was Marva. "I was about to call you," I said.

"Where are you?" she inquired.

"Leave me see," said I, "some where around Port Chester."

"Did you deliver my message to Swanee Wilks?"

"As you instructed," said I.

"And he said?" she inquired.

"He said a direct quote as follows," I replied. " 'The letters of her name spell musical chimes in my ear.' "

"That is old Swanee for you. I suppose Scotty Burns said about the same."

"About the same," said I.

"Remember that he is on California time," she said. "There fore he might not call you in till as late as 3 A.M. in the morning. I am sure you got a telephone by your bed. If not, sleep in your car."

"I will be exhausted by 3 o'clock in the morning," I said.

"We are never too exhausted for triumph and victory," she replied. "With your World Series money think how many horses you can come down and buy. You tell me you are in your car, but how do I know you are not driving to Iowa? Think of how many ball records will be broke in 125 years. But do you know the only record that will be left standing?"

"Which is that, Marva?"

"Your own triple historic first."

"Not if I go in the ice."

"If you are down around Port Chester you will not make it to Iowa by air time. She will bury you in your absence. Did you ever stop and think how much the interest will add up to in Mr. Alexander's bank book in 125 years?"

"Quite a sum," said I.

"You will be seeing my Jack by the end of the week," she said. "There is no need telling him you and me spoke, no need of confusing the picture. Good night, dear Author, although not for long."

We all settled down in front of the TV for the program from Iowa. The frost rose up from the ice if it was ice. I don't know what it was. It was a small swimming pool with a plastic cover. The light was not too good and she would not leave Suzanne get in too close because of the terrible deep emotions "Mr. Henry Wiggen" was going through. He was so broke up he was not permitting any body to see his face. I admire how she put it all together, she completely done it her self, dreamed it up, promoted it, worked up a lot of interest in it, and seemed to be having a good time besides. She could not get enough of the camera. She was feeling a lot more successful about her self than the hour she spent in Perkinsville.

Suzanne rotated her shoulders, winding up and firing questions at the freezer girl. "How do you count for the fact that Henry Wiggen is at home this very minute. Can a person be in 2 places at once?"

"Of course not," said the freezer girl, "the Henry Wiggen at home is a fake."

Hilary laughed in till the tears come in her eyes, and her mother and her sisters laughed a good deal, too.

"As for the real Henry Wiggen," the freezer girl continued, "here he comes now moving ever so slowly because of the deep emotion he is feeling."

From out of the shadows beside the swimming pool come a fellow wearing a baseball hat. His hair hung down his neck in my very own style, and as he walked along he swung his left arm by his side. Now, what always puzzles me is why do people think a baseball pitcher swings their arm like a gorilla? Does a foot ball quarter back walk along swinging their leg? No, they walk like other people, and so does a baseball player.

Once more Suzanne rotated her shoulders for a question. "I realize he does not wish to show his face. But unless you show us his face we can not really believe this is Henry Wiggen, the famous baseball player, entering the ice for 125 years."

"You may see his face any time you wish," said the freezer girl, "as soon as he wakes up fresh as a daisy and recovered from his grief and pain and prostrate trouble. At that time his face will be covered in smiles of bliss. He will be rested. Right now he is hiding his face from the world because it is covered by sadness and misery at the end of his baseball career and the troubles of his family. He is depressed by the cruelty of the corporation he once worked for, which he considered as a family, and as you know he suffers terribly from the pain of prostrate disease."

"No, I did not know that," said Suzanne. "He did not seem to be in pain these last 10 weeks."

"Good by to this mercy less world," said the fellow in the baseball hat, "but only for the present time. Good by 1971, hello 2096. Good by to my lovely family, to my many friends in the TV world, good by to the New York Mammoths Baseball Club which was always such a family to me, I am happy to be joining Walt Disney and President Eisenhower."

We all sat up and took notice hearing his voice. It was a very good imitation of mine, and we all got a great bang out of that. Hilary was squirming and doubling over laughing. He pulled aside a curtain beside the swimming pool and the frost poured out like you seen it pour out of those tremendous ice cream freezers in certain ball parks. May be she made it with dry ice. When we were kids we loved dry ice you could press a nickel in and make it sing.

"You do not look like Henry Wiggen to me," said Suzanne.

"You do not look like Suzanne Winograd to me," he said.

"You have not looked at me," said Suzanne. "You heard on the telephone his very own daughter is sitting on his lap back home in Perkinsville."

"He is a fake," said the freezer girl. "They can do great things these days with theatrical make up. They fooled the poor child."

"Please leave me ask 1 question as time runs out," said Suzanne. "As you enter the Iceoleum to be prepared by physicians to live 125 years, thanks to the miracles of science sponsored by Life After of West Des Moines, please answer this 1 test question."

"All the wars will be over," said "Henry Wiggen." "Life will be games for every body. All the races and colors of man kind will play together while kissing and dancing."

"You have heard of famous parks," said Suzanne. "In New York City you find the location of Central Park. In San Francisco we have all saw the famous and beautiful Golden Gate Park. In what city do we find Henry W. Wiggen Mini Park?"

"Chicago," said that galoot, stepping in to the cloud of frost.

"This is Suzanne Winograd, Friday Night Baseball," said Suzanne, "in some body's back yard in West Des Moines, Iowa."

The girls went to bed 1 by 1. I sat up and waited. "You do not need to wait either," I said to Holly, but she waited. We been through certain exhausting and nerve racking waits together, mainly medical, mainly children, and 1 long wait when Michele and several friends and Patricia Moors's son and several boys we did not know went and 85 other people were high jack and flew to India and back and forth 2 or 3 times in an air plane wired for dynamite. The high jackers were Japanese mad men.

When they heard that Michele was on the air plane they said they would bargain only with her father. I sat 47 hours in the control tower in New York talking and laughing with those high jackers, and Holly waiting with me talking now and then as well. I promised them if they defused the dynamite I would teach them how to throw curve balls and screw balls and make their motion to first base. I would introduce them to famous American ball players. I would play in Japan and tell the Prime Minister or the Emperor what I thought of them. I did not enjoy that wait at all. Those 47 hours in the control tower may of been the reason my prostrate was damaged, for I did not dare excuse my self or they might blow the fuse.

Tonight we ate crackers and cheese and drank some D'Agostini red wine the Petrotones sent us from a winery built in 1856 in northern California. For awhile the telephone rung and I sat with it in my lap. It was friends around the country saying they were glad I didn't go in the ice. But they were not close friends and they were not too *sure.* Some people think to the present day I am sleeping on ice in Iowa. We kept the conversations short, saying we were waiting to hear from California. Midnight come and went and the telephone quieted down. I took it off my lap and put it on the table. I was a little chilly. I was nervous.

"Did you see any body you knew tonight?" Holly asked.

"Do you remember Swanee Wilks from very early?"

"Faintly," she said.

"Do you remember Scotty Burns?" I inquired.

"Equally faintly," she said.

"I threw 18 strikes in a row," I said.

"Was that necessary?" Holly inquired.

"No," said I, "and I am ashamed of it and I do not really care to talk about it. I was advertising what good shape I was in. Will you think I am vulgar if I remove my contact lenses?"

"I will try and be broad minded," she said.

"Of course," I said, "we *could* go to sleep and leave the telephone wake us."

"Do you think Marva Sprat knows what she is talking about?" Holly inquired. "It is my impression she has a hard time telling a straight story. That is why I never wrote her up for *Baseball Wives*. According to Marva, 50,000 men are knocking down her door over come by a desire for her which maddens them beyond belief."

"May be she lives in a dream world," I said, "for I live in 1 my self, dreaming that I can continue playing baseball. May be it is all wrong. I will telephone Suicide and tell him it is all off and go to bed."

"I am on the border of tears," Holly said. "You are making a wrong decision if you play, but I can not be responsible for telling you other wise. Maybe dream worlds come true. Something got in you and reversed your mind after you all ready knew better. Time after time you told me how glad you would be if it was over. You hoped you would break a leg and end it. But you are too good a ball player to break a leg. You telephoned me in the morning from distant hotels saying 'I can not get out of bed 1 more day.' If you pulled up the window blind and seen that it was raining you cheered, no game today, no game today, you wished Noah would come with his ark and flood every ball park in the league. You ached in 14 places. You could not eat 1 more meal in 1 more bad restaurant, after 20 years in baseball you left on road trips *packing your own food with you*. I could cry. You had no friends on the ball club any more. Every body you ever knew quit or was fired or cracked up and 1 or 2 died. You were all alone. You sat in the front of the air plane and Dutch sat in the back and neither of you knew any body in between and now even he is dead. Your team mates annoyed you. They were like children exchanging wrong information. You seen them making the same mistakes over and over again which you thought by now no body made any more. They lacked experience. They told you what their high school coach told them and you did not have the heart to tell them their high school coach was wide of the mark. They threw to the wrong base. They had strong backs and weak minds. They run like naked mad men on slippery floors snapping wet towels at 1 another. You told them they were ruining their beautiful bodies and lives and careers by drugs and dope and they told you behind your back you were a case of senility and they called you 'Mr. Clean.'"

The telephone rung. It was Suicide Alexander from Newhall, California. "Author," he said, "Alexander here, just giving you a little ring a ling. I hope it is not too late for you."

"Not at all," said I, "it is never too late in the night for a friendly voice. Have you got your tape machines going?"

"Rigged to the ceiling and ready for business," said he. "I just now caught a glimpse of you on TV set me to thinking."

"You seen me go in to the ice?"

"Ice?" he inquired. "No, I seen you dancing back and forth with the tennis player. How does she do that acrobatics with her shoulder? What were those words wrote across her chest? Where are you now? Are you in your car? Do you know that you and I could start out from 1 end of the country talking all the way if only I had a telephone in my jalopy and smash up head on in the middle of Nebraska?"

"That does not strike me as 1 of your *more* creative ideas," I responded.

"Any how I seen you say you were ready to throw your glove away. I was awfully sorry to hear that."

"Not at all," I said. "I pitched 2 innings tonight and struck out 6 people."

"*For who?*" he asked, mighty alarmed.

"It was only an exhibition," I said.

"Because it is possible you will remember you and my manager Jack Sprat conferred regarding you pitching for us yet. Some time after that you and your lawyer dropped out here and we conferred further in greater detail, this factor and that factor."

"And you showed us your fantastic bank book," I said.

"Beg him to get to the point," said Holly. She held her wine glass at her forehead, twisting it left and right, this side and that, with her head bent forward and her eyes closed. I think she did not wish to see my face if the news that was coming was bad. She wished to be alone behind her eye lids. I remembered her in that same position from other waits we waited together.

"Back at that point in time," said Suicide, "I was ever so slightly worried about your *motivation*. I did not want some body working for me unless they really needed the money and cared about it."

"I felt that we answered that point at that time," I said.

"I know that we did," he said. "I been turning it over in my mind ever since. Jack been on me. You remember Jack Sprat. I should of trusted you. You are a great pitcher that his *motivation* is the pleasure of pitching as well as the money."

"I congratulate you on having the sense to wait in till the trading dead line was past," I said. "From a dollars and cents point of view that was the only smart thing to do and there is no point of view except the dollars and cents point of view."

"Pity poor me," said Suicide. "No body will trade with me. No body loves a winner or gives them a helping hand. As of tonight we lost the ball game and we have fell a ½ a game behind and I been thinking better and better thoughts of you as time went by."

"I am in a state of the most awful suspense to learn what those improved thoughts might be," said I, "and my wife is like wise in a state of suspense."

"Tell the son of a bitch to *spit it out*," said Holly. She opened her eyes at me, and she must of believed good news was on the way, for she did not close them again. "Tell him I am dying to know a little some thing which will tell me when we are going to begin to live the rest of our life."

"Is she addressing me?" asked Suicide.

"She is waiting to hear your good thoughts," I replied.

"These better and better thoughts lead me to the following," said Suicide. "What a fool I was to worried about your *motivation*! I could kill my self the time I wasted. Acting promptly we would of been 2 games ahead tonight instead of ½ behind. But the year is early and I can correct my mistake. Any 39 year old millionaire that will steal a ½ a bag of gold clubs off me at a dead man's funeral is my kind of a man."

12

I was a ball player again. It was not easy to believe. For 6 months I been living like a leaf in the wind, blew here, blew there, released, Japan and back, New York and back more times than I counted, Washington and back, California and back, up and down to Tozerbury, 10 times out with Friday Night Baseball, and once to Iowa by pinch runner. Now I was no longer a leaf but a man in charge of my self. I had never before wore any big league suit but "New York." Now my uniform was "California" and I was use to it in 10 seconds or less. I knew here I was and all the moves and all the people and who was who and what was what and where I stood in all matters.

I walked in to the visiting clubhouse in Montreal. "Gentle men," said Jack Sprat, jumping up in the air, "here comes the flag walking in the door," and he leaped on me like we all ready won it, like I just threw the last pitch on the last day, and every body crowded around or stood on chairs and benches for a glimpse of me. "How long will it take you to be in shape?" Jack inquired.

"I been in shape for months," I said, and the boys all shouted and applauded and set off their hair blowers. They were big league ball players but they were kids and I felt a little bit out of place in the beginning. This was Wednesday night. Old Timers Day Tuesday night, Montreal Wednesday, 2 innings vs. the visiting Old Timers Tuesday night, ⅔ inning vs. Montreal Wednesday. I entered the ball game 1 run up and 1 man out in the bottom of the ninth inning. They had a man on second base. He was a short, broad chested left hand hitting fellow. He was a hard target to pitch to and we had a hard time getting him out all through the series. He really *whacked* the ball like he was batting with a paddle.

The first fellow I ever faced in any suit but a New York Mammoths suit hit the first pitch back at me and I threw him out. Then right away I become lucky. The batter was anxious. He was way up on his toes leaning forward, if you threw him a bucket he would of hit it with a mop. He kept reaching out across the plate, and the farther he reached the farther out I threw in till finally after he fouled off 4 or 5 he missed all together and that was the ball game and we were in first place. In the clubhouse the boys all yelled and cheered finding them self in first place. Nothing you could tell them would quiet them down. They had no idea yet of the rhythm of it, they would be up and down several times yet before any thing was definite. If June was the time for cheering you would see old men like me cheering in June.

Some of the young pitchers crowded around asking questions. They asked me how come I never looked at the runner advancing to third base. "Why did you not *challenge* him?" asked 1 young pitcher. "I went directly to first base," I said, "out of old habit, I guess. It never occurred to me other wise. Was there not 1 out? Suppose I went to third base and the runner give us a hard time between the bases. The other fellow might *still* of got to second. Worse yet, some body might of threw the fucking thing away. Where would we of been then?"

"You just *give* the runner third base?" asked 1 of the young pitchers. "I was taught other wise."

"What was he going to *do* with it?" I inquired. "Nothing is going to bring him home except a base hit, which would of brang him home from second base as well. No body has *stole* home on me since child hood."

"I can see where you are coming from," said the young pitcher.

"I am going to have to think that 1 over," said another.

The thing I did not mention, how ever, was that the ball come back at me faster than I expected. I don't know. Of course, whereas I was in very good shape I still had not threw to any actual hitters in till the night before, and that was hardly actual hitters. I was all most surprised that I fielded it at all. I did not know I had it in my glove. I mentioned to Jack I thought may be the lights were a little dim in Montreal, but he said he believed I could field in the dark. "Having you aboard," said Jack, "I am the happiest man the world ever seen. How I campaigned for this! How I burned up the telephone connections between me and Mr. Alexander!" Jack was excited and high. He could not sleep very good that night after having slept very bad the night before. "I walked the gol darn floor all night wondering if he phoned you. He lives the life of a fortress. This morning he phones me from his little house he believes is in Spain and begins by saying, 'Say, Jack, do you remember we been discussing Wiggen?' Do I remember? We had 35 discussions on the subject."

But that was past and Jack now seen himself definitely managing a winner all the way. "Do you know what I see?" he inquired while riding in the taxi cab back to the hotel. "I see a family photo in the magazines where I am surrounded by my family. My arm is resting on the chair. The TV sets are all moved out of the way for class, the piano drug more in to the center of the photo, the fire place is blazing." Only 1 thing bothered him. "I felt sorry for the boy I sent down while clearing my roster," said Jack. "He was full of high hope, showing me photos of his wife and child. Tell me what you think, Author, did any manager ever sneak an extra person or 2 on to his club? Who *counts*? No body ever actually comes over and *counts* the number of men sitting on your bench for the gosh darn sake."

The club assigned me a room alone. How ever, the situation

was such that Tom Roguski was hoping to room with me if by any chance I did not object to rooming with him. "Why should I object to rooming with you?" I asked Tom.

"No reason a part from my personality," he said. "I will bet this is some sort of a record for the Hall of Fame, you roomed with my father and now you room with his son."

"It is a historic first," I said, but what I did not say was that I never roomed with his father, all though it was clear his father told him so. Close buddies yes. Roomies no.

Tom Roguski made me think of my daughter Michele. Every thing he owned he threw on the floor in till 5 minutes before check out he picked it all up and stuffed it in a duffel bag like he was off to summer camp, except his battery drove electric hair dryer that he carried with him at all times in case of an emergency such as a young girl approaching 9 blocks down the street. His wardrobe was small. From Montreal down the east coast we had bad heat, and Tom traveled comfortable, wearing by actual count 5 pieces of clothing as follows. A T shirt. A pair of street shorts. A pair of jockey shorts under his shorts. 2 open toe flaps, 1 for each foot. He carried a comb. He begun kidding me once we knew each other better, saying, "What is all the belongings you carry in your suit case? Do you steal the hotel TV?"

"No," I replied, "it is only that I dress in regular clothing instead of running the street like a savage. You your self will wear such clothes some day." He also took advantage of me regarding both my suit case and my clothes, often asking me to carry things for him, which of course I done. His T shirts carried printed messages. The 1 I remember best said.

When I Grow Up I Want to Be a Baseball Player

He urinated torrents. He woke me in the middle of the night coming in from drinking beer. I thought he would flood the hotel with his powerful stream. He did not suffer from prostrate trouble. He did not suffer from insomnia neither. From the time he rose in the morning in till the time he went to bed at night he kept going full blast. 2 minutes before bed time he was *still* going full blast, following which he collapsed on the bed and slept like a block of cement. He never woke up by him self. I had to wake him. "Who would wake you," I inquired, "if you did not have a fucking old man millionaire as a roomie to wake you?"

"The fucking desk," he replied. But he never heard the telephone if it rang.

He had a temper, like his father. I told him I did not believe bad tempers made good ball players. He would need to learn to control it. May be you think I was vulgar and coarse referring to my self as a millionaire when I woke him in the morning, but I can tell you it was effective among the boys on that baseball club. Jack Sprat done the same, telling them how rich I was, for it seemed to be the only way they respected me and believed in me and listened to things I passed along about the secrets of playing ball. Just being good, just loving it, just saying "Play for the love of it and leave the dollars fall where they may" is not enough for the mind of young players. I begun to see the secret in Suicide Alexander showing people his bank book. Young fellows can not simply enjoy them self. They are too tense. They press.

Tom soon noticed things about me I almost forgot about my self. I still come very early to the park every day and I was still nervous and excited entering the park, for I still expected every minute some chap with a badge would come up behind me and say, "Hey, kid, no body but players allowed in the clubhouse." And this was after 20 years and more!

"It is hard to believe you," said Tom. "If you said to me it is only routine, it is only another day's work I could believe you. That is what my father said, it is just a job, Tom, do not take it too serious. He thought I signed on too cheap. My enthusiasm cost me money."

"He got 9 children," I said. "You got only 5 articles of clothing."

Jack Sprat thought I done wonders for Tom and for several other boys on the club, specially pitchers. It is true I talked to them a lot all though I did not hang with them. I hung with Jack and the coaches. It did not seem to me very much to do. "It is a lot," said Jack, "it is giving them a big picture of them self. Henry Wiggen is a winner and he is on their club with them and he is ready to converse with them just like a regular fellow on every day bases. Think how important it is for the spirit of these boys. It gives them a family feeling. Good Lord, most big stars give the cold shoulder to younger fellows, but not you. You are different. Rooming with Tom is a golden kindness. You should be knighted in to saint hood."

Every night I begun warming in the sixth inning. I needed to be warm enough with out giving away too much strength. As the heat increased I was even more careful than ever about over doing it. The second night in Montreal I come in in the eighth inning with 2 men out and 2 men on base and the tie run at the bat. "Keep the tie run from coming to the bat and you can never lose," Dutch Schnell always said. The hitter was the same little broad chested fellow that been on second base the night before. He was a left hand hitter, which was why I entered the ball game exactly then, and he wished to pull the ball so bad he was positive I would never throw it where he wished. There fore I threw him my fast ball as hard as I could inside and low, which surprised him.

That was my fast ball for the inning. I was ahead of him and that was what I wanted. It put me in a good position, for this was not the old days when I could fall behind the batter. In the old days I always had the fast ball in reserve. I curved him very sharp on the out side corner. He was very strong. With that broad chest he could of hit it to the opposite field. But he did not know his own strength or trust it, and trying to pull the ball he only hit it 3 miles in the air and we were out of the inning on

2 pitches. "Oh, what a blessed man am I," Jack Sprat exclaimed, hugging me with both hands on the dugout steps. "I have struck a gold mine in the rough."

That was the eighth inning. The ninth inning was very easy and very pleasant. With a 3 run lead I could throw fast balls like I had plently of confidence in them. Take a chance. Leave the word get around that I still trusted it. No body knew that in my heart I wished I had worked harder on the knuckler with those 2 boys name of William in Perkinsville in the spring. I *showed* them the fast ball but I never come in too big with it in till I was down to the last man. Leave him hit it out of the park if he cared to, the tie run was still in the dugout. Instead he poled it on a line in to my outfield where 1 of my nice young new friends was waiting for it. I had now retired 6 men in a row in 2 nights.

The third night in Montreal I stood ready but was never needed. A young boy pitched for us name of Alvin Tibbles, who was very strong and fast but also threw many more curves than he should of been throwing so young. He won 18 games for Jack that year and begun disappearing from view by the end of the next. He threw his arm out. "An inflamed elbow tendon" I seen in the news paper, but "threw his arm out" is what I call it. I told Jack on the air plane out of Montreal the boy was pitching too many curves too young and Jack said he would raise the question with Tibbles and with Don Bello, who was the pitcher coach, and I am sure he did, and might of raised it with Suicide Alexander, too, and got the same answer every where he raised it, "This is our year, Jack, we will pour every thing in to it now and worry about every thing else in the future." We left Montreal 1½ games in first place and all the boys hooting and hollering and counting up their future money.

I knew that Ev McTaggart knew that I would be coming in with the first pitch and get ahead of his hitter. There fore I did not come in with the first pitch as good as Ev told his hitters I would, and they went after pitches just out of their range and never got much of a piece of any thing. Ev stood leaning up against the dugout wall with his hands in his ass pockets and not much of any kind of an expression on his face. With 2 men out in the ninth inning 1 of his boys slammed an out side pitch up against the fence for 2 bases. It was the only hit off me in 2 innings, first game of a double header, we now won 4 in a row since I joined the club.

Ev never said "Hello" or "Good by" to me 3 days in New York. Well, we were never close. I felt right at home in the visiting clubhouse. For 20 years I almost never seen the in side of it, but now I seen it twice with in 1 week. "You will start doing a lot of things you never done before," Jay Pringle told me Old Timers Day. Between the double header the boys conducted a little ceremony. They were so tired hearing me run down T shirts with printed messages they presented me with 1 my self with the message wrote across it, *Dirty Old Men Pitch Relief.* "I will wear it with pride," I said, "underneath a regular civilized shirt," and every body laughed a good deal.

Sitting side by side in front of our lockers Tom Roguski said to me, "I believe I am living in a dream." He drunk 1 of them orange drinks that rot your teeth and put sugar in your blood and make you so thirsty you finally crawl away looking for water. "I and you rooming together," he said. "I and you throwing in the bull pen. I and you sitting like this in the locker. This is like 1 of the miracles of the Bible."

"I never notice you reading the Bible," said I.

"No," said Tom, "my mother reads it for me." Oh yes, his mother. I remembered her from the days when Coker was courting her, but from what Coker mentioned she was not at that time too deep in the Bible. I could not remember her name. "You were a hero in our house. When I was a kid it was Henry Wiggen this and Henry Wiggen that. You were held up to us as a person of quality character. He was very proud to played with you and told us many incidents. We heard every incident 9 times, once for every kid in the family."

"1 night," said I, "your father give us a phone call coming down from Albany. He said he would drop by and we threw another steak on the fire."

"And then he never showed?" inquired Tom.

"Right," said I. "Why would he of did a thing like that?"

"Because he got too many memories to handle," said Tom. "He grew odd when he left baseball. We all hope we are never as odd as him." He did not seem to wish to talk further on this subject, and we never done so.

From the telephone in the visiting clubhouse I telephoned home. Holly and Hilary were suppose to come down that day if Hilary got free of her horses in time. They thought if they missed the first game they would arrived for the second game any how, and Hilary remain with me in till at last she seen me play. All her sisters seen me play, so why not Hilary?

"You done good," said Holly. She listened to the ball game while flowering the garden. She told me various bits and pieces of news. "Ed Lewis come down and finished your fence around Depot Park," she said. She never got over calling it "Depot Park." "It must be a very strange feeling pitching against the Mammoths," she said.

"Ball players are ball players," I said. "They put their pants on 1 leg at a time New York Mammoths or any body else. The thing I am wondering is when will Hilary see me play. I feel that I went to a certain amount of trouble on her behalf."

"You will need to consult Ms. Hilary her self," said Holly. "She is out of the house at present."

"Where?" I inquired.

"Horses," my wife replied.

"I am just thinking she might wish to catch me before we go west," I said. "She can zip up to Boston beginning Tuesday, or Friday and over the week end in Washington."

"She got your schedule prominently posted on her bulletin," said Holly.

"You have got to explain to her," I said, "that she has got to plan on coming for 2 or 3 days at least. You know, she can not be sure which day I will pitch even when she *does* come. The life of a relief pitcher is some thing else again."

True, I was a bull pen man now and stood there all the time, keeping loose, hanging on the fence watching the game it self, playing catch with our outfielders between innings, and talking to Tom Roguski. I could see his father's face in his and hear his father's voice and it carried me back many years. Tom and I were now playing ball in parks I and his father played in 10 years ago and more. We threw back and forth 2 nights in the bull pen in Boston with never a call for our services. Our winning streak was broke the first night up there but resumed on the second, and on the third night I and Tom both got in the action. Tom pinch hit and done very well. He could truly powder the ball. This 1 he hit on a line in to the seats with 2 men on the bases. It was still on the rise when it passed over the bull pen sailing into the sky like a bird.

His hit put us 2 runs ahead. He stood in the game, and I my self pitched for the pitcher Tom hit for, and I wondered if his father knew or was listening or watching, Wiggen pitching, Roguski catching. I thought he might give us a call on the phone. I made up his conversation for him, "Hey, what *about* that, you and my kid playing ball together after all these years, this is not some thing that happens every day." I thought he might also explain why he never showed up in Perkinsville that night, and I would reply, "Forget it, Coker old pal, I never give it a thought my self, that steak is always waiting."

I was never more loose, never felt better, never threw sharper stuff. True, no fast ball. It was such a pleasure to see the ball go where I sent it some times I almost hated getting my hitter out if you can believe me. Yet no sight is so fine to my eyes as the sight of a hitter swinging and missing. Or popping up. Or grounding out. I liked Tom back there, too. I had confidence in him. He was a good target and a good arm and a good head. I pitched 2 innings to him that night and give up no runs, no hits, and 1 base on an error. The error was my own and can be explained in the very simplest way. The ball was hit back at me and bounced off my glove. It was the first error I made in many years. They really dug back in the records to figure out when. It suddenly changed the game around for the moment. Instead of 2 out and none on in the ninth there was 1 out and 1 on and the tie run at the bat and me kicking my self thinking "Keep the tie run from coming to the bat and you can never lose" in the voice of Dutch Schnell shouting up from the grave. It is a voice I will hear all my life.

Another thing Dutch might also of said was, "Do not be thinking about too many dead friends when you are pitching baseball." True. Concentrate. He could tell when you were not concentrating. I wished to save this ball game and go out of Boston with the series won.

Boston pinch hit. The hitter was a veteran name of Buddy Zubrow. I and him once represented baseball players in certain Congressional hearings in Washington, D. C. He would be too cool to go after bad pitches, and he knew I knew he would never go after bad pitches. There fore I threw him a bad pitch, which he must of thought was good since I would never throw bad. It was a low curve, very sharp, breaking down with every thing I could possibly put on it, and he hit it in the dirt like a shot past me so fast I never seen it go by, and my infield gobbled it up, double play. I had now pitched 6 innings since June 16, give up no runs on 1 hit, saving 4 games for Jack, not bad for an old man. Of course it was not the same thing as doing it all in 1 day.

Hilary did not appear in Washington over the weekend and Coker Roguski did not telephone. "Here we sit feeling neglected," said Tom Roguski in the bull pen.

"Then let us stand," said I, "and change our luck," and we stood and threw but nobody needed us. When you are a relief pitcher you are in a peculiar position. You would like to get in the ball game, but you are never going to get in except at some body else's expense. Alvin Tibbles won the first game for us and a boy name of Chester Wackenhut won the second, 2 complete games back to back. You do not see too many complete games any more. Sunday, how ever, was 1 of those long, raggedy affairs full of hits and errors and cock eyed flukes resembling a high school game. We won the game, 11-8. I my self done very well, putting an end to all the nonsense. In such a game, when every body is hitting, the hitters become over confident. They think that if they just get wood on the ball the hits will fall in. They will lunge. Leave them lunge. For the last 2 innings I give Ben Crowder's young fellows plenty of time to go lunging at baseballs while they drifted to the plate. Notice how big and fat those baseballs were and how slow they approached during the lazy afternoon. The only thing about them was that the hitters could not get much of a piece of them with their bat. Did I hear young fellows shouting and hollering from the Washington bench that I could not throw hard enough to pitch out of a paper bag? May be that very paper bag fell down over some body's eyes while at the bat. Did I hear them calling out to me that I threw only junk? But of course we all heard of junk men that become very rich at their trade. I pitched $2\frac{1}{3}$ innings and give up nothing and we flew out of Washington $3\frac{1}{2}$ games ahead of the pack. We now had a 5 game winning streak going. We won 11 out of 12 since I joined the club on June 16.

We were greeted very big in California by several 1,000's of people at the air port hoping for a glimpse of Alvin Tibbles and a second glimpse of a boy name of Jimmy Leeds that hit nothing but doubles and home runs for us all during June. Jack Sprat and I walked through the air plane gate and through the crowd it self. All eyes were staring past us for the sight of real ball players. The weather was cool and perfect. We were glad to leave the east behind.

I was also personally greeted by Hilary wearing a T shirt saying *Let's Horse Around* across her chest with a picture of a horse's head in case you were weak at reading. She was sitting in the lobby of the hotel reading a book and when she seen me she said, "Would you mind sharing your room with a lady?"

"I will *enjoy* sharing my room with you if you are the lady in question," I said, "but I am curious how come you managed to come to California whereas Boston and Washington were difficult. Of course you come first class so as to enjoy maximum leg room while reading. Do you not think it was slightly extravagant?"

"No," she replied, "because I was planning to be here for your birth day. How ever, it turns out that I can only stay in till Thursday."

"Why must you return on Thursday?" I inquired.

"That is when my reservation is for," she replied.

Poor Hilary, she did not figure in the fact that Monday was a day off, and there fore she ended up seeing ball games on Tuesday and Wednesday only, when I was not needed. She watched me stay warm in the bull pen, but that was not the same thing as watching me pitch in an actual ball game, and I felt sorry for her. She was bored. To pass away the time she sold stock in our winery to the wives of several ball players and $25 in stock to Tom Roguski 1 night. We went to dinner with Tom at the Hamburger Hamlet again. She was interested in him because he was the child of a baseball player. "I can under stand your problems," said she to Tom.

"I am glad that some body can," he replied.

"I have never yet saw my father play baseball," said Hilary. "My mother and my sisters have all saw him play more than once. Do you consider that fair?"

"I would agree with you," said Tom, "except that I never saw mine either. Once we almost done so. The whole family drove to Pittsburgh for a ball game and when we got there it rained. We all cried and went home again."

"But now at last your chance is come to see me play ball,

has it not?" I inquired of Hilary. She would see me pitch Tuesday, or if I was not needed Tuesday she would see me Wednesday, or if not Wednesday certainly Thursday. No, not Thursday, said Hilary, her air plane left too early in the day.

Why could she not take a later plane back Thursday?

Because of a certain engagement regarding horses in New York on Friday. "I all ready bought tickets," she said.

"I hope you did not buy tickets with the stock holders' money," I sarcastically said. "Can you tell me the price of the tickets?"

"$3," she replied.

"What I am not able to understand," said I, "speaking as frankly as I can, is why you can not make a sacrifice of $3 tickets since you spent several *100's* of dollars coming here for another purpose. I would think you would remain and see me play even if it took in till Friday or Saturday."

"You are putting me on a terrible spot," she said.

"I am sorry," I said. "Your face is beginning to resemble the Speckled Mouthbrooder from the aquarium in San Francisco. Do you remember him?"

"Of *course* I do," she replied.

"I do not know why poor Tom should be dragged in to the middle of all this," I said, "but I am just wondering if you do *remember* that it was not entirely my idea to come back and play ball once she released me. I would as soon stood home and helped mother flower the garden and 1 thing and another. Are you aware, Hilary, that I done it all for you? That is why we went all over creation from Japan to Washington and California and back trying to make the connection which I made with great effort."

But when I mentioned California it only made her think of her strong desire to visit her friend Cynthia Petrotone who now also owned 2 horses. "My whole life is horses now," Hilary said.

"My whole life was baseball," I replied.

"That was *your* life," she said.

"Sweet heart, do not cry," I said, giving her my hankerchief. "How about we all drop in again on the Wax Museum?"

A lady in the ball club office give me several possible apartments to look in to, and I and Hilary spent Monday afternoon running some of them down in till I clearly seen they were not for me. They were perfect for ball players age 22 with 1 infant child and their wife was pregnant with number 2. These apartments offered such special features as baby sitters, diaper services, and free charcoal for your barbecue. Free charcoal. It been a long time since I worried about the price of charcoal. I felt very sorry for young ball players the rents they were asking.

I decided I would buy a house in Beverly Hills instead which I could always get my money back plus when I retired from baseball. At that moment it did not look like that might happen for years. I give a call to my old friend, Lisa Mayflower, the actress, who strangles her self with a diamond necklace in the movie in title *Lonesome*. She now sold real estate around Los Angeles sounding as sweet as ever and delighted to hear from me and we made an appointment to look at houses in Beverly Hills the Monday after the Fourth.

We beat Oakland the first night they come to town and they beat us the second. Hilary sat down the third base side 1 night with 2 wives of 2 young ball players and enjoyed her self a great deal. She sold them several shares of stock. On the following night they sat down the first base side. She seen me stay warm in the bull pen, but she did not get the chance to see me pitch in the actual game since I never done so. We got very good pitching from Alvin Tibbles the first night and very bad pitching from 3 or 4 pitchers the second. I was not needed the first night and there was nothing I could of did the second, and on the following day after lunch we drove off to the air port.

"I am sure you are aware," said I to Hilary, "that a relief

pitcher is not on rotation like I was when I was a starting pitcher. As a relief pitcher I might pitch several days or nights in a row and then not be needed for several days or nights and so forth."

"I under stand perfectly," she said. "You stay in the bull pen and wait in till the manager rings the alarm. That is why they call relief pitchers *fire men.*" She learned these things from the wives she sat with.

"Exactly," said I, "and I hope in the bottom of my heart that you are not too terribly disappointed missing seeing me."

"No, I am not," she said. "I will see you play in the east."

"That is the spirit," I said. "Of course you will, for I am hoping you do not plan on making too many trips across the country as they are slightly extravagant."

"I got your schedule on my bulletin," she said.

"Good going," I said. "New York, Pittsburgh, Boston, Washington, pick a town in the east, they are all the same to me, come and watch your father mow down the batters left and right where ever they dare to step in against him. I can see that schedule this very minute amongst the color photos of many fine horses from many noble families on your bulletin."

"And the list of stock holders in our winery," she said. She was proud of all the stock she sold, all though the winery it self still never planted Seed Number 1.

I pitched ⅔ of an inning Thursday night vs. Oakland, entering the ball game in the ninth inning with 1 man out, 1 man on base and their 2 strongest hitters hitting. Very soon it was 2 outs later and the fellow was still standing on the base where he been when I entered. No body hit a base hit off me since the boy doubled in the first game in New York. I now pitched 9 innings or 1 complete game you might as well say, stretched over time from June 16 to the first of July.

The fans of California were now becoming aware of my present business address and the way I was saving ball games for Jack. The following day was a long article in the paper on the importance of short relief. That night I entered the ball game vs.

San Francisco in the situation very similar to the night before. It was the eighth inning, 1 man was out, 1 man was on first base, and people begun to rise and move towards the exits like people do when things look definite. What happened was that word got round that as soon as I entered the ball game every thing was over, no body in the world could hit me in short relief, I was the master, I was the secret of it all, clear the decks, expand the ball park, California was winners at last. A fellow on the TV signed off saying, "Mr. Alexander, be ready to start up a new bank book."

The hitter was a boy name of Muddy Rivers. I never seen him before and never heard of him since except when I played him over and over again for a couple years on my TV cassette machine. He was a left hand hitter. It looked to me from the film that he was waiting for the fast ball. I threw him a low curve ball in side and a low curve ball out side. He left the first 1 pass and he went after the second 1 with very little enthusiasm, but they were strikes and he was in trouble.

It entered my mind when ever I watched the film that I might of blew the fast ball past him even so. The same idea must of struck me while I was pitching, too. After awhile I can not remember what things I remember from the film or what I remember from life or what I remember from only remembering. I did not throw the fast ball, how ever. I threw another curve ball breaking down and away to a left hand hitter, and it was like I said to Hilary the day she screamed after hearing the news, "Every ball player arrives some time at his last pitch, and I have arrived at mine."

I come up singing. So they told me. I was singing,

> When your head has turned to splinters,
> I will love you just the same . . .

which I sing and whistle yet while writing up these events in the form of a book.

I was laying on a stretcher in a corridor. My head was X rayed several times. Later, when Holly arrived, she made them do it again. A doctor waved many lights in my face and said he believed my focus was derailed, possibly the impact of the ball against my skull jarred my retina loose. When I felt the stretcher wheels rolling under me I took the notion I was heading down the corridor in to major eye surgery. I thought to my self, "How many days out of action will you be due to major eye surgery?" I sat up and looked around. "Lay back down," the doctor said, which I done with out complaining, for my head ached beyond any head ache I ever had before. In my opinion my skull was split in 2, the back ½ of my head was hanging down my back like Bertilia's pig tail. "In deed," said the doctor, "you been struck a definite blow."

"Are we rolling in to eye surgery?" I inquired.

"Not to the best of my knowledge," said the doctor.

"My brains been boiled," I informed him.

"We will cool them with plenty of ice," he replied.

"I suppose if I had any brains to begin with I would not of been playing ball with those young savages," said I.

"That is not my department," said the doctor.

My brains were boiled, my retina was loose, several teeth rattled in my mouth, it took my mind off my prostrate. After awhile I was no longer on a stretcher but a bed. "We do not advise sleep," said the doctor, but what he advised I never remembered. Off and on I slept in spite of my self.

After the ball game Jack Sprat arrived, asking me how I was but never waiting for an answer. He needed only 1 glance to see that I was not well. He stood at the foot of the bed studying my face and asking him self the same question, "How many days out of action will you be due to major surgery of the eyes, ears, nose, and throat?" How ever, he said only, "May be you better not leave on the road right away."

"I have come to the end of the road," I said.

"That is not what I said," said Jack. "I have faith in you. I believe in you."

"There was 2 of us believed in me," I said, "and now there is only 1."

"Not at all, Author," said he, flying around from the foot of the bed to my side. "I am as full of faith in you this minute as I ever was in the depths of the winter. Do not think I am 1 of those fair weather friends."

"I know that you have faith in me, Jack," I said. "It is I that have lost faith in my self."

"Accidents can happen," said Jack.

"This was no accident," I replied. "This is Nature speaking."

"This could of happened to any body," Jack said.

"No," I replied, "it could not of happened to me 5 years ago or even 2 years ago. I think I should of knew the night in Montreal when the ball come back so fast."

"The light is bad in Montreal," said Jack.

"Or if I did not know in Montreal I should of knew when I made the error in Boston."

"You were not yet in shape," said Jack, "because that consarned dolgolly Mr. Alexander took so long to hire you."

"He was right and we were wrong," I said.

Jack brang a chair to the bed. The sound of the chair scraping the floor tortured my skull. "Sleep on it," said he.

"You must not sleep," said the doctor, entering the room again with his flashing lights. "Why did you not tell me you wore contact lenses in your eye."

"Contact lenses who?" Jack Sprat asked.

"Him," said the doctor, fishing in 1 eye and then in the other and finally finding a contact lens smashed to pieces. He removed it with an instrument. Suddenly my eyes come back in focus and every body was relieved, especially me.

"You never told me you wore contact lenses," said Jack. His face begun to disappear. My eyes kept closing. Then his face returned. Then disappeared. Returned. My jaws locked in place. People were climbing in and out my skull with their shoes on while the nurses kept waking me up and saying, "We do not advise sleep, do not sleep," and good old wonderful, faithful, loyal Jack Sprat kept disappearing in till he disappeared for ever.

Before long I thought I saw Hilary sitting in Jack's chair, but it was not Hilary, it was Holly. "You took Jack Sprat's chair," I said to her. She leaned close to me to hear me speak, all though I thought that I was speaking very loud. How ever, I was not. My jaws were locked on their hinge. Soon I begun taking a powerful medicine to unlock them. A *relaxant.* 2 days later I was babbling like a mad man.

"Jack is long gone," Holly replied, drawing her chair closer to the bed and holding my hand supported on our elbow like 2 arm wrestlers. Later she drug her chair to the other side of the bed, and back and forth again from time to time, I forget why. When my jaw relaxed I could feel all the teeth that were loose in my mouth, and I did not like that feeling. Little by little I sat up higher and higher as my head ache got less and less. The time was Saturday after noon. I thought it was still Friday night. My face was blue, red, yellow, orange and numerous other colors down the left side from my eye to the opposite jaw bone.

"Holly," I said, "answer 1 question. Did it hit me on the line or on the bounce?"

"That is what every body ask," she said, "all though no body knows." It is a question I am often asked, "Did the ball hit you on the line or on the bounce?" I do not know. No body knows. Tom Roguski does not know. The film was shot from behind Tom, and you can see him coming up out of his crouch, and you can see my shortstop and my second baseman running towards the middle, for that was where they thought the ball was going. You can see how much quicker they seen it than I seen it if ever I seen it at all.

Holly filled many ice packs with ice for my head. She fed me ice cream through a metal straw wired for pressure in till my swallowing come back. When I begun speaking again I inquired, "What are we going to do with the rest of our life?"

"Now is our chance to do a 1,000,000 things," she replied.

"We will watch our girls grow. We will flower our garden. We will move to warmer climates which are better for the aches and pains of younger older persons like you and me. We can try out life in Paris or Europe as discussed."

"We will own a winery," I said. "You can force wine down my throat with pressurize metal straws. Hilary is very eager to own a winery and has sold several 100's of dollars in stock to interested parties on 2 coasts."

"I am sorry to say I believe that Hilary lost interest in the winery," said Holly. "Possibly we must give people their money back."

"If there is 1 thing I hate," said I, "it is giving people their money back."

Prior to leaving my hospital room I telephoned Lisa Mayflower asking her for a rain check on a house in Beverly Hills. Down below, in the press room of the hospital, I announced to 1 and all that I was now finally retired from baseball for ever, Nature was Nature, I talked back to Nature once too often and Nature slammed the door. This brung a great laugh from the writers. A TV fellow asked me, "Are you considering managing?" "Oh, yes," I replied, "I got baskets full of offers pending but I will reject them all. I will raise wine and horses in a spot I picked out in sun swept California ½ way between the desert and the ocean," and so forth and so on at the rate of 2½ lies per minute due to the relaxant unlocking my jaws.

"Why did you come back in the first place?" some body asked.

"Mr. Suicide Alexander made me do it," I said. "He put the pressure on Jack Sprat. I only done it to help out several mutual friends and my daughter."

"Tell us the location of your winery and horses in California," some body said.

"My financial director asked me to keep it confidential."

"Who is your financial director?" the same person asked.

"She is a business woman of the east," I replied.

On the air plane my head ache returned some thing awful. Holly give me pills to relieve the pain and coffee by the bucket to keep me from falling asleep. I was not suppose to sleep too much. In years past I flew 1,250,000 miles by air plane sleeping most of them. My head was full of noises such as Marva Sprat's TV and Ben Crowder's furnace and Tom Roguski's hair blower and the telephone ringing in my car and the hoofs of horses stampeding around and around in the stable of the horse lady of Tozerbury. Worst of all was the noise of the air plane motor tearing loose from the wings. Holly informed the captain, and the captain come back and rest assured me I was mistaken, we agreed it was my *teeth* were loose, he expected to see me back in action very soon.

We drove direct from JFK to Dr. Howard Pointer, dentist, brother of Dr. Frank Pointer the famous prostrate doctor. It was the day after my 40th birthday. While I was in Howard's chair Frank popped his head in the door and said "I told you you could not do it" and popped his head out again. "This is no impossible problem," said Howard. "Tightening loose teeth is a specialty of the house, although to tell you the truth these are *very* loose teeth. It might take several visits. Tell me, did these cannon balls strike you on the line or on the bounce?"

Up we come from New York City, up the Taconic I drove so many times that winter. In to Perkinsville we drove, and through town and up the drive way to the house. We live there yet. We never bought a winery in sun swept California or took up residence in Paris or Europe. You ask your self a 1,000 times, "What will I do with the rest of my life?" but when I walked in the door the question begun to melt away. Baseball was over. For the first time in my life I was no longer a baseball player and had not been a baseball player since the eighth inning Friday evening in California. The rest of my life all ready begun. It was here. "Where has every body went?" I inquired.

Michele went to a deep sea diving camp in Florida, guaranteed no sharks. Rosemary went to a school friend's place in

Maine. Millicent had a small summer job at that time in town. Hilary went horse back riding, and I went some where, too—I went up stairs and give a look around. Naturally I am not 1 of those fathers that prowl around in their daughter's room looking for secrets, although I could not help noticing on Hilary's bulletin board the California baseball schedule and the color photos of many fine horses.

On Hilary's desk I seen the list of stock holders covered by a pile of checks and green cash they had give her on 2 coasts. It would lay there for months if I left it. I picked it up. Standing with the money in my hand in Hilary's mirror I looked like a prize fighter collecting the loser's purse. I returned all the sums to the various parties, and the winery slipped out of Hilary's mind little by little like baseball it self.

When Hilary first heard I was released the previous December she screamed the bloodiest murder attracting a crowd from all over the house. She must see me play ball! She never did. After July I issued many invitations to her to stroll down with me in my fire proof room and watch me on film, and she said she would, but she never quite made it. The 2 of us eased out of baseball together.

Now and then, with a small glass of sherry, I use to run California 1 more time through my TV cassette machine in the belief that may be that boy name of Muddy Rivers would change his mind about my third pitch. He never did. Strike 1. Strike 2. Then smash, and the next thing you see I am flat on the ground unconscious. It give me the head ache. I turned off the machine, popped an aspirin, washed it down with sherry, and strolled up stairs to bed. After a while I no longer required the film but give it to the Hall of Fame at Cooperstown, N. Y., along with many other silvernears of time gone by.

The End